Meet Me At
The Barbershop

Meet Me At The Barbershop

PART 1

Rashi Dildy

Library of Congress Control Number: 2021903440
ISBN: Hardcover 978-1-6641-5944-0
Softcover 978-1-6641-5943-3
eBook 978-1-6641-5942-6

Print information available on the last page.

Rev. date: 02/19/2021

To order additional copies of this book, contact:
Xlibris
844-714-8691
www.Xlibris.com
Orders@Xlibris.com
814139

Prelude

One year. That's all Jujuan could think about as he waited in the barbershop to get his hair cut. This can't be life. One year, and everything in his crew seemed to have changed. Looking back, no one could foresee the things that happened in this short amount of time. Was this what college was? Four years of drama, regret, and changes? Who could have seen this coming?

His crew was in bizarro world or something. Rashi the flagrant player and Rashad "Mr. I'm scared to get into a relationship because of karma" were the ones in stable relationships. Rashi and this Stacie girl he was with was becoming a headache. She was a model for one and for two she was so down to earth it was like Rashi was given a blessing for being a jerk for so long. Seeing Rashi in a relationship was sickening in itself, but watching him with this girl and the way they were together was enough to make you want to puke.

Then there was Rashad. He was with a girl on the women's basketball team at the college he was attending. Her name was Jackie. She and Rashad fit like puzzle pieces, sort of like Jujuan and Carrie used to fit. They almost didn't happen because when they met, Shad was with another girl, which was unlike Rashad in the first place. Now he was happy too. Every time he saw the crew he was somehow talking up Jackie and that was starting to get a little sickening as well. "Me and Jackie this, Me and Jackie that." It was just getting a little unbearable.

As for himself and Nehi, life had basically taken a 180 degree turn. Jujuan was the good one in the crew until college. As he sat here and waited for his turn in the chair, he couldn't help but think about this. The school year was almost over and he honestly couldn't recognize himself. His hair was different now and the way he acted was like another person.

Actually, it was another person. Tired of being known as the good guy, Jujuan decided to create an alter ego. Someone who did all the things he didn't do. Another version of Rashi, but part time. This seemed like a great plan at the time, and now, less than a year later, he was regretting it. Trying to "have fun" in college, he knew now that he'd messed up a good thing. All Jujuan could think was that he was happy a year ago and just didn't know it. He thought he wanted something else out of life, instead of being the good guy.

Even with that, Jujuan was happy that he wasn't in Nehi's shoes. Nehi was having an even worse first year of college. Yeah, he made a little money, but in the current situation he was in, he was going to need it. Nehi's problems got so bad that he'd basically abandoned the crew and became a bit of a loner. Aria, his girl, was a BIG part of the problem though. When she put him in a crazy situation, the crew was the only place he could really turn, and now he was back. Bigger problems than everyone else, but back in the circle. So a year from the time they got back and almost two since they finished high school and the whole world was on its head.

The two from the crew who you could not pay to be in a relationship, were in the most stable relationships. While himself and Nehi were dealing with a laundry list of problems. A pregnancy, an alter ego, a crazy old broad, and a love triangle, these would seem like Rashad/Rashi type like problems, but apparently in just one year, things can change and for some people things can change for the better while for others not so much.

Jujuan was in utter disbelief as he sat there and thought about the things that transpired in just a year. Even as he sat there in the shop with his crew, he knew they weren't as tight as they were one measly year ago. It was nobody's fault, in Jujuan's opinion this was just college. In his one year there, he went from being the Freshman everyone loved to just a freshman in college trying to survive. All of this in just one year, it left Jujuan thinking, does the first eighteen years of your life just not count or is every year of college going to be like this …

Chapter 1

"How many girls you think Rashi has slept with?" It was in Rashad's head, and since Nehi was here, he figured he'd put it out there.

"I have no idea, bro. But I know it's a lot. I mean did you see dude in Europe? I'm surprised he ain't caught something by now." Rashi wasn't Nehi's favorite guy in the crew.

Rashad was driving Nehi to his girlfriend, Kionna's, dorm. She was mad at Nehi for spending time with his ex-girlfriend, Aria. On the phone, Nehi couldn't get a word in edgewise with her, so he was on his way to grovel in person. Rashad was there cause Nehi needed a ride, needed someone to keep her roommate company, and most importantly for jokes at the shop next week. You beg for forgiveness, you get clowned. That's like a shop rule.

"Whatever, son. You did your thing too, Shad. I counted at least six different girls." Nehi's girl went with them on the trip, and Jujuan's girl was in Chicago. So while in Europe, Nehi spent his free time with his girlfriend. But Jujuan was there to see the sights. While Rashad and Rashi spent their time meeting girls and partying.

"It's the experience, Bro. Your chick was with you, but think about it from my point of view. I got to smash a few European chicks as well as travel abroad with my guys. Ain't too many people saying that on the south side of Chicago. Plus, I'm single, clown. I can smash whoever, whenever. With that being said though, I just met a cutie recently. She's a dime, too."

"Who?"

"This chick named Caryl. I was in the mall the other day looking for some kicks and I found her instead. Good trade off, if you ask me."

"Caryl, huh?"

"Yeah, son. She was with a bunch of girls, and I had to handpick her. She was standing in the food court and I just walked up like, 'Here's my phone, you should put your number in it.' After she put her number in, I grabbed her hand. Honestly, I thought she was going to resist, but she walked with me. When I got a few feet away from her friends, I just told her I had to pull her away from them to properly introduce myself. She tried to hit me with the whole, 'I don't give my number to gang bangers' speech. I had to let her know I'm a college student. Couple tats here and there, but no guns, knives, brass knuckles, enemies, none of that. I'm a smart dude. I'll do your taxes before I'll rob you.'"

"What'd she say to that?"

"Come on now. You know what she said to that. She said, 'We should go out on some dates and make sure you're being honest' That wasn't exactly how it went, but when you're with your guys, small, boring details usually get skipped. Plus, this ride was about Nehi and his current situation. "So what happened with you and Kionna, son?"

"This whole situation with Aria got her losing her damn mind. We're getting close to her place, so I'll tell you the rest when we leave here, Shad. We should be out of here in like an hour or so. I'm gonna need you to go ahead and keep her roommate company while I talk to Kionna."

"Oh hell no, Nehi! You didn't tell me I would have to deal with her roommate. I told you. I just met a chick. What does her roommate look like anyway?"

"Shad, you ain't been in a relationship in over a year. You just met this Caryl girl at the mall recently. Cool out. I'm not asking you to marry her. I'm just asking you to kick it with her for an hour or two while I get things straightened out with Ki."

"Dude, I'll kick it with her for an hour or two, but that's it. And I noticed you didn't answer my question. What the hell does the roommate look like?" Nehi was trying to avoid the question the first time Rashad asked it. Rashad wasn't really a big fan of the big girls, a personal preference of his, and he stood by that. Kionna's roommate was kinda big, maybe five pounds over Rashad's limit —maybe a couple more.

"She's cute as hell. Smart as hell too. Shorty can cook, too. And she's healthy."

"How healthy? Heart attack healthy?"

"Dude, she ain't that big! Plus, it ain't like you're impregnating the broad. I just need to you to kick it with her for an hour or two. We're in, we're out. I just need to clarify some things with Kionna. It shouldn't be too long. Shouldn't be long at all ..."

* * *

"You aren't tired?" Rashad was tired as could be, but he was trying to be a good friend and stay up and alert. It was four ten in the morning and Rashad was ready to hit the sack.

"Give me like fifteen-twenty minutes, I'll be ready. How are things going with her roommate?"

"Seriously? We've been here for like nine hours. I feel like I've been entertaining this big-ass girl for a full shift." Rashad's mind was actually on Caryl. Rashad hadn't told Nehi, but since getting her number they'd talked that first night from eleven until five in the morning, and on the next night they talked even longer. "I don't even know why she's still awake, I tried acting like I was sleeping at one point. She just keeps going. Cookies this, cakes that, this broad should be in culinary school."

"Kionna is mad, cause according to her, Aria shouldn't have been there at all. I told her she just showed up without my permission. She doesn't believe me."

Actually Nehi invited her. Nehi told Kionna that he hadn't talked to Aria in over six months, the thing was, Aria was his Kryptonite. He saw her and told her basically everything. He told her where his dorm was. Told her where Kionna'sdorm was. Then even kissed her.

Nehi was getting sloppy. They actually kissed in his dorm room just one week earlier. Aria actually helped him move in. That's when they kissed and although it was known that Nehemiah was taken, he let it happen. Tonight's mission was to fix all of this somehow.

The kiss just confused Nehi. They broke up because she was getting attention from Nehi's barber and good friend, Rashi. Aria had dumped Nehi when she thought she was going to get with Rashi. Rashi, this so called friend slept with Aria, then he shot her the deuces. Nehi moved on and was happy with Kionna. They traveled the world together and were getting super close, then the Aria situation happened. He was always with Kionna or hanging out with his friends Rashad, JuJuan, and Rashi. Yep, he stayed cool with Rashi. The helping with the dorm thing was the first time he was alone with Aria in over a year and things happened that shouldn't have.

They ended up alone together when he moved in because for the first time really the whole crew was apart from one another. JuJuan was at school in Iowa. Rashi was cutting. And Kionna was at school —in Dekalb, Illinois, the same school Aria was attending. So she volunteered to help Nehi move. He was the only one without a car, cause he spent his money on vinyl. He's a DJ. She drove him, she helped, and after all that time together alone, they ended up kissing.

"I'm ready. You know what—she's tripping. So Aria knows where I stay. It ain't like I'm giving her the pipe work." Nehi was talking rather loudly, but that was just in case Kionna was listening. He told her nothing happened, and that his mom had given Aria his info at school. Aria and her family lived two doors down from his parents, and now she lived right across campus from Kionna. So not only were they exes, and they'd known each other practically their whole lives, but his current girl and his ex—who he might or might not still want to get back with—went to the same university.

"That's cool. Let's roll." Rashad was more than ready to go. He was fine talking to Kionna's roommate, but Caryl was heavy on his brain. Although it was four thirty in the morning, Rashad was looking forward to calling her.

"So what exactly did you tell her happened with you and the Big A?" Aria was a bit heavy set, hence the name "The Big A."

"I told her Aria came over last week and I had one of her nips in my mouth! Fool, what did I just say when I got in the car? I didn't tell her nothing. She's already insecure about Aria to begin with. I'm just trying to get to a point where she's speaking to me again."

Rashad was speeding, ready to hear Caryl's voice before he hit the hay, but the conversation was pretty good so he kept it going. "So not only does she not know that The Big A helped you move, she don't know you slobbed her down? How in the hell she think you got to school?"

"Rashi."

"She believed that? She already knows you don't really trust him like that. If he didn't already know her, I wouldn't introduce him to my mother. That's my guy, but you know how he gets down. If the opportunity presents itself, you know he's on top of it. Literally."

"I know, but before Jennifer dumped your ass, I hate to say it, you were the same way. You gave Jennifer's sister the pipe work! ***Her sister***, what was on your mind, clown?"

"Same thing that was on your mind last week. It wasn't like that was the plan. Jennifer left us alone one too many times. I wasn't as bad as Rashi though. He doesn't have boundaries. He'd smash your momma while your daddy was asleep in the same bed."

Nehi couldn't help but laugh at that, cause it was funny as hell, and cause it was true. "Shad, two years ago that was you in high school. I ain't gonna lie, I thought you were going to catch like ten different diseases."

"High school is just that though, bro. It's teenagers in a building trying to figure shit out. Yeah, I was a bit of a ladies man, but I wasn't trying to be married either. People always made it seem like Jennifer and I were supposed to be married, but it was a high school relationship. Yep, I slept with her sister, and I know I was dead ass wrong, but at the end of the day it happened and its over with. I'm on to a new chapter in my life bro, as is she. And tonight isn't about me or Jennifer sir. Its about DJ Neo and his lady problems. What you gonna do? You going to tell her? Before you start, I think you should. Of course she's going to be mad, but if she finds out from you it'll be much better than Aria rubbing it in her face, cause you know she will. Tell her she helped you move in. That's how she knows where you stay and that she kissed you when you were off guard. Just don't tell here you kissed back. ***Did you kiss back?"***

"Not only did I kiss back, my hands wandered, and I was holding all kindcs of buns. I don't know why, but kissing Aria kinda felt right. I mean I enjoyed the kiss from the beginning to the end. If my roommate hadn't walked in, I don't know how far it would have gone. Kionna was the furthest thing from my mind."

"Of course it felt right, y'all been a couple since y'all were ten and this ain't a movie. Of course another woman wasn't on your mind when you were in the middle of a kiss. Look, you're only 19, you're going to make some mistakes. She will too. My granny of all people is always telling me that I'm too young to commit to just one girl and that I need to experience life. Nehi, you and Kionna ain't married. You made a mistake, man up. Would you want her to hide shit from you?"

"I don't want her to hide nothing but I get this feeling that she is. I don't know what, but, I just got this feeling in my gut."

"That feeling is you, clown. You're hiding something. So you trying to put your guilty conscience off on her. Cool out."

Nehi took that point and let in sink in. It made him feel a little better, but something just wasn't right to him. He'd had a feeling like this before, but it was a while ago. This was how he felt around the time Aria broke up with him. He honestly didn't know if it was something going on with Kionna or if it was the fact that Aria was back in his life.

"You know what? You might be right. I ain't telling Kionna though. She's already upset and I just don't feel like that type of information is really going to help us. I know if I told her, this would just mess everything up as far as us trying to stay together."

"Ok, well ask yourself this. Is Aria even worth it? A couple of years ago y'all was hot and horny, then look what she did. From what Rashi says, ***she*** approached ***him.*** The worst part is, she knew the deal. She knew he wasn't just your barber. You ask me, she's a dirty broad."

"Come on now! She was bogus, I'll give you that, but a dirty broad?

"You know what's funny? When she first let your boy Ra hit, you was calling her all kinds of broads, bitches, and hoes too. Quite frankly, until you kissed her last week, she was a dirty broad to you. Guess grabbing them buns changed your mind huh?"

"I don't know. Ever since I kissed her, I've been thinking about her all the time bro. It's like she put something on me. Aria of all people. Shad, I was upset with her for months. Now, out of the blue, she's back. What am I going to do?"

They were back in the city and the sun was coming up. Rashad was ready to head home and give Caryl a good morning/ goodnight call. "Ok, look. We're here so I'm going to leave you with this. You say you're feeling her now and I don't know if you really do, but if you feeling her more than Kionna how you gonna feel the next time she's with you and you have to get a haircut? Just think about it."

"Aiight then clown, Holla Back!" Nehi got out and he thought about what Rashad said. He knew he'd think about it cause it was a good point. He ended up losing sleep thinking about it. He was up all night just going through scenarios and situations in his head. He didn't get to sleep until noon.

"Hello?"

"What's up Caryl, you up?" Rashad was relieved to be in his dorm room now. He'd been thinking about calling Caryl during the whole ride home. It was 6:15 a.m.but he knew he was calling. Even if she was asleep, he was going to make this call a goodnight/good morning call. To Rashad, Caryl was something different. His reasons for this were 1. He's not a phone person—meaning most of is calls lasted on average three to four minutes. He found himself talking to Caryl for hours on end. And 2, he wasn't looking, but somehow he found her. Ever since the whole Jennifer situation he'd been trying to avoid dating. He knew he was wrong and somehow he felt that by not dating and getting involved, he could make up for what he did to Jennifer. Lastly, he was really feeling Caryl. Although he hadn't been dating or kicking it with anyone, the opportunity had presented itself plenty of times. In his words, "pussy had been throwing itself at me and I'm blocking it."

Rashad wouldn't say this to his guys, but he felt that until the whole Jennifer thing, he was a genuinely nice guy. He felt that he tarnished his "nice guy" status, and with the constant comparison to Rashi, he knew his guys thought so too.

"Barely, I just about gave up on you, Rashad. What you been doing all night?"

"My bad Ms. Lady, I was out with my guy Nehi. He dealing with some shit so I'm trying to help him out. He ain't got a car so I gotta help him out. We drove all the way out to NIU, and for most of the night I was talking to his girlfriend's roommate"

"What's up with him? what's he dealing with?"

"I can't tell you that, but I gotta talk to you about a couple things before I go to bed."

"What's up, Baby?" That slipped. That was the first time using the "B" word to him, but she'd been calling him "my baby Shad" to her friends since the first time they talked. She was slipping a bit. Hopefully he didn't notice.

He did, but he ignored it. "Caryl, remember the first time we talked and you wanted to know why I didn't have a girl?"

"Yeah. Don't tell me, you got a girl."

"No, not yet at least. I just wanna tell you the real reason why. I mean chillin with Nehi, watching him deal with this shit, I just wanna be open and honest with you. I think you have a right to know this before you decide if you want to be with me or not."

"What is it?"

Rashad could hear the nervousness in her voice. This was going to be harder than he thought. "Okay, let me tell you a little about my past. In high school, people thought I was a player or whatnot. The thing was, I was very popular. I'm a Hooper. I was second on the team in scoring, and me, my guy JuJuan, and my barber pretty much ran the school." He was very careful and made sure he said Rashi was his barber. If this was going to be his girl, of course she was going to meet Rashi, but not too soon. Rashi is Rashi. Does he really need to meet another female? NO!

"So the general consensus was that we were just giving every female in the school the pipe work. I know plenty of girls and I went out all the time. Not with the same girl for the most part, but these girls were my friends. I'm not going to sit here and say I didn't have sex with any of my friends, but I wasn't nearly as bad as people thought. And then came Jennifer."

"Who is Jennifer?"

"Jennifer is the girl who pretty much made it look like the whole player thing look like the truth. I met her, I dug her, I decided to date her. Now things were going great until right after prom. Jennifer had a sister, Lisa, and Lisa was older than us and she was in college. So for the first six months we were together, I knew nothing of her. That May she came home from school, we met and from day one there was a very strong attraction."

"Oh you didn't, did you?

"Hold on, let me finish the story. Well, that summer while she was home I'd find myself with Lisa all the time. She got a summer job. Guess who was her ride to and from work? When Jennifer was off getting her hair and nails did, guess who was keeping Lisa company? It came to a point where I was spending more time with Lisa than with Jennifer. So that August I'm taking Lisa back to school in Indianapolis and Jennifer can't go. So it's just me and her on this long trip, and while we were there at her apartment, one thing led to another. I ended up sleeping with Lisa."

"So what happened? Did Lisa tell Jennifer?"

"Nope, but I did. I had to. I loved Jennifer so I couldn't just keep something like that from her. She snapped out. She slapped me, called me all kinds of bitches, said I let me know that I wasn't a man. It came to a point where she was saying she hated me. She was a junior so when she got back to the high school, although I wasn't there, I had become what I had been trying to avoid, a player. I was getting all kinds of messages from people I'd gone to school with. Some hated my guts cause I hurt Jennifer. Others were females trying to get with me since they heard that Jennifer and I had broken up."

"What?"

"Yep, when we got back in the country, those same females who were supposed to be Jennifer's friends were trying to get with me."

"So you get with any?"

"You're the first girl I've been interested in since Jennifer." That was true, but he didn't answer the question. Rashad hadn't been interested in too many girls, but when he was in Europe, he did make good use of his time there. "So that's what this call is about. I'm digging you and I just want you to know what you're getting into before you actually get into it."

"So let me get this straight. You loved Jennifer, but when you met her sister, you were attracted to her. So instead of telling her this, you just kept spending time with her sister and ended up sleeping with her?"

"Basically, yes. So do me a favor, just think about what you wanna do as far as you and I are concerned. I'm going to go ahead and go to bed. I'm going to call you later today when I get up and we'll talk more. Remember that I told you for a reason though. I'm feeling you and I want you to know everything there is to know about me before we go any further."

"Okay talk to you later then."

"One."

Rashad was sure before the conversation that getting all of this out in the open would make him feel better. It didn't. It was the way that Caryl said the last thing she said to him. The way she summarized the whole situation sounded so negative to him the he was sure that this was one of his last times talking to Caryl. He was prepared for the worst and he figured no Caryl was the worst. That was the last thing on his mind as he fell asleep.

Chapter 1.5

THE CREW
Rashi M Holla AKA Ra
Age: 19 Occupation: Barber
Reputation: Ladies' Man Personality: Funny/Smooth

Rashi M Holla, known as a ladies' man and a bit of a back stabber. The back stabber bit came a year ago when he slept with one of his closest friends', Nehi, girlfriend. The truth of the matter was that Rashi was actually the complete opposite. Until Rashi's growth spurt at 13, he was 5'3, 290 pounds. He was short and fat. This growth spurt seemed to be over night. At 5'3 most girls say you are too short and at 290 pounds fuhgedabout it. He was now 6'2 220 pounds. He wasn't trying to get over a lifetime of rejection. He was actually just trying to make up for lost time. He knew what his friends -his foes as well- thought of him. He'd done his share of dirt and was aware that it was killing his rep and some of his friendships. He'd slept with Aria Nehi's girl, Rashad's sister, and three of JuJuan's cousins. Rashi could honestly say that he hadn't purposely initiated any of these encounters. Rashi really was just used to being around a lot of women, he had 13 sisters (Angie, Lanae, Qualita, Gretchen, Eisha, Mihjara, Danai, Jacienya, Hannah, Tamara, Terri, Aubrey, and Triniti), and he really just liked women.

Rashi became a barber because he knew as a freshman that he didn't want to go to college. His father owned a barber college, so as a sophomore in high school he began going there part time. By the middle of his senior, year he'd finished and started working in a shop. He'd had a large clientele since his junior year in high school. He started off cutting heads on the basketball team for much less than professionals and it just grew from then on. When colleges came with scholarships from his time on the basketball court, he declined. He looked at it like he could either be a broke college student/athlete or barber with a large clientele and constant cash flow. To him that was an easy decision. No matter how successful his friends got, "everybody needs a barber." At least that what his pops was always saying.

Rashi wasn't living the easy life either. Being the only one in his circle of friends with his own apartment also meant he was the only one with bills. He wasn't regretting his decision to skip on the college thing, but he did feel that cutting heads was sometimes a little overwhelming. He wouldn't express these feelings out loud, but they weighed heavy on his mind.

Rashi's biggest problem by far though was his single status. In all honesty, he wanted a girlfriend. But with the girls he met, somehow his reputation preceded him. He thought that his perfect girl was going to be easy to find, all he wanted was a girl who was going to laugh at his jokes and who liked to chill. He was tired of going out all the time. Plus all of his guys had steady girls at some point in the last year, he realized he wanted the stability.

Rashad D Burkes AKA Shad
Age: 19 Occupation: Student/Athlete
Reputation: Ladies Man/Hooper
Personality: Funny/Always joking

Shad, known as a ladies' man, had been missing in action lately. Physically Rashad was 6'4, 215 pounds. Tall, slender, and on a college basketball team, that equaled lots of temptation. He had a hard exterior, but deep down, he really did care what people thought about him. At some point or another everyday he worried about if he'd be known as the cat that slept with his girl's sister for the rest of his life. His constant joking and laughing all the time kept his friends in the dark about his feelings and worries.

He knew exactly what made him go after Caryl in the mall: her looks. She was cute and thick so he knew that when other people saw her with him, they would know who he was and how he got down. She was his arm candy, if you saw him with her you just knew he got the cuties and settled for nothing less. It wasn't until after their first conversation that he started thinking of her as more than just a trophy.

Shad's favorite words on the phone were, "let me hit you back later." And for the first time since Jennifer, he was on the phone for more than an hour when he wasn't forced. Caryl looked good, but she had other qualities. He didn't know what they were exactly, but knew that he wanted to find them out. She had a good head on her shoulders. With her looks to go with her smarts, that put her in the elite, made her a dime (a 10 out of 10).

It was actually something Rashi said that had Rashad really trying to do the right thing as far as Caryl was concerned. Of all people, when Rashad broke up with Jennifer, Rashi took him aside and told him his great one theory. According to Rashi, "In your life you get three great ones. Some cats marry the first one cause they know a good thing when they see it. Others marry the second or third while some cats use the first as the standard and find a great one based on that. Then you have the majority of us. We have a great one and we blow it. I know I've probably killed my chances of finding a great one, but I knew from jump that for you, Jennifer was one. You gotta take this and learn from it. You're due for another one, so do two things for me. Keep your eyes open. You could meet another great one today, and don't blow it. Consider yourself lucky when you land a great one, cause you are."

Rashad felt that Caryl was a great one. He wasn't trying to blow it, so he decided to start off as truthful and honest as possible. He knew the risk, but was using this whole open and honest approach as a measuring stick. Either she was going to be with him or she was going to take this info and run.

As far as academics went, Rashad was on the right track. Out of his main group of friends, he had the highest GPA. In his opinion though, he was the second smartest. (He felt like this cause Rashi had the lowest GPA but only because he didn't take school seriously. He'd seen Rashi answer almost every question on Jeopardy plenty of times.) Carrying a 3.6 GPA, leading the school basketball team in scoring, and scoring well on college entry tests had Rashad in a great position as far as going to a good school. He chose to stay in the city cause DePaul showed interest in him as a sophomore. He figured going DePaul University was being loyal. He did have to work out for the coach plenty after his year off, but they still wanted him so it was an easy decision. Because school was being paid for by scholarship, his parents let him travel abroad for a year before going to college. They let him use his college fund.

Nehemiah Carter AKA Nehi DJ Name: Neo (When it comes to DJing he says he's, "The ONE")
Age: 19 Occupation: DJ/Student
Reputation: The Sweet One Personality: Funny but Sensitive

Nehi was in a good relationship, but lately he'd been doing some things that were out of character. He was happy with Kionna. She was smart, funny, and she even took him out sometimes. Kionna, in Nehi's opinion, was almost perfect. She'd been around all of his friends, even to the barbershop. Nehi felt like this could be love, but then there was Aria.

Aria had been out of Nehi's life for a while now, but had been in it much longer. Aria grew up with Nehi. She'd been his neighbor for 13 years. He didn't notice that she had grown into a beautiful young woman until his sophomore year in high school. They flirted a bit, but didn't get together until they were juniors. He lost his virginity to her, so Aria had a special place in Nehi's heart.

The one flaw with Kionna, according to Nehi, was that she was kind of clingy. They met in May the year before when he was with Aria. He was DJing at a house party for a friend and she was a friend of a friend. They ended up talking about hip-hop, and their mutual love for it. She stuck around until the party was over and they exchanged numbers. Aria broke up with him in July. He and Kionna were a couple almost immediately after that, before August came around. By September when they were getting ready for their year abroad (really 10 months) she'd planned on going with. At the time it was a good idea to him. He'd just gotten into a relationship with her and a year apart wouldn't help. She came from a wealthy family so paying for the trip wouldn't be a problem for her. While out of the country, they grew closer and everything was going great.

When Nehi got back, he wasn't expecting Aria. When he left they weren't even speaking, so when he got back and she was in his house cooking with his mom, he was surprised to say the least. Aria being there really brought out the clinginess in Kionna. She always tried to be there so that Nehi and Aria couldn't be alone together. In Europe, this was fine, but at home Nehi just wanted a little privacy. He was starting college soon and missed just hanging with his guys. Kionna talked about hanging out with her girlfriends as well, but when Aria came around, her girlfriends slid out of the picture.

Kionna being on the block all the time was starting to get annoying to Nehi, and for some strange reason all of his anger towards Aria began to fade. By late August, Kionna had to focus on getting everything ready for school, and in her absence Nehi and Aria started hanging out. There were days when she was at his house until almost 5 a.m. and other days when they fell asleep in his bed after a long night of just talking. He liked sharing his many adventures from his trip with her. Unlike Kionna, Aria wasn't there so he told her stories and she listened.

Nehi was starting at UIC, he lived on the southside and the University was on the west side. An easy train ride, but he was moving so a train wouldn't help. When Aria offered him a ride to school, he said yes, knowing deep down that it would cause some trouble with Kionna. He didn't plan on kissing her or letting anything happen, but she was Aria and there would always be strong feelings there.

In his 19 long years, Nehi had never been in a situation where he had to choose between two women. He didn't know what he as going to do. Six months ago this was an easy decision, but now Nehi just didn't understand. Six months ago, Aria wasn't on his mind at all, there wouldn't have been a choice to make because he was with Kionna, and that was what he wanted.

JuJuan West AKA Preach
Age: 19 Occupation: Student/Athlete
Reputation: The Quiet One
Personality: All Business/The Serious One

As a joke, people always told JuJuan he was lucky to have the girlfriend that he had. She was actually Rashi's cousin so he didn't have to worry about an Aria situation. Rashi hooking up with his girl was out of the equation. It was funny to Jujuan, but Rashi stealing any of his girlfriends was the least of his worries.

JuJuan just didn't fit the mold as far as who his friends were. Of course he was on the basketball team. That was one of the things he had in common with Rashi and Rashad, but he was also very into church. Even when they were on their trip abroad he visited several cathedrals and even wanted to visit the Vatican. He knew it was going against the grain to want to do those things, but his faith was strong.

JuJuan, like Rashad, had a free ride. He'd gotten a scholarship for college as well, but unlike Rashad, he had to go to school out of state. He was being recruited by five schools and all of them were out of state. He wasn't planning on going into the NBA or anything, but he did feel like basketball served a purpose for him. It got him into college, for free.

JuJuan wasn't so into the church life that he didn't have fun. He enjoyed hanging out with his friends. He just wasn't into the same things they were into. As far as he was concerned, all of them had at one point slept around. He wasn't into that. His girlfriend, Carrie, had been with him for three years and he planned on marrying her sometime soon.

JuJuan was the point guard at 5'11, 165 pounds. He wasn't the biggest guy, but he was probably the toughest. That and his no-nonsense demeanor led people to believe he was this mean ass, bible toting preacher. JuJuan wasn't as uptight as people thought, he laughed a lot while hanging out with his friends. He just felt like if he didn't crack jokes on you, don't crack jokes on him. His guys did every once in a while, but it was pretty much a known fact—don't mess with Preach.

Jujuan got his nickname from being the guy who says the team prayer before the games. He didn't have sermons, but he made sure his pre-game words were heard. His church actually paid for him to go overseas for a year. He played drums and volunteered for the church for almost his entire life. The Church funded his trip as a graduation gift and to show how proud they were of JuJuan!

JuJuan and Rashad knew each other the longest. They met in kindergarten, so their friendship spanned nearly 15 years. JuJuan going to school out of state was going to be hard on everyone, but especially Rashad. All his life, he'd lived down the block from JuJuan. They could chill, go out, or just kick it on the block with each other whenever they wanted. Neither one would say it out loud, but JuJuan leaving Chicago was a big blow.

Jujuan going to school out of state wasn't going to be a problem for his relationship. Carrie was going to be in Iowa as well. She chose to go to the same college. This was their plan from the time JuJuan graduated. She'd finish up her senior year, and if her grades permitted, she'd go to school with him. This was her idea and he agreed to it. Both wanted this because of the trip to Europe. They'd be spending almost a whole year apart and figured going to the same college and spending time together would make up for it.

THE TRIP

During their sophomore year, the seed for this one year get away was planted. It was Rashi's idea. He was going to do it alone since college wasn't in his future, but talked the others into it. "Who ever heard of four black cats taking a year off and traveling Europe?" Somehow just that statement convinced everyone else. In movies, books, and sitcoms it just seemed that going to Europe was the "white" thing. Rashad was excited to go because basketball took him all over the country, but he was thinking "more." He wanted more than just to be able to say "I've been there. We were playing ..." whenever someone mentioned a city or state. He wanted to be able to say, "I've been to London to shop, not hoop."

Nehi wanted to go because he just wanted to get out of Chicago. He'd been in Chicago since he was two. Aside from being born and living his first two years in Washington D.C. (which he didn't remember) Chicago is where he'd spent every minute of his life. No car meant that just getting up and going places wasn't an option. For him when it came down to his final weeks in Chicago before heading out of the county, he was worried because he'd be leaving his new love interest Kionna. When she decided to go on the trip, he was all for it. (Even though his guys weren't as enthusiastic.) But they changed their minds quickly when they found out they'd be staying at her family's home in England. That saved all of them a ton of money. From that point on, everyone was cool with Kionna being there.

As everyone expected, Rashi really enjoyed himself while in Europe. There was a girl who was around for almost a month, by far Rashi's longest fling. He kept everyone looking good. (***He is a barber***) When they weren't out partying, he actually made money on the side. Their last couple of weeks Rashi spent a lot of time writing and reading. This wasn't a surprise to any of the guys, but Kionna definitely noticed. She originally thought he was making a list of the women he'd smashed, but it was actually Nehi that told her Rashi read plenty of the old philosophers like Freud and Nietzsche, and that he wrote his thoughts and ideas down.

Rashad had the time of his life. He played ball with all different types of players and got to see what the real difference was in the European style of play. He knew he was only there for a year, so having a girlfriend in Europe was out of the picture. He didn't sleep around as much as Rashi, but he did get a couple "cutty buddies." These were women that were okay with being friends and smashing on occasion, no girlfriend talks. Going out and being seen together in public was optional. Rashad got over the language barrier pretty quickly. He'd taken Spanish four years and gotten nothing less than a B. Two of his "cutty buddies" were Spanish and he met a black girl from Paris, France. Rashad was the only one of his crew to get smacked in public, although he couldn't figure out how Rashi wasn't getting smacked every night. Rashad's "buddy" from France happened to see him with one of his Spanish "buddies". She did not like that at all, and things got physical. His friends clowned him for weeks for that, but by the time they left, the French girl was back to being his main "cutty buddy."

JuJuan's reason for going to Europe was to see how they lived on the other side of the pond. In his mind, aside from different languages, these different countries were just like America, rap music, saggin jeans, hanging out at the park/basketball court, almost everything was the same, except for the food. Everyone of them missed Harold's Chicken. It was the best chicken in Chicago and they would be going damn near a year without it. JuJuan couldn't believe it.

As far as the ladies went, they were beautiful to JuJuan. But two things kept him honest, his love for Carrie and Rashi being her cousin would tell her if he slipped up. He wasn't worried about Rashi telling Carrie because he wouldn't do that to her anyway, but Rashi was her cousin. JuJuan was the only one in the crew who went to church every Sunday in Europe and for a large part of the trip, he was doing his own thing. He never missed a party, but made it clear that he was there for more than just the females. Yeah, the beach was fun and all but JuJuan wanted to see the places he'd read about and experience the whole European thing.

Nehi became "Mr. Cool" while there. He always seemed to be walking around the house in this smoking jacket like Hugh Heffner or somebody. He was feeling good because Kionna was there with him. He could have been away from Kionna for a year with no problem, but when the trip got closer, he'd have chosen to stay in Chicago to be with her. Since she came, he was feeling good in every way. He was way out of Chicago for once and he had his girlfriend with him. He thought it couldn't get any better. But then his girlfriend gave them all a place to stay, threw parties, and he even got to do some DJing. He didn't really trust Rashi around Kionna but after a while he started thinking, "who would want to be with this clown after seeing him with all these different women?" Not Kionna. So Nehi loosened his grip and enjoyed his time in Europe.

Chapter 2

Rashi was sitting in his mom's living room after church on a Sunday. She knew he hadn't gone while he was in Europe, so every Sunday since he'd been back, she asked him to go with her. That meant that he met up with his "supreme clientele" (what he called his crew when they met with them when the shop was closed) at 3:00 pm on Sundays. Instead of meeting, having breakfast at 9, and then going to the shop, he was now meeting them at the shop. Whenever he got finished with Nehi's head (Nehi had the longest hair, had specific instructions, and was anal about his haircuts) they went to dinner or downtown to kick it.

"So how you feeling about all of your friends going to college? Still happy with this decision you made? Rashi you're so smart, I don't see how you let your daddy talk you out of going to school."

Rashi knew that no matter what he said or did, him not going to school was always going to be his dad's idea in his moms head. "He wanted me to go just as bad as you. I just knew what I wanted to do, Ma. College is where you go to become who you're going to be. You know, get your career started. For me, going to a university isn't going to make me a barber."

"But a barber, Rashi? You wanna be like your daddy that bad?"

"Once again Ma, it ain't like that. I wanted to be a barber cause I do my job right here in the community. I get to help people, and the money is good. Ma, I can go anywhere in the world, and with my training, I can make money. Anywhere! I did some cutting in Europe. When was the last time I borrowed or asked anybody for money? The girls call me when you ain't got it." The girls were Rashi's 13 sisters.

"I know, but is this really what you want to do for the rest of your life?"

"I don't know, but I'm happy doing it now. I mean, even if I want to go to college or whatever later on I'll have money saved up for that. Ma, I make $25 a head and I cut pretty fast. Even on slow days I'm making at least $50 an hour. Who's doing that, Ma?"

"Yeah, but don't you even want to experience college? Your friends are."

"I know, but I didn't even like being in high school, Ma. School just ain't for me. I know most of the stuff they teach and it just doesn't hold my interest. Why can't you just be happy for me? I was cutting heads back when I was living here, Ma. You knew what I was going to be."

He knew why she couldn't be happy for him. He was a barber like his father, for one. And he had a lot of lady friends like his father. His dad ended up cheating and his parents split up right after his youngest sister was born. He was just too much like his dad and he knew that was a problem for his mom. He didn't plan on being like his dad, but he knew at a very young age that he wanted to be a barber. He basically grew up in the barbershop, and he loved everything about it.

"Rashi, I just want what's best for you."

"So, being a barber isn't best for me? Even though it's what I want? Come on now Ma, we have this same discussion every week. Damn!"

"What?"

"Ma, I'm just saying. Is there anything else we can talk about? I mean, you didn't even ask me how my trip was. All these weeks and you don't even know what I did when I was out of the country. I could be wanted in every country in Europe right now." The fact that she hadn't asked was kind of weird to Rashi. Usually if he wasn't around for a week she'd be all over him. But he'd been gone for nearly a year and she didn't seem to be the least bit interested in his trip. "What's up with that? You don't wanna know what I did while was out of the country? I wasn't in Indiana, Ma. I was in Europe."

"I've heard things. I just didn't want to know cause what I heard ain't how I raised you." She did hear things. Ever since he smashed Aria and stopped talking to her, Aria made it her business to talk to Rashi's mom weekly. When Nehi got back, he talked to Aria. He made Rashi's adventure in Europe ten times better than what it was. Nehi was exaggerating to make Aria jealous, and Aria was taking what Nehi told her and exaggerating those stories to his mom.

"What you hear? I mean you couldn't have heard much. Alls I did was travel, party, and cut hair. No drugs, no drinking, and I even went to church a time or two while I was there." He didn't actually go in, but he did go to church to pick up JuJuan once or twice.

"Why am I hearing that you slept with every girl in Europe? Rashi, I know you and I know your father. Explain to me why I'm hearing you went over there and acted a damn fool, Rashi. Tell me that."

Rashi was speechless. How in the hell did she know what he was doing in Europe? Kionna? Couldn't be. She only met his mother once, and that was more than a year ago. He knew that none of his guys would have told her, so how did she know?

"Who told you that ma?"

"Does it matter who told me? How about you just tell me why the hell I heard it. How bout that? Tell me how you sleeping with every girl in Europe is crossing the Atlantic and ending up here."

Rashi didn't know, and lying was the first thing that came to his head. So that's what he did. "I don't know what you talking about."

"Really? So you didn't sleep with a bunch of girls while you were over there? And don't lie again."

"Ma, let me ask you a question. How many is a bunch?" He was joking and buying time. Joking to cut some of the tension in the room and buying time so that he could do some thinking. Who could have told her all that? He knew she hadn't talked to any of his guys. Who could she have talked to about that? Who the hell would tell her that anyway?

"Rashi, I'm not joking. I wasn't there, but my resource is very reliable. Why would this, of all things, be the very first thing I'm told about your trip?"

"Ma, I don't know what you talking about. I went over there, kicked it, and met a few new people. I cut a few heads and I did a little shopping. Aside from that, I saw the sights and tried to learn a thing or two. I don't know what you talking about as far my sexual activity. Anyhow, I gotta go meet my guys at the shop, so if it's okay with you, I gotta go." He knew this was going to piss her off a bit, but he didn't care. The fact that somebody told his mother his personal business and she wouldn't say who, was pissing him off.

"What time do you have to be there?"

"Now."

"Is there a reason why you have an attitude?"

"Ma, look how long I been back. This is the first time you've asked about my trip, and when you do finally ask, you're talking about something you heard. That's why I have an attitude. You don't care that I was gone for a year and that I met new people and did new things. The main thing that's concerning you is who I was fucking!"

She slapped him.

Rashi left almost as soon as her hand made contact with his face. She was trippin. Rashi was super close with his mom and now she was slapping him over some he said she said? It was a twenty-minute ride to the shop from his mom's place, and the slap was getting to him. He decided to call. She answered after one ring, like she was expecting the call.

"Hello?"

"What was that about Ma? I know I cursed, but I have cursed in front of you before, and it's never resulted in you putting hands on me."

"I slapped you because what you were saying was getting under my skin. I missed you more than you know while you were gone, but since you got back, it's like you've changed. Something about you is different. Maybe your leaving the country for a year has shown me that you really are your own man. Maybe it's you not going to college and being out here in the world working and paying bills. Maybe it's the girls asking about you all the time. I don't know, but I'm so sorry for reacting like that. I'm glad you're back and I'm glad you're being responsible Rashi."

I know Ma, and I wanted to call you everyday I was gone. No hard feelings about the slap, I'll call you tonight after I hang out with the fellas. Love ya"

Rashi felt a little better after talking his mom as far as the slap went. What was still on his mind and what he planned on calling her about that evening was who told her that. He was careful at home and around his sisters as far as his business being out there and them hearing it. He was like 5,000 miles away, this felt like an inside job.

When Rashi got to the shop, nobody was there. He sat in his chair and thought about who could have told his Mama about Europe. Rashad? Nope. He'd been busy getting ready for school. But his mom was asking a bunch of questions about college, too, so maybe it was Rashad, or Nehi. He was getting ready for school, too. Nehi hadn't really been the same since the whole Aria incident. But if he didn't say anything to his mom about what went down with Aria, why would he tell her about Europe? It couldn't have been JuJuan. JuJuan hadn't even been in the state lately. Maybe JuJuan told Carrie and Carrie let it slip or something. There was the off chance that Aria said something, but how in the hell would she know?

Rashi let Aria meet his mom once before he stopped talking to her, but for some unknown reason, Aria kept in touch with his mom after he let her go. He figured she kept in touch for one of two reasons: she wanted to use his Mama to get back with him or revenge. But how would Aria know about anything he did in Europe?

3:00 was fast approaching, so Rashi did a little last minute cleaning. While he was sweeping, Rashad walked in.

"What up, my guy? JuJuan in town for a cut or is he still at school?" Rashi hadn't heard anything from Preach, so he figured Shad knew.

"He's here. He's just running a little late. He had to pick up Nehi. This clown has some real drama these days, but I'll let him tell you himself."

"Come on bro, you brought it up. What's good?"

"Can't. This is his drama. I can't be telling everybody. Alls I know is this clown is juggling women like an actual clown."

"Not Nehi! The way he lectured me forever when I was messing with his girl Aria? And the way he was all up under Kionna in Europe? I know he ain't cheating on her."

"Since you brought it up, let me ask you a question. Why did you get with Aria? You knew she was Nehi's girl. That was super dirty my guy. I mean, when the whole thing was going on up until now, I never said a word. I have to ask now cause I don't even know if I can bring a girl around you. How do you sleep with you best friend's girl?"

"How you sleep with your girl's sister?"

Rashi was taking offense to the, 'can I bring a girl around you' part and spoke a little hasty. He knew he was wrong for what he said. "My bad Shad, that was way out of line. I'm going to tell you like I told Nehi. I slept with her cause she ain't worth cuffing." Cuffing meant making a girlfriend of, dating exclusively, spending quality time with and not just looking of sex. "To me, she's like the girls I smashed while we were in Europe. Small naps." Small naps or quick lays. "I could have just told him, but we both know what would have happened."

"He would have taken her word over yours and somehow y'all would have gotten into it." Rashad knew the answer to this because that's almost what happened. Rashi told Nehi to watch Aria. Aria told Nehi that Rashi was the aggressor. Nehi believed her, until he caught Aria at the shop. She dumped him the next day and the rest is history.

"Exactly. So I showed him, plus I wasn't really getting "Great One" vibes from her anyway. You know her stalking ass is still in touch with my Mama?"

"Seriously?"

"Yep, she was visiting and calling her when we were gone. It ain't like I'm leading her on, she knows the deal. I flat out told her that I got what I wanted from her so we didn't even need to be around each other. She did the whole crying thing, but at least I was honest with her."

"You didn't think that was kind of bogus? Just telling her like that?"

"Shad, the fact of the matter is that she did Nehi wrong. Was I supposed to give her a chance to do me wrong? You gotta look at it for what it is. I did it to show him what he was dealing with. If I just told him, he wouldn't have believed me, and then we would have got into it anyway. With me proving she was dirty, yeah we got into it, but he's over her and he's found a new girl. I think as far as Kionna goes, Nehi finally has a Great One."

Rashad knew Nehi was back to his old ways, and was dealing with Aria again, but he didn't want to tell Rashi. He didn't feel it was his place. Rashad wasn't very big on keeping secrets, but he wasn't into overstepping his bounds. To him, telling Rashi that Nehi was back with Aria again, would definitely be overstepping his bounds.

Just as he was thinking this, Nehi and JuJuan came through the door. Nehi didn't seem to be in the best mood, but Rashad and Rashi soon realized why. "Yall ain't going to believe this, but Aria goes to the same school as Kionna. Kionna has seen her on campus like five different times. I don't know what to do."

Rashi thought it was funny, but before he could laugh he realized that Nehi was talking about Aria in his presence. "So Aria's at school with your girl, what's the big deal about that?"

"Ra, let the people in college actually deal with the college problems."

That was a low blow. "Seems like you've been holding that one in sir." Rashi was still sweeping up the shop. He was about to say something low as well, but decided to keep it light. "Right, so how many of these college cats got bald spots?" Before everyone had a chance to laugh, Rashi decided to throw in the low blow. "And just so you know, I knew where Aria was going to school way before your lame ass walked through the door. She's been inviting me on campus pretty much since I got back into the country. What you didn't get any invites?"

Nehi looked like he'd been hit in the stomach. Rashad knew he had to intervene, but he really didn't want to. Honestly he wanted to see where this was going. He knew it would be better for all parties involved if he said something though.

"Chill, clowns! Rashi cool out! Nehi you too, you started it bro. You know we need cuts, so chill." He turned to Jujuan who was just watching with his mouth wide open. "Preach say something."

Any other time JuJuan would have said something, but there were two reasons why this time he didn't. Number one, the whole "Preach" thing. He was actually tired of people looking at him like he was a 19 year old preacher. And number two, this was a situation that needed to be addressed. When Rashi and Nehi got into it the first time about Aria, they didn't really settle it. They just kind of acted as if it didn't happen.

"You heard Nehi start it, sometimes when you start stuff like that, you need to deal with whatever comes back. I think that if Nehi didn't want to hear this, he shouldn't have said what he said. Seriously, what did you expect to hear when you said that?"

"Chill, okay. Everybody just chill. I came to get a haircut, can I get one?" Rashad, like JuJuan, wanted to see what was going to transpire, but didn't want there to be trouble in the crew. Also, he knew that Nehi was wrong too.

"Nehi, you started that, bro. You got some animosity toward Rashi or what?"

Rashi didn't even wait for his answer. He had his cape in his hand and waved Rashad over. "If you do, can you get out of my shop? I told your ass when it went down with me and Aria. I didn't tell her to leave you and the reason I did her like I did was because she pulled that garbage on you. It's come to a point now that either you believe me or you don't. If you don't then get out of my shop, my guy. I've looked out for you probably more than anybody, so if you think I snaked you like that, then do you." Rashi was serious. He knew what people thought of him for the whole Aria thing. He didn't care, but he knew he wasn't wrong for what he did. There wasn't any doubt in his mind that smashing Aria was going to be seen as wrong, but he knew what he was doing. He needed to show Nehi and everybody else what kind of girl Aria was.

"Okay, this is the deal. I'm kind of messing with Aria again."

"WHAT?" Rashi was shocked.

"WHAT?" So was JuJuan.

"So, talking about her around you is kind of awkward."

"But you know how she is. You know for a fact that she'll pull some bogus shit for the next cat to show her some attention." Rashi was honestly trying to understand what was going on.

"As a matter of fact, I wasn't even showing her attention. She just basically asked for the pipe work.

"Don't you got a girlfriend? As I recall you had a cutie named Kionna the last time I checked. And why don't you seem phased at all by any of this, Shad?" JuJuan noticed that all the questions and looks of surprise were coming from him and Rashi.

"I knew. This clown had Aria at his dorm when he moved in and she stopped by again unannounced when Kionna was there."

"Word? Ever since I moved, I don't know. It's like I'm out of the loop."

"Me too. Rashad was the only one he told, and to be honest, I don't even think this cat would have told me anyhow."

Rashi was actually right. He would have been the last person Nehi told.

JuJuan wanted to know what was going on with Kionna more than anything. "So Nehi, what's the deal? You still with Kionna or what?"

"Ever since the whole Aria thing, I don't know. She ain't really spoke to me since."

"Duh, your ex popped up at your dorm while she was there. What was she supposed to do?"

"Dog, I don't even know what to tell her. The thing is that I know Aria shouldn't have been there, but at the same time I'm glad she was. I've talked to Aria like everyday since and not to Kionna once. I went to her dorm with Rashad and I couldn't really get her to talk much then."

JuJuan heard Nehi say that he'd talked to Aria like every day and took it one way, while Rashi heard it and took it another. Rashi didn't want to interrupt or anything just yet, and he wanted to see where their conversation was going. He saved his question for when Nehi and JuJuan were done with their conversation. JuJuan took Nehi's talking to Aria everyday as a terribly bad idea.

"So, let me get this straight. You said you're talking to Aria like every day and not talking to your girl? Shouldn't you be trying to talk to Kionna every day and not so much to Aria? Everybody in here knows that Aria is a bogus broad and we all know that she did you wrong. But ever since she rolled up and upset Kionna, you've been talking to ***her*** everyday? Do you even want to be with Kionna? Cause from what I'm hearing, this whole talking to Aria on the daily is going to cause more problems than anything else. Have you even tried calling Kionna everyday like you're doing with Aria?"

"That's the thing. I really don't know what I want. I mean this has been a fun year with Kionna, and don't get me wrong, I think she's a good girl. But Aria gets me."

Rashi couldn't help but say something at this point. "Gets you? Was she getting you when she was sleeping with me? Was she getting you when she broke your heart and had you walking around looking all depressed and shit? I mean really does she get you? Or are you on some ole 'I'm whipped' type shit?"

Nehi was ready for any question except for the one he just got and from the person he'd just gotten it from. Rashi had been pretty cool about not mentioning the situation in Nehi's presence and he had been extra careful not to get on Nehi's bad side since then either. "When I say's she gets me, I mean we can talk about whatever and even though she did what she did, I dig her."

"And since you say you talk to her every day, let me ask you a quick question." Rashi knew that this question would cause some drama if the answer was yes, but he had to ask. It had been bothering him since he'd left his mom's place earlier that morning. "Have you mentioned my vacation activities to Aria? Please tell me that you didn't cause if she's the one that said something to my momma, that falls directly on you. If you had something to do with it, then I just might have to beat yo ass!"

"We talked about you a time or two but I doubt she said something to your momma. The only reason I said anything about you to her was to kinda let her know that you weren't thinking about her. You know, to kinda keep a repeat performance from happening."

"I hear you my guy, but I'm serious, Nehi, if I find out that Aria had anything to do with my momma finding out about Europe, it's going to be forget the whole walking on eggshells thing I've been doing around you since me and Aria. I'm gone flat out beat yo ass, Nehi."

This was getting way too serious as far as JuJuan was concerned so he decided to try and change the subject. "I think I want a double lining this time, Ra. Just to do something a little different. Especially since I'll be out of town for the next couple weeks. You know, stand out and maybe get you a little clientele in the process."

Rashad obviously didn't catch that JuJuan was trying to change the subject. "Yeah, yeah, yeah, you want a double lining. I'm trying to see where this is going. I know I ain't said nothing to Ra's momma. You ain't said nothing. Nehi says he hasn't, and I know for a fact Rashi ain't said nothing himself. So basically all fingers point to Aria. She's the only one who knows Ra's momma and since Nehi's been running his mouth, she's also the only one who knows about Europe. I mean the ***real*** story that goes along with Europe. By the way, she know anything about me in Europe? Or you for that matter, cause you were there with Kionna."

Nehi was once again speechless, because he knew deep down that Aria had to be the one who told Rashi's mom. And as if Rashi was reading his mind he said, "dude if she told, we boxing. Then after that everything will go back to normal. I mean the fact that my momma knows about what I was doing in Europe is dirty. Since I can't do nothing to her, I gotta get at you. So don't take it personal You're my guy and after I beat that ass, I'll even keep cutting your hair."

Ever since the barber shop incident, Rashi had been feeling a little uneasy around Nehi. He called Rashad and they decided to hang out the next night. First he had to figure out how he was going to get the information out of his mom as to who told her about Europe. He wasn't very comfortable about the idea of lying to his mom, but he knew he was going to have to lie to her in order to get it. Rashi was working on different ideas and had close to 15. Of the 15, just three of them really seemed to make real sense to him.

1. He could approach his mom like, "What did Aria tell you? She told me she told you a few things jokingly, and when I told her you'd taken whatever it was seriously she told me to just ask you what she said." That sounded okay, but he seriously doubted his mom would believe that.

2. There was the, "You know Aria hates me. What did she tell you that was so bad that you would take her word over mine?" This idea would work better than the first seeing how Rashi's mom knew how Rashi felt about Aria and vice versa. The only thing about this idea

was that, although she did know about their brief history, what were the chances that she would tell Rashi what was said about him by Aria? Would she not tell what was said thinking that she was somehow protecting Aria from him?

3. There was finally the, "I've talked to Aria and she said some things to you that were kind of exaggerated. I can tell you what I did in Europe, but I need to know what you were told by Aria." The only drawback from this approach was that he'd have to give up some info. Everybody knows that you have to give a little to get a little, so Rashi was leaning toward this idea. He felt that although this wasn't a very good idea from the giving of information standpoint, he'd gain more than just the knowledge that Aria was the person who told his mom about Europe. He felt that by giving information he'd be opening the lines of communication with his mom, letting her feel like she's included in his busy life, and he felt that she would trust him again.

It was when he was about to call his mom when another idea crossed his mind, call Aria. He hadn't talked to her in ages, and if he lied to her it'd be a lot easier than lying to his mom and easier to get the information he needed. If he called Aria pretending to be upset because his mom "told me what you told her," he felt that Aria would crack and pretty much confess. Rashi hung up the phone and began to look for Aria's number. It had been a long while since he called her so it wasn't just hanging around in his cell. He was in deep in his top drawer going through sheet after sheet of scrap paper when his phone rang. He didn't immediately recognize the voice on the other end:

"Hello, is Rashi available?"

"Speaking, um, I don't recognize the number, so can you tell me who this is?

"I don't even know if I should be calling you but I had you number and I needed someone to talk to so I called you. Rashi, this is Kionna."

"Kionna? Kionna as in Nehi's girl Kionna? You aren't Kionna cause Kionna would know to call JuJuan, Rashad, or one of her friends if she needed someone to talk to. Anyone but Rashi. So really, who is this?"

"Rashi this is really Kionna. Am I bothering you?"

"Nah, I'm just shocked to be hearing from you, shorty. How you doing?"

"Not so well. I haven't talked to Nehi in like three and a half weeks. For the first week, I wasn't speaking to him. Then I noticed that he just hasn't been calling me period. I know you aren't the tightest with him, but just from being around you I know you're the most honest. Even if it means hurting someone's feelings. So I called you looking for the truth. What's going on with Nehi?"

"I don't know if I should get involved. I mean, to be honest I'd love to tell you, but the fact of the matter is that if I do get involved it'll look like a revenge thing, and I'm not into that."

"Revenge for what? You slept with his girl. Why would you be trying to get revenge on Nehi?"

"Damn, I know I'm going to regret this, but I'm going tell you everything. To be quite honest, I think you should have already known all of this by now anyway. But since no one has bothered to tell you, I guess I will. Here is the deal, Nehi is confused and at this point he says he doesn't know what he wants as far as you're concerned."

"What?"

"Well since the whole Aria situation went down, he's been talking to her on the regular. Now when he came to my shop talking about that, we all tried talking sense into him cause we all know you're a way better woman than Aria. His exact words were that 'Aria gets me.'"

"Aria gets him?"

"That's exactly what I said. I mean I know from personal experience that she's a bogus chick, and that she will do him wrong at the drop of a hat. Kionna, I'm one of Nehi's best friends, or at least I used to be, and I can tell you first hand shorty, you deserve better. I mean this cat obviously wants to deal with the girl who did him wrong. You're worrying about him, and even pretty much called the one dude he wouldn't want you to ever call trying to understand what's going on. He, on the other hand, is chasing after the wrong girl. You stormed off because you were justly pissed off about the situation, and instead of giving you the time you needed to recover or even apologize, he went running after the girl who basically shit on him. I mean we both know I don't deserve a girl like you, but if I had one, I wouldn't leave her for a girl who did me dead wrong."

"So he left me?"

"I'm not saying that. But I wouldn't even leave that up to question. I mean I think the fact that he's talking to Aria every day is the exact opposite of what he should be doing. But that's just me. I mean I've never heard you speak badly about Aria so I always figured he's bad mouthed me to you enough that you thought that it was all my fault. I'm fine with that. The fact of the matter is, I think that even you know that if I initiated the whole Aria thing, she'd have to be dirty to let it happen. By the way, I didn't initiate it and I went through with it cause at the time I actually thought that Nehi deserved better. In my own sick and twisted way I thought that I was doing the kid a favor. Even after all this time, I've always tried to respect him after that. And up until yesterday at the shop, I've pretty much walked on eggshells around him. I was okay with the fact that I met you last and that around me he has you in handcuffs. I mean I wouldn't trust me just yet either, but from the moment I met you, I knew you were a great one. I was happy that Nehi was finally over Aria and found a dime on top of that."

"Whatever Rashi, I know you don't really think I'm a dime."

"I do. Ask Rashad. When I finally got to meet you, I told Rashad that I thought you were a dime. My exact words were something like 'Nehi found a dime, bro, but I'll just take five twos.'"

"You're kind of funny, Rashi, and I believe you on the five twos thing. You did your thing in Europe. So can I ask you a personal question?"

"Of course."

"The revenge thing, what was that about? What did Nehi do to you?"

"That's part of the whole Aria thing, too. It's an ugly situation. This is how I know Aria ain't changed at all. Somehow in this three weeks that your guy and Aria have been talking, who I'm sleeping with just so happened to come up. Now I understand that I did Nehi wrong a long time ago. Apparently that was enough for him to go around spreading my business. And to Aria no less. Anyway, he tells her and this broad goes and tells my momma. The thing is, my mom, as strong as she is, had serious issues with what most people call playas or whatever. I personally feel like I'm just enjoying my youth. I do want to eventually settle down and get married. So I go and see my mom and all of a sudden it's like I'm the enemy. She's yelling and telling me how I ain't shit. I took offense to it cause me and mom dukes are pretty tight. I couldn't figure out for the life of me who could have told her. I asked Nehi, JuJuan, and Rashad they all said no. Nehi let it slip that he'd been talking to Aria every day and I just put two and two together. I actually told Nehi that I was going to beat his ass. I mean I also told him we'd still be cool, but for this, a beat down was in order. Now I can't even do that."

"Why not?"

"As concerned as you sound, the fact that I told you this will probably make it look like a revenge type thing and then it'll appear we're even."

"Rashi, I know it's Monday, and the shop is closed, but I was wondering if you were busy. It ain't like you're thinking. I just want to talk to you in person about Nehi and I need your advice as to what I should do."

"I'm chillin all day, so I guess we can go and maybe have lunch or something."

"How's three o'clock?"

"Fine with me, shorty. I'll pick you up or do you want to meet somewhere?"

"You can pick me up, but I'm kind of far from the southside."

"It's cool, I'll see you at 2:45, woman."

Rashi took the address and then knew what he had to do, cancel with Rashad. That was easy enough. Rashad would understand, especially since he'd been chillin with Caryl basically every minute since they got back. But what was he going to tell him? Rashi didn't like to lie to his guys, and in situations like this where he was just meeting up with a ***friend*** to talk, he thought that the truth should be enough. He wasn't stupid either though. He'd had a huge blow up with Nehi on Sunday and now Monday he's going out with his girl? That's bound to look fishy, even in Rashad's eyes.

"Here we go," thought Rashi, "I just know that when I call this clown and I tell him that I'm having lunch with Kionna he's going to lose it. Especially after yesterday in the shop. All that shit I talked and here I go again alone with a girl who's messing around with Nehi. Damn, what's wrong with me? Am I really as bogus as everybody thinks I am? Let me quit trippin. It's only lunch. At lunch, I'm going to tell her to get back with Nehi. So, I'm actually doing a good thing. Even after this clown did me bogus, I'm going to tell her to forgive him and try to rebuild their relationship. I don't agree with him talking to Aria every day and not talking to his girl, but I ain't his daddy so I can't tell him what to do. I'm going to go to this lunch, talk up my boy Nehi, and hopefully for once, I'll be the reason two people come together. My main goal today is to talk up Nehi. Kionna is a friend and she's a good fit for Nehi. She called me as a friend and I'm going to make sure I treat this situation the same way she does. Let me call this clown and cancel."

"What up, clown?" Rashad knew who it was before the phone even rang. "What you doing? Getting ready to hit this Harold's? I was just about to call and ask if Caryl can tag along. She ain't really doing nothing today and when I told her we were chillin, she asked if she could roll with us."

"That's why I'm calling, Shad. I don't think I'm going to make it. Something came up."

"Oh, okay, I feel ya. Ra got a freak lined up for the day, huh? Who is it this time?"

"It's yo momma!!! Nah, I'm kidding, but it really ain't like that at all. Something just came up"

"Really? Damn, you going to fight Nehi ain't you? I don't wanna miss that either. I was telling Caryl about it and neither does she. Dude, you really gone box him over something Aria said?"

"It ain't like that either, clown. I'm having lunch with a friend."

"What friend?"

This was the moment Rashi was trying to avoid, but since Rashad asked he had to tell him. "Dog, when I tell you this, don't be taking it the wrong way. I ain't doing this as revenge or nothing like that. I'm not a snake and I'm doing this to make things right. I was actually about to call my momma when Kionna hit me on my cell. She wanted to talk about Nehi and of all people, she wanted to talk to me about him."

"Oh shit! You know what, don't do it. You bone another female that's with Nehi you're going to clear up like a million things. Like you didn't smash Aria just to prove that she was a bogus chick. You've been saying that trash since it happened. You do anything with Kionna, it's going to be clear that you were on some bullshit and that you're the bogus one. It's going to be clear that you got something against the kid cause this will be his second girlfriend that you clearly crossed the line with. It's going to be obvious that you're the one who needs his ass beat. Ra, you should cancel the Kionna thing and just meet us at Harold's."

It ain't like that Shad. I mean you know how I feel about Aria and you know what I think of Kionna, so-"

"Exactly, I know what you think of Kionna and the thing is that I don't put you giving her the pipe work past you. Nehi is a little confused these days, but you know he's feeling her. I can see you giving her the pipe and moving on like it never happened. Plus he's been running his mouth to Aria, the girl you hate so much, about you and she's been running that information to your momma. I don't know if you are or not, but it looks like this is some getting even type shit."

"Dog, it ain't like that. I know what happened yesterday, but I'm looking past that. I'd rather see Nehi with Kionna than Aria. I ain't his daddy and I can't make him get with the female I want him to be with, but I do want him to know that he is my guy and that I do have his best interest in mind. Plus if this works out and he knows I played a part in it, he'll finally be able to trust me around his girl."

"Like I said, I think you should cancel, but you're a grown ass man. Do you, clown. Just don't make shit worse cause of Aria."

"Shad, on everything, I'm going to talk up Nehi and try to get them back on some together type shit. You know I'm all about love and bringing people together."

"Right, and I'm all about unicorns and rainbows and shit. Whatever clown, just don't make matter worse."

"Aiight my guy, I'll get at you as soon as I get back from lunch with Kionna. Maybe we can go bowling or something, me, you, and Caryl."

"We'll see. One."

"One hundred."

After getting off the phone with Rashad, Rashi felt okay with what was going down. Although Rashad was all about caution and making sure he didn't make things worse, he was ultimately cool with the lunch. Rashi wasn't trying to get Rashad's approval, but knowing that his friend trusted him made going to this lunch easier. Rashi was on a mission and he was planning on doing the unexpected even after yesterday. He was planning on doing something good for Nehi.

"I think you should call him." Up until he'd said this, the conversation between them had been pretty light. Rashi was letting it build up to this, while he also found it hard to ignore the big pink elephant in the room. "The thing is, if you aren't speaking to him and he doesn't know how you feel, what should he do? I know you probably think he should call you, but men just aren't that smart sometimes. Also, you aren't really answering his calls and what not. I don't have a girlfriend. It's not cause I can't find one, but because you have to do a lot of thinking when you have a girlfriend. Even times like this, when the answer is obvious and staring you in the face, are harder when you do have someone. I'm sure Nehi is somewhere thinking that by not calling you for all this time, he is somehow giving you your space. You know, letting you vent a little bit. The two mistakes he's made, from what I hear, are that he's waited way too long to call you and he's been calling the Big A instead. When he stopped calling though, you admitted that you weren't trying to talk to him."

"The big what?" Kionna couldn't help laughing. She knew he was talking about Aria. She just wanted to hear him say it again.

"The Big A, that's what we call Aria. Behind her back of course. I wanna call her that to her face so bad it's ridiculous. I just know that I'd never hear the end of it."

"So, you think that I should call him? I mean he has to realize that he hasn't talked to me since he came by my dorm a couple weeks ago."

"He knows. It's just that as long as he's talking to Aria all the time, talking to you just hasn't really occurred to him. You know, out of sight, out of mind. You call him tonight and he'll forget about Aria's big ass by tomorrow."

"You think? I mean it's been three weeks."

"Take it from me, shorty. You call him and let him know that everything is good and he'll come around. For the most part that's what he's waiting for. Since he's been not talking to you I think it's been because he feels like you need your space. Think about it, he came all the way out to DeKalb just to see if you were talking to him. You said no apparently and now it's one of those things where he's waiting on you to be ready to talk."

"What about Aria though?"

"What about her?"

"You've seen her and you call her the Big A yourself, so you know she outweighs me by like 60 pounds. I just don't want her trying to beat me up cause I called my man. I like Nehi, but I ain't trying to fight no big broads for him."

"Don't even worry about her. She knows she in the wrong and on top of that if she wanted to beat you down, she would have been beat you down."

"What you mean by that?"

"You do know she goes to Northern too, right?" He could tell by the look on her face that she knew. "Damn, Nehi ain't even mentioned that to you? He knows. We all know. We knew when he first met you cause she was there before you. To be honest when he first met you, I thought that he was up there trying to get at her and he saw you. I still think that. Now I see that he ain't even told you that you and the Big A are like a rock throw apart. That's crazy, I mean she could have rolled on you at any time now and he ain't told you to watch your back?"

"I know she goes here, I mean you can't miss her big ass. We just haven't been talking much, so maybe he doesn't know that I know. I'm sure I've mentioned it though when he came by. Your boy is kinda bogus. Not to be in your business again, but what exactly happened with you and Aria?"

"So he mentioned that but couldn't mention that you were at the same school as Aria? That's cool. I ain't ashamed of nothing that I do, I can tell you. I just basically exposed her fat ass. She was with Nehi and they were doing their thing and she met me. She knew I was Nehi's guy and she still wanted to sleep with me cause I was making a lil dough cutting heads and stuff. She just kept coming at me behind Nehi's back. Don't nobody know this, but I told Nehi what was going down and he didn't believe me. Now you saw me in Europe, so you know I get a variety of females. Aria just ain't in my league. Anyhow, he believed her when she said that I was hitting on her so eventually I just slept with her and exposed her fat ass. Me and Nehi ain't been the same since and I know Rashad and JuJuan think that I'm bogus as far as that situation goes. I still say I did it for a good reason. I knew he needed somebody more like you. By more like you, I mean a girl who has his well-being in mind and ain't just looking for a come up."

"So you had sex with the Big A?"

"Yep, had to. I had to put her out there. The only problem with that was that during that time she was coming to my crib all the time behind Nehi's back and she met my people- my mom and all my sisters. My sisters can't stand her, but since she liked to eat, she got on my mom's good side. I think she actually told my mom about my escapades on our little trip. I mean, that's bothering me, too, Nehi is at a point where he's telling Aria everything cause he's not talking to you. We had a big ass fight in the shop Sunday. I kinda told your guy that I was going to beat his ass."

"What? Why did you tell him that?"

"He told Aria about what I was doing in Europe and she told my mom. So of course my mom comes down on me about it. I told you before that I'm not ashamed about what I do, but I don't want my momma to know. I was little upset Sunday so instead of just asking, I told him I was going to beat his ass. I was serious at the time, but after talking to you I just want to do some good for a change. I like you and I think since I can't have you, at least my guy should."

"And why can't you?"

"Girl, stop playing!"

Chapter 3

Rashad was having lunch with Caryl while Rashi was out starting trouble. Rashad had cooked for Caryl and although he loved cooking for his girl, he was hoping all the time that she wouldn't mention it to his guys. Since getting back, Rashad was busy with school and playing ball, but he made sure he made time for Caryl. He didn't know if he was in love or not, but he was definitely feeling her like no other. He told himself he loved Jennifer when they were together, but this was something better. He was older for one and for two, Caryl didn't have any sisters. The whole dorm was smelling good, one of Rashad's many recipes he got from his mom. She was definitely going to be impressed with this.

"So what's going on with you and your guys? I'm not trying to be nosy, but we've been dating a few weeks and as much as I hear about them, it sucks that I haven't seen them yet. You hiding me Shad?"

"Man! Drama, drama, and more drama! Rashi got into it with Nehi at the shop on Sunday- Also, I wouldn't hide you at all. Once you meet these clowns, you'll be seeing them more than you want. For now though, I just want you to myself."

"Rashi is the barber, right? I mean does your barber hang out with y'all?"

"Okay, I should tell you. Rashi is not only the barber, but he's part of the clique. He's what you call the player in the crew. He boned the Big A a while back. That's Nehi's ex girl. He said he was doing it to show Nehi what kind of girl she was. Nehi says he did it cause he has sex with anything that walks."

"So which is it?"

"I think it is a little bit of both. I mean Rashi told me something a while ago and every time I see this cat talking to a new girl it comes back to me. He took me aside one day and was like, 'Barbers are some pussy getting ass cats.' And ever since he said it, I've noticed that it's true."

"Wait, so let me get this straight. Rashi slept with his friend's girl, and you slept with your first love's sister? Y'all crazy. I mean when you told me that, I figured that would be as bad as it got. Shad, I know we talked about it and I accepted it cause I figured that the whole sister thing was bad enough. So you give the pipe work to the sisters and he gives it to everybody else?"

"Caryl, I dig you a lot kid, but you gotta chill on that whole Jennifer situation. I mean yeah I did that, but how long ago was that? I dealt with the situation when it happened. Do I gotta relive it every day? You seem to mention it every damn day, shorty. Up until you said that, I was enjoying spending time with you. Caryl, it's come to a point where I think you have a decision to make. Either you can deal with my past or you can't. I already lived through the situation and look how you reacted. You think I'm going to want to talk about other shit from my past with you when you won't even let that go? I mean you make it seem like I cheated on you. The thought ain't even crossed my mind and I need you to know that. Instead, you just keep focusing on my past and that kind of pisses me off, kid. So like I said, you got a decision to make. It seems like you believe that bullshit saying 'once a player always a player.' By the way, that saying doesn't make sense with anything in life so miss me with that shit. I hate to do this Caryl, but I'm going to ask you to leave."

"What?"

"You have some thinking to do and I don't think that you should be doing it here. Hit me whenever you make your decision, kid. I mean, Caryl, females throw it at me basically every day and I steadily stay faithful to you, and for what? I have no idea. If you want to be with someone you feel like you can trust then I suggest that's what you do. Sorry shorty, but I can't be in a relationship where everything I do is going to be viewed under the microscope. So, like I said, I'm sorry, but you gotta roll kid."

"You serious, Rashad? You can't be serious."

"I am. Caryl, hit me when you've made up your mind." Rashad got up from the table and started walking towards the door. When this first happened, he wasn't sure how he was going to feel doing something this dramatic. Now that it was out and he'd said what was on his mind, he knew that it was the right thing to do. "Sorry Caryl, but I need you to be sure that you want to be involved in this relationship. I want to be with you, but I can't just let you constantly remind me of my past mistakes. It's been three weeks woman and at this point it's starting to feel like years. If you think about it, you'll realize that's not helping the relationship either."

At this point he was standing at the door with it open. Caryl was getting up from the table with a look of utter disbelief on her face. "Like I said kid, just hit me when you've made up your mind. Either way, let me know what the deal is. I'll Holla!"

She left, with all the delicious smells in the air and food everywhere. Rashad would just share it with his roommate or something. He threw down though, cooking was his thing outside of hooping.

After Caryl left, Rashad had a lot of thinking to do. Not just about him and Caryl but about him and the way people looked at him. Why do I even care? People are going to think what they want to think anyway. Had I not slept with Jennifer's sister, and we broke up about something else, it still would have shocked people. People thought we were the so-called perfect couple, but we had our share of problems just like anyone else. Trying to get people to think this or that about me, I have passed on a few nice broads. I was worried about what this person or that person would think. I didn't cheat on my wife, I cheated on a girlfriend from high school. I have a whole lot of life in front of me.

Look at this dude, Rashi. He messes around with whoever and I guess the people who like him, they like him regardless. I know broads that he's given the pipe and everything, and then flat out done wrong, and they still cool with him. I'd have guessed with what went down with Aria that him and Nehi would be at each others' throats, but somehow they're still tight. Not as tight as they were, but they're still guys and you gotta respect that. It's been years and the same broads who thought that I was a dog for what went down with Jennifer think that I'm a dog to this very day. I don't know, I guess that whole not caring mentality just doesn't work with me like it does with Ra. For some reason, it bothers the hell out of me when Caryl starts on the 'you and Jennifer' bullsh-

He couldn't even finish the thought before someone was knocking on his door. He knew who it was before he even asked. Jackie from the women's basketball team had been paying him a bunch of attention lately. He'd told her about Caryl, but she was persistent and didn't really seem to care much about her.

"Who goes there?" Rashad's cousin in Florida answered his door like that and for the last couple years, Rashad had been answering like that too. At home in his room, the buzzer at his mom's apartment, in his dorm room, wherever, "who goes there" was hot to him so he used it all the time.

"Jackie. I was stopping by to see if you wanted to go to the café with me."

"Come on in, woman. I just cooked, but I'll go with you if you want to kick it for a lil while."

"Damn, I still can't believe the way they take care of yall. The men's hoop squad is aiight, but damn this is ridiculous. A kitchen, kid? How the hell you get a kitchen?"

"That's what you get when you're one of the most recruited players in the country, big head. They wanted my guy Rashi up here as well, but they couldn't convince him to come to college."

"He a D-boy or something?"

"Nah, nothing like that. He's a barber. He's been cutting hair forever and that's basically what he wanted to do. He always said that college wasn't nothing but extra classes and he wasn't trying to take no extra classes. Anyhow, if you want, you can eat some of what I made. Me and Caryl got into it so we ended up not even finishing lunch or whatever."

"What you make? I ain't trying to die from food poisoning."

"You grew up on the Westside, kid. Ain't nothing here capable of killing you. Anyhow, I made fried chicken, mac and cheese from scratch, none of that out of the box shit, and some broccoli. You want some? Or you wanna go to the café?"

"I'm going to go with the café. I'll have some of your cooking when it's meant for me and not Caryl. Don't need her all in my face about some mac and cheese. And what did you get into it with her about today? I mean if my man cooked for me I'd at least save the argument for another time."

"First, I'm not her man. We're trying to work on that now. And second, it was basically about a couple things from my past." Rashad could have easily discussed this with his guys and told Jackie that he didn't want to talk about it, but for some reason he wanted to talk to her. It was at this moment that Rashad realized that he might be attracted to Jackie. She was cute, tall, and even that walk that made it obvious that she was a hooper. "She was taking a situation that had nothing to do with her or me and comparing it to my past situations. Don't get me wrong. In the whole scheme of things she may have had a small point, but the way she brought it out was like she was trying to judge me or whatever. Anyway, if we're going to the café, let me put this food away and grab my keys."

"All you're having is a Gatorade and cookie?" They were at the café and Jackie was about to pig out, that is until she saw Rashad with a chocolate chip cookie and a Gatorade. "You ain't about to watch me eat all this and you eat just that. Take one of these wings or something."

"I'm good. I'll just bother you with my presence and ask a couple questions while you do you."

"What kind of questions?"

"Shit I wanna know. Like first off, you got a man or are you dating?"

"Neither, I was with my high school boyfriend for like a year and a half. To be honest, it got to a point where I just wasn't feeling Big Josh like that but stayed with him cause I just wasn't trying to be by myself. When we graduated since we were going to be in different states as far as going to school was concerned, we just decided to call it quits. I honestly think that he was ready to call it quits, too."

"Seriously? Why were you ready to call it quits in the first place?"

"We were just two different people. I mean we make great friends but a not so great couple."

"Okay, I feel ya. So are you dating currently?"

"Nope, waiting on the right guy to come along and I guess sweep me off my feet."

"Sweep you off your feet, huh? How would a guy sweep you off your feet, they're so damn big?"

"Shut up stupid! Anyhow, I don't know exactly, just do something that requires some thought, I guess. I've been to plenty of movie and dinner type dates so that's not going to do it. I'm not saying it has to be extravagant, but something thoughtful and fun. Keep me smiling and you've pretty much got me in the palm of your hands."

"You got a certain type?"

"Damn, you got a lot of questions, shorty. Let me ask you a few … that's okay, I've seen Caryl, I know your type."

"Do you? Then tell me cause I don't have a certain type. To be honest I've been out with more Jackie's than Caryl's. I mean physically you basically fit what I'm looking for, excluding that manly ass walk and the way you sit …"

"How do I sit?"

"Like you're ready to go into the game. There are times when I wanna blow a whistle just to see if you jump up like 'I'm going in for Suzy!' So like I was saying, Caryl didn't get my attention based on the way she looked, kinda like you were saying, when I first met her I couldn't stop smiling."

"What about now?"

"Not so much …"

Chapter 4

"Can you believe that clown? He said he was going to beat my ass. I mean I wanted to fight him when the situation with you went down, but I know we've been friends since the stone age so I let it slide and dealt with you. Now he's talking about boxing me. That's ridiculous, kid." Nehi was kind of thinking out loud and talking to Aria at the same time. Since the incident at the shop he'd been through this in his head like a hundred times. Although Aria was in his dorm room, this was one of the few times as of late that they weren't all over each other.

"So what you going to do?"

"No idea. Let me ask you this though. Why you go to his momma anyways? I mean you say you're over him and that you want to focus on us, and then as soon as you get a little information, you at his momma's? Were you hoping to see him or something?"

"I don't know why I went to his momma's. I guess I just wanted his mom to know what kind of person that he is. He's a dog and I just don't like that fact that in his eyes I'm this dirty broad. In school he had everyone believing that I came at him and cheated on you."

"What exactly happened then? I was under the impression that he was kind of ballin in high school so you focused on him instead of me."

"It doesn't really matter now what happened. What matters is that we should be back together. So when you going to tell your so-called girlfriend that she's out the picture? I see her all the time at school. I can tell her for you."

"I'm good. I'll tell her that when you tell me what happened with you and Ra. Until now, I was never really interested but seeing as to how I'm almost back in the situation I was in when I was in high school, I think I need to know. You know, so that I don't make the same mistake twice."

"Okay Nehi, I'm going to tell you everything, but you can't get mad. You have to remember that it was the past. Okay, baby?"

"Okay."

"Well of course I knew y'all were friends. Who didn't? At first I wasn't really attracted to him like that and I was focused on us. Then you and I started to have little fall outs and we weren't really doing anything. One Friday night we went to a basketball game and I think that was when the attraction started. I had a couple classes with him and didn't really know him like that. We spoke, but basically because you were his guy and he knew that I was your girlfriend. I noticed that he wasn't a dumb jock, so one day I asked him to help me out with my history and then that lead to you know ..."

"Nah, I don't know." Nehi really did know. Rashi had told him the whole story before and so far she had been honest. Rashi's version just went into a little more detail, which was exactly what he was fishing for. The whole tutoring thing had been on point with Rashi's story, but in Ra's story, while helping Aria with her history at her house unsupervised, Aria got a little friendly. Aria got hot, took off her sweatshirt, and right in front of Ra, she took off her jeans and put on some shorts. From there, according to Ra, Aria offered him a massage. Things got a lil freaky during the massage and they ended up having sex. "Ra says you came at him and so far from listening to your story he wasn't lying. You were just saying that he's a dog. Make me understand why."

"He was helping me out and he started feeling on me. One thing led to another and we ended up doing it. I know I should have stopped him, but I didn't. I didn't think it was going to go as far as it did."

Did she just lie to me?" That was the first thing to go through Nehi's head. "I've heard Ra's story and it ain't like he just a liar. He approached me and told me about the whole situation with Aria. If he hadn't told me, I'm sure she wouldn't have mentioned it. Why would she lie now, though? I mean now's the time to come clean and somehow she still seems to be hiding something.

"Aria, let me run to grab some food, I got some thinking to do. You can stay here and chill if you want, but I honestly have some thinking to do. I don't want you to leave yet, but if you want to or if you aren't comfortable while I run across campus, you can leave and just hit me later."

She'd sat in his dorm plenty of times before so he would be surprised if she left. He knew that he had to get away from her for a little while because things were on his mind and he just couldn't ignore them.

"I'll be here when you get back. Can you grab me something to eat?"

"Of course, but I just want you to know that this conversation isn't over, kid. I mean, I have some questions and some observations that I need to address. I mean I'm really serious about us and I just need a few things clarified because listening to you tell your version of what went down kind of makes this decision a hard one. Here's something to think about while I'm gone though. If you were in my position, would you be willing to give up a good girl, a girl whose proven to be almost everything I need, for you? You, Aria. A girl who cheated on me with my best friend and from what I can tell isn't even being 100 with me right now. I'm not saying you're lying kid, but from Ra's story and yours, some things add up while others don't. I need time to think cause I honestly don't know if you're lying to me and I'm not comfortable questioning that. So think about it while I'm gone. I'll be back in like 30 minutes, woman."

"Okay, Nehi. I wasn't completely honest about some things that happened that day. It's just that I want this again too and I really don't want you to take that part and judge me or decide that you don't want to be with me because of it."

"Whatever that part is kid, Rashi probably already told me and where am I now?" With those words he walked out. He knew what was coming and in all honesty, he felt like he was ready to hear it come out of her mouth. Knowing all of this from Ra and having time to think about it, even against his guys' words and wishes, he was here still dealing with Aria cause he knew that the history they had was worth more than one mistake. It's just when she started lying about the mistake or making things into something else that it started to look a little funny. "She probably didn't know that Rashi told me everything." Nehi was talking to himself now on the way to the Café. "She probably thought that I was still in the dark about this. That still ain't a reason to lie though. I mean had it been the other way around, would I have lied? I doubt I would, son." Nehi decided to make a phone call since being honest was in his head.

"Hello?"

"Wassup kid, what's good?"

"Nothing, was just thinking about you."

"Were you? That's a good thing. I was thinking about you too, kid. Hence the call." Nehi was getting nervous now, thinking maybe he shouldn't have made the call. Aria was getting under his skin for real. "Kionna, I called cause I have some things on my mind and I wanted to get them off my chest."

"Well you know you can talk to me, Nehi. Wassup? And I've been thinking about some things too that I want to talk about. A friend actually told me to call you and tell you how I'd been feeling with you pulling this disappearing act lately. I know you've been talking to Aria. What's the deal playboy?"

"That's what I was calling about now. I've been spending time with Aria and-"

Before he could finish his sentence, Kionna said the first thing to come into her head, "Well I've been spending time with Rashi. We had lunch this afternoon."

"What?"

"Nothing, Nehemiah. I didn't say anything. So you said you are spending time with Aria?"

"What? What did you just say to me? I'm hoping I heard you wrong. So let's hear what you just said to me one more time. I said I've been spending time with Aria and you said what?"

"I didn't say anything, Nehi. I was listening to you tell me about you and Aria. Whatever you think you heard me say, it's not as bad as you not spending time with me to spend time with an ex. How am I supposed to feel about that?"

Nehi was seeing red now. "Deuces!" He hung up on Kionna and started to pace in a circle. He wasn't hungry anymore and was thinking about just heading back to the dorm. He'd totally forgotten that Aria was there, so when he walked in, the fact that she was staring at him made him even more upset. He grabbed her and started kissing her as passionately as he could. He was determined to get back at Kionna, thinking about all the things should could have done with Ra and how Ra had just threatened him. He stopped. Do I really want to do this with her? He was thinking to himself, She did the same thing Kionna did apparently.

"What's wrong? Why did you stop? Felt like you were finally making the right choice and coming home."

"Get the hell out, Aria!"

"What?"

"Yeah, you gotta go. I got somewhere to be and you being here isn't helping. So get all your shit you got here and just go. If I wanna talk to you later, I got your number. Otherwise I don't see a reason for you to call, so don't."

"What?"

"I gotta go and I need you out my dorm. Nothing personal, wait, it is personal. You could have been honest with me and just lied. I got some real thinking to do and I can't do it with you around. I got some running around to do as well and I'm trying not to be rude, but I need you out now. I don't really care about that look right now kid, you gotta go." Nehi started devising a plan as soon as she left cause at this point, he was just flat out pissed.

Rashi did the same thing twice. What kind of friend is that? He threatened me at the shop, then it turns out he's sleeping with my girl? I have to do something to get back at this clown. He thinks he's untouchable cause of his stupid lifestyle. People won't say anything to him? He's a lame and I'm going to make sure he knows what's good."

Nehi left the dorm not sure where he was going, but with bad intentions. His phone rang. It was Rashi. "Dude don't call me, bitch!

You say you gonna beat my ass? I ought to beat yours! You're a fucking coward. I see you outside the shop, inside the shop, where ever B, I promise you're going to be heavily injured, bro. Ra, I'm not kidding. I swear to God if I catch you slipping, you will never cut another head again!" He hung up on Ra, and knew what he needed to do. I have to do something to his hands.

"What kind of friend, or so-called friend, sleeps with your girl? Who does it twice? This is crazy to me. What did he call me to do, apologize? He thinks I wanna hear that shit?" Nehi was talking to himself now, trying to really understand what was happening. "This clown Rashi can't keep it in his pants to save his life. And my girls? I have a way different type than this dude and still this clown keeps doing the same thing. I should have done something when the Aria situation came up, but I wanted to keep friendship. I'm the idiot. He's piping my girl and I'm still hanging out with this judas. I'll get my haircut somewhere else. Screw Rashi, bro!"

"Hello?"

"What up, B. This Nehi, I had to call somebody, I was over here talking to myself."

"Why was you talking to yourself, fool?"

"This dude, man. This dude Rashi. He wants to get beat down, B. I mean, I gave this dude the benefit of the doubt and he did it again, B. He screwed me, Preach. This so-called friend screwed me. He said he did me a favor by showing me Aria wasn't shit. It was a lie B. He did that shit to me again!"

"Calm down, Neo." JuJuan was shocked by what he'd just been told. He'd been with Rashi's cousin for a while now and the one thing it seemed Rashi regretted more than anything was the smashing the Big A. "Neo, that's crazy son. Did he tell you that himself?"

"Nope, Kionna told me. She was mad I was hanging out with Aria and she told me cause she knew I would lose my mind. Now I don't even regret getting back with Aria cause Kionna is even worse. Dude, she knew what went down with that clown and Aria and her lying ass still slept with him, kid. Dude, she a dirty broad and I'm glad I'm done with her, B. She can kiss my ass."

"Neo, calm down. You're using a lot of 'dudes' and 'Bs' right now. Take a breath, and calm down. She told you she got the goods from Ra? Were y'all arguing or something?"

"Nope, she wasn't even expecting my call. Dude, I don't need you trying to stop me, but I'm breaking his hands, B."

"What?"

"Yeah, he can't keep his damn hands to himself. I breaking them flat out. You were there last weekend when he threatened me and now I find out this clown is once again on that BS? I'm breaking his hands, Preach. Let's see this clown cut hair with casts on. Dude, he's a bitch flat out!"

"Neo once again, calm down. I know he didn't sleep with Kionna. He just wouldn't do that to you clo-"

"He did it before dude. He did the exact same thing with Aria. What you mean he wouldn't do this me? He just did it a couple years ago acting like he was doing it to show me that Aria was dirty. Bullshit! I ought to beat his clown's ass, but I'm breaking his hands, B. I don't care what you say, Preach. Ain't no way I'm letting it slide this time, B. I'm so tired of this clown and all of his BS! He reads a book or two and thinks he can just do whatever he wants. Dude, you know he's full of shit, B. You know and now you're trying to take up for him! You sleeping with his cousin so you don't got nothing to worry about. But the rest of us, we don't trust him and I still can't figure out why we hang with him in the first place!"

"Neo, it ain't cause I'm with his cousin that I don't care, he's been trying to keep it quiet, but he's been dealing with a female for a couple months now. She was like a model or something, met her in Paris. Carrie knows, so of course I know. So that's why I don't think he would do it, at least not now he wouldn't. He's been taking this new girl seriously and pretty much keeping her under wraps. From what I heard she's, some broad he thought was a going to be a cutty buddy, but turns out she lives here. She's supposed to be from Cali or something. Stacie or something like that, kid."

"What?"

"Yeah, bro. Word is, he's been caking it with her real hard son. I mean from dinners and movies to walks on the beach, all of that. And you say Kionna told you she slept with him?"

"Basically. Anyhow I gotta roll, B. Deuces" Nehi wasn't about to let Preach change his mind. He was breaking Ra's hands and if he could find this chick Stacie, he was planning on smashing her too. His mind was on payback. Rashi, in his eyes, was no longer a friend; more of an enemy now, a snake.

"Stacie is just another broad on this dude's list. If she is real, somebody he cares about, I plan on killing that." Nehi was talking to himself again and he didn't care. He was just so upset.

"Dude, you bogus as hell, B! You dirty, son. How am I hearing about all the bull you doing all the way here in Iowa, son? I'm chillin with Carrie and Neo calling me like he wants to do some bodily harm to you, kid. If you did what he said you did, I doubt I can even stay friends with you, B. That's just bogus." JuJaun called Rashi as soon as he got off the phone with Neo. He was the peacekeeper and knew what he had to do. Neo called him for this very reason. "Kionna, B? Seriously? I mean first Aria, and I don't know what you were thinking with that, and now Kionna?"

"What the hell are you talking about, dude? What I do now?"

"Neo say you slept with Kionna and that Kionna told him this. But why? I mean after the Aria thing, and the barbershop thing, dude, what's the deal with you?"

"Preach, you know I wouldn't do that to Nehemiah. You can say what you want Preach, but we both know I wouldn't do that again. I took Kionna to lunch."

"What! Why would you even do that? And it had to be more cause she told Neo that you slept with her. Ra, I always take up for you, but look at you, kid. You keep doing the same shit that has people disliking you in the first place, dude."

"First of all, I don't care. Secondly, dude, I'm dealing with a chick and I'm trying to keep it 100 with her so whatever you heard is a lie."

"He talking about breaking your hands clown!"

Rashi was laughing now. "Is he? What an idiot, son. I didn't give her the goods. We went to lunch and talked about how much I regret sleeping with Aria and how she should be calling Nehi letting him know how she feels."

"Right, and I would believe that because?"

"Cause I'm telling you, Preach. I'm a jerk and I know this, but I damn sure am not a liar. Even this new girl Stacie, I told her to think about if she wants to be with me. She knows I've been with 122 girls and that I haven't had a real relationship."

"But the thing with- wait, 122 girls? Dude you're like 20 years old! How the hell have you had 122 females in this short amount time? What are you, a gigolo? You do need to slow down. That alone makes this look worse. I ain't saying I don't believe you, Ra. It's just that Neo is upset and talking crazy right now. He's really talking about hurting you, bro. You need to call him and say something."

"Fool, I called him! This idiot hung up on me. He was talking crazy, calling me all outta my name. He hung up so I haven't called his lame ass back. He got real tough today, kid. But at the end of the day, I didn't do anything with Kionna, Preach. I called her and had lunch with her cause I actually felt bad about threatening him at the shop in front of y'all. And she said we slept together? I doubt that son, cause she's nice, but I have a shorty I'm working on right now. I wouldn't lie to you, Preach. You know how I get down and you gotta know that I wouldn't do that to Nehi again, son."

"Dude, I feel ya, but Neo is upset. Breaking your hands, B. He's serious about going after your hands. You're laughing, but dude is hurt, Ra. You need to talk to him ASAP."

"I just told you he hung up on me. He's not talking me, I'm over here chillin. I figure he'll call me when he's calmed down a little bit and then we can talk like men."

"Whateva, B. Deuces."

"ONE."

Rashi wanted to call both Nehi and Kionna, just to get them both on the phone and straighten all of this out. She couldn't have called Nehi and told him that of all things. It was tough, but Rashi talked Nehi up the whole time he was at lunch with Kionna. From talking about how good of a DJ he is to his endless knowledge of black culture. Rashi felt he was being a real friend and the payout was terrible.

Nehemiah on the other hand was still seeing red. He just couldn't believe that of all the people in the world Rashi would do this to him again. They were trying to rebuild a friendship and now it was basically over again. He'd never trust Ra again, and all the ways he was going to get him back was going through his head when his phone rang.

"Hello?"

"Hi Nehi. It's me Ki. I was calling to apologize about earlier. I was calling to clarify a few things, particularly about Rashi and I. I was mad so I said we'd been spending time together and that was kind of a half truth."

"Kionna, what do you mean a half truth?'

"Well, we did have lunch. But he told me about the barbershop, and how you guys kind of had a verbal altercation. His whole thing at lunch was me paying you more attention to keep you from spending time with Aria. He really doesn't like her much. But I just wanted to apologize for making you think any different. I was hurt and wanted you to be hurt as well."

"Women, I've threatened him at this point. I've actually talked about breaking his hands. I'm sorry I wasn't up front and honest with you Ki, but I wasn't expecting that."

"Expecting what? I told you nothing happened, Nehi. If you ask me, the day we had lunch, Rashi wasn't being a dog. He was actually being a friend. He was looking out for you and although I knew you were chilling with her, he had me actually ready to fight for you."

"What?"

"Yeah, he was telling me what I needed to do. The funny thing is, Rashi was fighting for you and when we went out to lunch he was being convincing for your benefit. You know I think he's a dog, but I can tell he's a good friend, dude. So Nehi, do your thing with your girl Aria. I know she was in the picture way before me and I know y'all have a history and what not. So, I will be here though if you need me, as a friend or a shoulder, or even just someone to talk to. Tell Aria she's a lucky girl. You made your choice though Nehi, so we're really done. I had a blast this summer with you and your friends. So, thanks for the good times and all of that. And like I said, Aria is a lucky girl, don't forget that."

"She's really not, woman, and I already know that I'm making the wrong choice because I know you and I had something special. I did have the most fum of my life with you this summer. She's a lifer though, kid. She has been around forever. She knows my people. I don't know woman. I really don't know."

"Nehi, it's fine. I understand and I'd rather you be happy with her as my friend, than as my guy and unhappy cause you have a ton of unanswered questions in your head about you and Aria. I totally understand. Seriously, I do."

"Thanks for being so understanding, kid. I have to call Ra and apologize for earlier. I kind of hung up on him because I was mad. Also, Kionna, I never actually said we were over, I was letting you know why I'd been so distant lately."

"I know, but I had to keep it real with myself and realize that if you're spending time with her, most likely we were done. Like I said Nehi, she iss a lucky girl. Also, you made your choice without saying it was over. I gotta go, sir. Goodnight."

"Deuces, kid. Thanks for calling. I appreciate you understanding, Ki."

"Bye dummy."

Chapter 5

JuJaun, aka Preach, was doing what he usually does; keeping everything cool. But in Iowa, he was doing something else. He'd gotten bored with the Preach thing and until basketball season actually started, he had some time to be an unknown freshman. Whenever he wasn't with Carrie, it was on. He got the idea from Rashi, although Rashi wasn't aware. He would be a player since no one knew who he was, just a flat out in your face player. He wouldn't be as blatant as Ra, but it was the same idea. He would have the guerilla mentality when it comes to the opposite sex. Love em and leave em, right? JuJaun was just tired of the whole Preach thing. College was about living life, right? Realizing who you really are and partying it up, right?

The idea that Ra had given him was not supposed to influence Preach. It was just a story. One of a million stories that Rashi always told. Ra told this story one Sunday at the shop, "So yeah clowns I met this one broad named Jarren when I was out in San Diego last year, B. She was cute, but I knew I wasn't going to want to deal with her any time after I left, or even while I was there for that matter. I approached her on the beach in straight shy-boy mode. I walked up on her like I was lost, son. Once I got her to laugh, I knew she was bagged, bro. Now keep in mind I had just left the hotel. I approached her like I was straight lost.

"I was like, 'Excuse me, I know you're trying to enjoy your time alone at the beach tanning and what not. I'm not trying to bother you or flirt cause I know a lot of the guys out here are. But I'm Cory and I'm from Chicago. My reason for even coming over here is that I'm lost and

I need to get back to my hotel. She was like, 'It's cool, Cory. I'm Jarren'. I hit her with the 'I know I could have asked anybody out here, but who wouldn't ask you?' That got her to smiling and what not. So, she helped me find the hotel and I ask her if she wanted to kick it with me. You know, 'I'd hate to get lost again.' So of course, she hung out with your boy and we kicked it real strong. The next day, son, same thing. We basically chillin like a couple. I mean that first day we did a movie and dinner. She even stayed the night that first night and you know what happened.

"The second day, the same thing. We hit the beach. I splashed around in the ocean. She splashed with your boy. It was cool, but I knew when I met Jarren, it wouldn't be lasting more than a day or two, son. She stayed with me until like 4:30 that morning. The next day I checked out and went to another hotel. She called my cell like ten times that day. I knew she knew something was up when my voicemail was saying Rashi isn't available, but she kept calling. This is my favorite part, kid. I saw her at the beach the next day. She approaches me like 'Cory, I was looking for you yesterday. They said you checked out.' I'm like, 'Excuse me? Do I know you?' I could tell she was confused, and I just stuck to my guns. 'I'm sorry, ma'am. I don't know this Cory that you speak of. Maybe he looks like me, but I seriously doubt that as well.' She was angry as hell, especially with me calling her ma'am like she was an old woman. So, in one last-ditch effort, she called my phone. It rang right there in front of her. She thought she had me cornered. She actually got loud like, 'You see, Cory. I have your number and you're ringing as we speak.' You know me bro, I always keep my cool. I just said, 'I don't know how you got my number, cutie, but I'm Rashi. Keep listening and I'm pretty sure my voicemail says the same thing.' In the end she actually apologized to me and says maybe she had the wrong person. What a clown, b! Jarren knew it was me. The funny thing is, even after that, sometimes she would still call my phone, every now and again. Sometimes to talk to me and sometimes she'd call private and ask for Cory. It's hilarious, B."

This was the story that gave Jujuan the idea. No more Preach here in Iowa. Preach was a good dude, but up until this point, Jujuan just felt like he hadn't really lived. Preach was expected to do the right thing and Jujuan was just tired of it. All his life it was church, basketball, and school. Even now it was the same thing. He was in college through a basketball scholarship, and every other weekend he was getting on I-80 headed to Chicago, before he went back to school on Sunday, it was off to church with the family.

When Ra told that story initially, it was funny, but nothing Jujuan would consider doing. Jujuan was sure that Carrie was the woman he would marry. They were at the same school and although they stayed in different dorms, they were together all the time. He wasn't tired of Carrie by any means. He was just tired of always doing the right thing. It was like his life was a script, and that script was the most boring movie ever made.

It was time for change. It was time for Chris Gotit. The name was the hard part. When he finally decided to do this, he promised himself he wouldn't half-ass it. That meant that he would not start this until he'd looked at it from all angles and taken the precautions needed to make sure that he wasn't caught. He had to be sure that there was no way that Gotit could be linked to Jujuan. He and Carrie were strong believers in the whole keeping your life off of the internet thing. Carrie because she planned on running for public office someday, and Jujuan because in between school, church, and hooping, he never really learned the whole computer thing. He was computer illiterate, but he knew that and really didn't care.

Basketball got him into college free and he planned on taking advantage of that, but this Chris Gotit situation was the first thing on his mind. So, in a very un-Jujuan-like way, he put up a Instagram and a Facebook page as Chris Gotit. He was networking/flirting and figured if he met people on campus in person, he wouldn't have the heart to introduce himself as Chris, at least not yet. He put up a Instagram page as 'Gotit's Got It' and his Facebook page was just under the name Chris Gotit. No fancy taglines or anything, but he put up pictures and made up facts about himself.

It took a few weeks to learn and memorize these facts, but he was committed to the roll. At the end of the day, to Jujuan, this was about experiencing college. Lying to women was not his thing, but he really wasn't trying to get married to Carrie before experiencing any other women. Although it sounded good, and his people (friends and family) would know nothing about Chris, this was something he needed and wanted to do. Also, when if his friends found out, he was sure that they wouldn't disagree. Sure, Ra was pretty protective about his cousin Carrie, but not with Preach. He'd even asked him a few times about seeing other females and how he felt Preach was too young to be thinking marriage. Yeah, Gotit was something out of the ordinary for Jujuan, but he was chalking this up as a good life experience. At the end of the day, what was the worst that could happen?

Tia – The first girl Chris met. She was cute, but had a very low self-esteem because she didn't have a model's body. Preach would have looked at this and tried to help her; offer a hand of companionship or even try to open up lines of communication to make this girl understand that she was a catch. As a promise to himself though, Chris was about doing the exact opposite of what Jujuan would usually do, so Chris took advantage of this opportunity. Chris didn't know about her low self-esteem initially. Over the phone she seemed cool, calm, and collected. Once on the date though, it was obvious. Chris got there 15 minutes early and Tia was already there. As soon as he got there, she was showing signs of body image concerns and not too much confidence. Every time her sweater opened up she was quick to close it and wrap herself pretty tight. Whenever the conversation was about her, she'd say negative things ot just change the subject. By the end of the night it was an obvious thing.

"Wassup Tia. Pretty prompt, huh?"

"I live close by so getting here wasn't a problem."

"Oh, I stay on campus, so I got lost a couple times on the way. I'm from New York so the rhyme and reason of the streets here are kind of confusing, kid."

"Oh, well I was just here early just in case you saw me and didn't like what you saw. I was nervous. I wanted you to have the chance to see me first, just in case you changed your mind."

"What? Chris wouldn't do that." Since talking to her on Instagram, Jujuan had decided to make Chris into this guy who's kind of cocky. He talked about himself in the third person a lot. And as a complete opposite of Jujuan, Chris talked about himself a lot. "Plus, I've seen pictures of you on the Gram, woman. I knew what you looked like and like I said, you're a cutie. I mean you and I together, we're killing them shorty. We are two tens, what do you expect?"

"Chris shut up! You're so silly. Anyways Mr. I ordered a salad and a Diet Coke, what you having?"

"That's all you're having, woman? No wonder you don't have any meat on those bones. Salads and Diet Coke ain't a meal kid."

"I'm trying to lose a few pounds. I feel like such a fat ass sometimes. I've been eating salads lately. I already told you this, Chris. And is Gotit really your last name?"

"Well, from here kid, you're perfect. And yeah, I'm from the Gotit family. All we need is a Tia Gotit. Anyways, I don't want to scare you away, cutie. The longer you're here the more jealous the rest of these dudes are getting. You are fly to me and the last thing you need is a salad from where I'm sitting. Let me chill with the flirting though. Have you had the chicken fingers here?" Straight out of the book of Ra. Just from being around the clown and seeing him do his thing, Preach knew what to say and what not to say. This tidbit here didn't sound right coming out of his mouth to him, but by the time dinner was over and they were on their way to the movies, Chris was in full effect.

"I know you told me you were single, Tia, but now that I'm with you in person, I'm having problems believing that. I mean cute as hell, sexy in so many ways, and smart, too. You are either single by choice or dudes are just scared of this combination you got going on, kid. I mean lets be real, you're batting them with a stick aren't you?"

"Whatever Chris-"

"I'm serious, woman. I mean at dinner I was joking like we need a Tia in the Gotit family, but I'm loving this whole package. Only thing is, if I bring you to the house and the family meets you, I may have to knock a few of my cousins out for trying to steal you away, Tia. I mean, let me just say the fact that you're holding my hand right now has made a few dudes who have passed us jealous. I know the look and I've gotten that look a few times, kid."

"Well, I don't want to do that, but I do want to chill with you. I got movies back at my place. Let's save you a few dollars and you can have me all to yourself."

She was bagged and Chris, as well as Jujuan, knew it. "Sounds good to me, woman. But are you absolutely sure you trust me that much?"

He knew what was going to happen before they got to her place and this put the seal on keeping Chris around. "Am I sure? What does this tell you?" She leaned in to kiss him, and for the first time in his life, he was in a kiss with someone other than his future wife. She was just some random girl who didn't even know his real name, and even better, had no idea that he was known as "Preach," the good one in the crew.

Preach was spending time on campus with Carrie, but also leaving campus as well to chill with Tia. But after two weeks or so, he just ghosted her. It surprised him that he didn't care, but he knew that Chris had to be a "Cold Piece of Work." When it came to Tia, although her self-esteem was low, he was taking no prisoners. She was out of there, and the funny thing was, to Preach, it seemed like she saw it coming.

Next there was:

Jasmine; She was born and raised in Iowa, but wanted people to think she had a Chicago edge to her. She called herself, "Fresh." Going into this one, Chris was sure that this would be a problem. It wasn't. He met her on Instagram as well, and like Tia she was dealing with some poor self image issues. She played it cool on the outside, but he slowly got to see that she was quite needy. Spending time with her was actually cutting into his time with Carrie. Carrie wasn't making a big deal out of it, but she did notice. Jujaun's attitude seemed to be changing and he was talking in a way that reminded her of her cousin Ra. She didn't say anything though.

Chris, when he first met Fresh, was already in a bad mood. He'd gotten into a small argument with Carrie earlier in the day and it had him in a foul mood. Fresh had no idea he was upset. She just thought it was his New York attitude. They went bowling and by the end of the night, he was calm. He didn't stay the first night with her, but he also didn't get back to the dorm until after 3:30 AM. At 8 AM before his first class, Fresh was calling his phone, telling him home-cooked breakfast was on the table and that he should come over, have breakfast, and then go to class. He decided to go, and while there, he ended up falling asleep. They got up at 1 PM, had lunch and ended up spending the day with her. He liked Fresh more than Tia. She was fun to be around, and she continually texted when she was missing him or just thinking about him. He didn't go to class that day, and the next morning he was there as well, laughing it up and spending time with Fresh.

For a week straight, Chris put class on the back burner and made Fresh a main focus. There were two problems with that. Carrie was being pushed aside too, and the semester had just started. When Chris finally did get intimate with Fresh, she asked him something that Jujuan wouldn't have said yes to if he was really paying attention. She asked him if she start spending time with him on campus, and not thinking, he answered not like Chris, but like Jujuan. Chris wasn't looking for a girlfriend and Jujuan was used to having one. He answered like it was Carrie talking to him. He had hit his first snag as Chris. Either he was going to find a way out of this, or he was going to stop the whole Chris thing and be truthful. That night he laid there holding Fresh, but not knowing what to do or say at all. He decided that if he couldn't get out of this, Chris was dead. Calling Rashi was an option, but no a very good one. Thinking quickly, Chris grabbed his phone and dialed Rashad's number. He didn't press talk, but he had an imaginary conversation with Jujuan his "roommate."

"Wassup Preach?" One second pause.

"Nothing. Chilling with my girl, Fresh. what's good on campus?" five second pause.

"Yeah, she asleep. I was just letting you know I'd be there for class today so you don't have to take notes for me." He knew she was awake, but he had to pretend she was asleep. He prayed she was buying this. To Fresh, Chris Gotit was about to be dead either way. He wasn't going to do in one swift motion, but he did see an accident in Chris' immediate future as far as she was concerned. 11 second pause.

"Yeah I feel ya son, but look here Preach. I was really calling to let you know that you might get to meet my girl real soon, B. Don't be trying to flirt." Eight second pause.

"Aiight then, B. 100" Jujuan fake hung up his phone and got comfy with Fresh. "Damn," he thought, "I'm getting good at this Gotit thing." He went to sleep thinking of his diabolical plan for Chris and for Fresh. It was kinda exciting. No wonder Ra did it. Every day it was something new and fresh. Plus, when he wanted he could kill the kid, and bring him back a million times over. He was loving college …

Over the next week, every time Chris talked to Fresh, he mentioned he was making a trip home on the weekend. They hadn't really done any sleepovers since that last night, but school was important and Fresh understood that Chris had some catching up to do. Chris was delighted cause he knew that Fresh's time was coming to an end. Onto the next conquest. This "break-up" was going to take some good acting, but if anyone could pull it off, Chris could!

Finally, the weekend came and Jujuan called Fresh as himself, Preach, Chris' roommate and good friend sadly, as the bearer of bad news. "Hello is Jasmine available?"

"This is her. What's up Chris?"

"Ummm, Jasmine, this is not Chris. This is his roommate JuJaun. I was actually calling to talk to you about Chris though."

"Damn, y'all sound just alike JuJaun. I mean I was sure you were Chris calling to tell me you got back early."

"Oh, sorry, kid, but that kind of can't happen, I just talked to his people and the news ain't good, shorty."

"What happened? Is Chris okay?"

Jujuan, was trying not to laugh at this point. He was actually on the phone telling a girl that his roommate, who was actually him, was in an accident. "Shorty, I didn't want to call you, but I knew you'd be worried. Plus, Chris made me promise to tell you cause he can't call right now. It is pretty bad, though. He shattered his knee on the way to New York, shorty. Bad car accident. I mean he'll live, but he was really hurt. Asked about you a lot though. At least that's what his family told me. I really hate to be the bearer of bad news, Jasmine."

"What?"

"Yeah, it was pretty bad, so I doubt he'll even be back this semester. I talked with his family and they say all he's talking about is you and how he wants to come back. I don't know, kid. It seems like he was more concerned with you than with school, so-"

"You got a number on him?"

"Unfortunately, I don't. But let me do some looking and I promise I'll call you back with what's good. Okay?"

"You promise Jujuan?"

"Shorty, if I didn't, Chris would kill me."

"Thanks, Jujuan. I appreciate you looking out for me."

"Come on, woman. Had the situation been any different, you, me, and Chris would be hanging out all the time, shorty. So, you know I got your back. You ever need anything Jasmine, just hit me at the dorms. I'll keep you posted on Chris."

"Thanks, Jujuan. And you can call me Fresh."

"Alright then, Fresh. I'll most likely be calling you either later this week or next week with an update. Remember if you need anything, give me call or email and I got you. You're my guy's girl and by extension, I have to make sure you're good, woman. Deuces."

"Bye Chris-, I mean Jujuan."

And that was how Chris got rid of Fresh. Onto his next conquest. The older woman, Ms. CiCi-

Chapter 6

Jujuan hadn't been to the shop in four weekends. That was normal and to be expected. He lived in Iowa- away from the action, but this time it was different. It was like everything had changed. Rashi and Nehi were getting along and Rashad was talking about breaking up with Caryl. It was like everything from the last time he was in the shop was the exact opposite. He, himself, was having flings. Rashi and Nehi were as close as they were before the Aria scandal. Nehi was back with Aria and Rashad was unhappy.

When he walked into the shop, Harold's chicken was in the air. It smelled so damn good. Iowa was cool and all, but it definitely didn't have Harold's. The music was going through the speakers and everyone was laughing and slapping high fives. Football was playing on the TV in the background and the general mood was just happy. It felt like Europe, it felt like home, it just felt right.

"How's Carrie, son?" Rashi was concerned about his cousin. Carrie called him a couple times in the last two weeks about Jujuan. She said he was acting different and he was very rarely on campus. Rashi said he would ask Jujuan but to him it wasn't really necessary. Preach was Preach, she didn't really have anything to worry about. "She's been worried about you, so you know we were, too. She good? You good?"

"Everything is good, Bro. I've just been busy with homework and a couple projects from my sociology class. It takes me off campus a lot, but we're good. She knows that? I mean we spend almost every night together when I'm not too beat. I take my grades seriously, though. She knows that and y'all know that as well. And what are y'all worried about me for? What the hell is up with you and Caryl, son?" He turned to Shad, he had been hearing all the way in Iowa that the great Caryl was about to be downgraded.

"He got a basketball Jones, kid." Rashi had been using that ever since Rashad came into the shop talking about him and Jackie. "You know this dude and his ego. Him and Caryl got into it over some trash and he's giving her an extended silent treatment, bro."

"Nope, it ain't like that at all, B. She starting to make it seem like now that she knows a little bit about me that it's okay to judge me, and trusting me will be an issue. I'm giving her time to think about that as well as letting her see that time apart is just that, time apart."

"So where does Jackie fit in, son?" Nehi was just happy not to be discussing himself and Aria. Ever since he had gotten back with Aria and made it official, Rashi and Rashad had been clowning him like every day about it, at the shop, phone calls, everything. Now they were back on Rashad, and he was relishing this. "I mean what happens when you and Caryl get back? I mean if y'all break up or what not, is she going to be good? You and Jackie chill all the time, Shad. You get back with Caryl, you got school beef, clown."

"Nope, Jackie knows what's up. I mean as much as we chill, she still knows that Caryl is my girl."

"Dude, you cooked for her, bro. Quite a few times." Nehi was eating his wings and talking with his mouth full. He was glad the crew was back like this, tight.

"Calm down, Nehi. I cooked and she came by. It wasn't ***for her.*** She's on the hoop team, and since I ain't cooking for these dudes, I call her over to eat with me sometimes. Don't make it seem worse than what it is, Bro. I talk to Caryl, just not as much. I don't like being judged, for one and if she has to be with me every second of every day, then maybe we shouldn't be together. This is the biggest thing to me, y'all, I feel like she's on that buffoonery because I told her about the Jennifer situation."

"What?" Jujuan wanted to tell them about Chris Gotit so bad, but he couldn't. He was Preach. Preach wouldn't do that, especially to his best friend's cousin. "She's knows about that old Jennifer stuff, clown? What you do? Smash her sister too?"

"Ha, you got jokes, son! She is just suspicious now. I mean we were always together and we chill all the time. I put everything out in the open. Dude, I don't like the fact that she tried to play me like that after the fact. I trust her 100%, B, so that should be mutual. The funny thing is, I don't know much about her past, but seeing how it's her past, I really don't care. And for the record, clowns, there is no silent treatment or whatnot. We talk. She just knows how I feel and we haven't really gone out since she pulled that bullshit she pulled a couple weeks ago."

Jujuan, of course, had no idea what happened. With everyone telling stories he wanted to mention Chris and what had been going on in Iowa, but instead he just listened to everything he'd missed out on. "What did she do, kid? She talk to Jennifer or something?"

"Nope, she heard. That's it, she heard about what happened with me and J, and she wanted to try and make our relationship comparable. Dude, she tried to play me with some stuff I was on in high school. She brought Rashi up and all. Like every time we talk, she tries to throw you in like, 'Well look how Ra is. And on the trip this, and on the trip that.' I say the same thing every time son, 'Did I do any of that on the trip?' She gets quiet every time because she doesn't know what the hell I did. She'll probably never know at this point. I talked to her yesterday and had to break it down to her. I flat out told her. I don't know if I'm going to marry you cause that's something later in my life. Even if I do though, the time that we are together and we call ourselves a couple, I'm going to treat you as if you are my wife. I don't plan on cheating and if I do want to move on, you'll be the first to know."

"What she say to that, son?" Jujuan wasn't trying to sound nosy, but if this happened yesterday, he knew that Rashi and Nehi knew last night. Rashad was the kind of guy who'd call you at like 2:31 in the morning because of something that happened at 2:30 in the morning. He'd make sure you knew. Jujuan knew that Ra and Nehi got the news hot off the press. That was the downside about being in Iowa. Out of sight, out of mind. He hadn't heard from these fools in weeks. Last time he talked to Rashi and Nehi they were on the verge of fighting over Kionna.

"Nothing. she's a clown and hopefully she gets it together or she gets the deuces. I mean I like her, but I don't need that right now, bro. The season's coming up and with practice and class, I kind of just need her to be a good girlfriend. I actually started on this cooking thing because I was trying to get her to chill on campus with me more. You know feed her, keep her happy. She looks at what's happening with this fool and I get the blame. So I've been kicking it with Jackie. I mean she's cool as hell B. We hang out a lot, son. I like her."

"That's funny. What if her and Caryl are sisters?" Rashi was joking, but he'd entertained that thought ever since this whole Jackie situation became "phone call in the middle of the night" worthy. "I'm just saying, that is your luck, clown."

"It doesn't matter. Me and Jackie just chill and talk hoop, son. I mean I talk to her about Caryl sometimes and she mentions her ex, but aside from that we just talk hoop and watch movies."

Rashi pounced on this because his movie theory was something he stood by and believed was a time proven fact. "You already know what I say about girls and movies, bro. Dudes don't want to agree with this, but I say if you see three movies with a chick, that's your girl. You can deny it all day, but three movies equal a real status. I'm the two-movie king. If I take her to two movies and I ain't smashed after that, she will not hear from me again. I don't have the time nor the patience, B. I don't know why y'all got girlfriends any way. Shad, you need a girl like you need a hole in your head. Look at you stressing and right before the season? You and Jennifer broke up and I think you went like four games straight with under ten points. Had I not picked up your slack, I'm sure we'd have lost. I don't see why you were off your game, son. You still had her sister. Nehi, you and Aria are about as good as sweating perfume in jail, son. It seems sweet, but at the end of the day, expect to get screwed. Like I told you before, you're my guy and I'm going to support you. I can't choose for you, so although I think Kionna is such a better look for you, I gotta support what you do cause you are my guy. You know I'm going to make my jokes and be rude when I need to be rude, but like I said I support your decision. You, Preach, you're in a strange town so I guess you having a girl is a good thing. Me, I'd be at two movies a week, every week, different broad, cutting hair, and chilling. With that being said, I did take this chick Stacie out to a few movies. Turned out to be dead. I mean not totally dead I am feeling her and I'm trying to do the right thing, but I don't know.

Rashi trailed off. He'd been spending a lot of time with Stacie, but he'd also been helping Kionna deal. She wasn't taking the break-up with Nehi particularly bad, but she was calling him more and more since he took her to lunch and told her to fight, she was kind of putting a little of the blame on him.

"Yeah, I'm trying to take Stacie seriously, but I don't really trust her. You know how I am with my phone, but I've chilled on that cause when you meet a model son, you gotta pump the breaks. She's always on her joint though. Plus, she got the code names and all of that. I guess it could just be me. I've been with a lot of women and I don't know, son. It just doesn't seem right. When we're chilling, we're chilling. But when we aren't together, I'm never thinking about what's she's doing. I'm thinking about who she's chilling with. Like I was saying, the three-movie thing gives you a status, but I'm thinking I should have just stopped at two with her. I was actually looking at you fool's and I guess trying to do whatever you lames are doing. When I think about it though, aside from Preach cause he's damn near married, having a girlfriend is kind of stressful. I want to fly solo, bro. But walking in the club with a model on your arm is like walking into Nike Town with Michael Jordan. It demands immediate respect. I just don't trust her though, so it's almost dead. I mean she's supposed to stop by today because I want you clowns to see her. She is a dime, but I don't know if I can do the stress and drama you clowns are constantly complaining about. We're supposed to be college students and y'all sound like old ass men and I ain't even in college."

Rashi stood up from his barber chair and motioned Nehi to it. "Look at us, a DJ dating a bouncer. My bad Nehi, I was joking, but you know she's heavy. A clown cooking for a female hooper and doesn't see what's about to happen. You think you and Jackie are just hoop friends huh? Right, son, keep thinking that. Remember this Shad, dudes who can cook always get the girl. She might be cool now and act like the friend's thing is okay, but mark my words, B. Eventually she's going to want to get down. What are you going to do when she makes it known that she's trying to smash? Or even that the friend's thing ain't cutting it? Then we got Preach. He's been married since his sophomore year of high school. He'll never smash anyone other than Carrie and he's a freshman in college."

They were all laughing, but Nehi was the first to address what was said. "Dude, I know Aria is big, but there is something about her. I mean she knows me, and she's been around since I was a shorty. Don't get me wrong. This ain't no forever type jump off like Preach over here. I'm with her cause right now it just seems right. I got the same thing you got going. Do I trust her? I don't know. She let one of my best friends hit, and then damn near wrecked my whole crew. I know it ain't forever, but I dig her, Ra. I really do."

"Then the question is, what about Kionna?" They had this conversation before, but Jujuan wasn't there so Rashi was trying to catch him up.

"I told you, bro. I might be making a huge mistake giving Ki the deuces, but I think even if this with Aria doesn't work out, she'll give your boy a second chance. I didn't cheat or nothing bogus like that- that she knows of." He saw Rashad about to say something, so he decided to fix his statement before it lead him down another road he didn't really want to go down. "I honestly feel like if Aria gave me a reason to shoot her the final deuces, going back to Kionna would be a possibility."

"You're an idiot." That sounded crazy even to Preach. At this point in the conversation, telling the crew about Chris was something he wanted to do so bad he was shaking. Was this how even his closest friends looked at him? Was he the marred man out of the group? The most mature? And how would they react to Chris? Would they even believe him about Chris? "If it were me, after what almost went down with you and Ra and how you broke up, I'd just distance myself from Kionna for the time being and not put her through anything like that situation again." Damn!!! He was the mature one!

"Preach, I knew you'd say something like that, son. You and Carrie are like the couple on My Wife and Kids, so of course you want to do things the old married way. I'm just saying there wasn't a real bad break up, so you never know. We talk on the phone every now and again, and she seems genuinely interested in my well-being so you gotta respect that. It seems to me that she's really trying to keep the friendship whole cause like I said, you never know. She could have walked away and just shot the whole crew the deuces."

Rashad was listening and taking things in. From what Rashi had been saying as of late, not only had Kionna been calling Nehi, but she'd been calling Ra too. He wasn't going to say it now, but in his opinion Kionna was staying close to the crew for reasons other than keeping the friendship intact. He could be wrong, but it seemed like either Kionna was trying to get Nehi back, or she was trying to get Rashi. One way or another, to Rashad, Kionna staying cool with the crew wasn't a good look at all.

"I don't know, Neo, seems kinda fishy to me. Why in the hell would she stay cool with you when you did her that dirty?" It was like Jujuan read Rashad's mind and he didn't even know about the calls to Rashi. "Let me ask you this. Did you stay cool with Aria when she slept with Rashi? Why would she stay cool with you if you left her for the same chick she helped you get over dummy?"

"I stayed cool with Rashi, though."

"He's the one that told you what happened stupid. Had he not told you, not only would you have not met Kionna, you would not have gone on the trip. And Aria would probably sleeping with like five other dudes, clown."

"He does have a point. If I didn't tell you, bro, you'd be that dude. You know the 'he made a hoe into a housewife' dude, and I know you don't want that."

Preach was looking out for the crew. It had been a while since they were cool like this with no beef or tension in the air. "You gotta feel her out, Nehi. Kionna seems cool now, but I'm betting if she saw you and Aria together, she'd flip out. I mean think about it, she was a keeper and you shot her the deuces for an ex who did you dirtball."

"I asked her about that, bro. Can you throw a graphic in Ra? Anything graffiti will be a good look." Nehi liked to stay fresh with the designs in his hair. "She was like everything is cool. No worries. She's cut from a different cloth, son. I know she should be upset and she knows it, too. But she's not and I can't fault her for that. Only a fool would be like, 'hey, get angry!' She's a good girl. She didn't grow up in the hood like these chicks around here, B."

"You're a clown if you believe that dude. No matter where you grew up, a broken heart is a broken heart. She may not show it in public and get loud, but she's feeling it, kid." Rashi knew a little bit about breaking hearts and felt like Nehi was a little naive if he thought this was over. "You are basically having your cake and eating it too. Damn I hate that saying. 'Have your cake and eat it, too.' What the hell else you gonna do with it? It's cake. I mean, you give me a yummy piece of cake and tell me not to eat it, then we got beef. If I HAVE cake, I'm EATING it, too. Anyhow, I digress. I was just saying, son. In her eyes, she thinks you are having your cake and eating it, too. If you really think she'll come back if you break up with Aria, then you're basically going back for seconds, son. I ain't Preach, so ain't saying you should stop talking to her, but you need to know that just cause she ain't from the hood doesn't mean she's not hurt. She liked you a lot. I don't know why, but she did, and you snaked her son. You say I snaked you, right? You did the same thing to her and actually picked Aria, the other person who snaked you, over her." Those were actually Kionna's exact words. When she called Rashi, she described how Nehi used to talk about being snaked by his best friends and his girlfriend. He explained to her that their first lunch (they had three more since) was about him trying to fix what he messed up. "Preach is right, as usual though. Just because it looks like everything is good, doesn't mean that it is. I was reading something by Nietzsche that said, 'The advantage of a bad memory is that one enjoys several times the same good things for the first time. 'I think that is why you're with Aria, bro. You forget how bad y'all were as a couple. Your only bad memory of her is when she was with me. So yeah, you might get that good feeling you're looking for again, but at what cost? Just because she's been around for years doesn't make her the right one. It just means that she knows how to get to you. I ain't going to preach but think about it. Yeah, it's been nice the last few weeks. But did you have any disagreements or loud ass confrontations with Kionna since you've known her?" He knew the answer to that as well. Kionna told him about this break-up hurting even more because of the lack of beef and arguments they'd had when they were together.

"When do you find time to read that stuff, son? Nietzsche? Who in the hell just sits and reads Nietzsche in their spare time? I mean, even when I told Carrie, your own cousin, she didn't even believe me. You amaze me Ra. As much as you read and all that you need to be in college, fool. I still don't know why you aren't."

"You paying for this cut today, Preach?"

"Nope, I ain't never had to pay before so I didn't really plan on paying now."

"No, what I'm saying is, do you have $20 plus a tip if I did decide to charge you? I'm not going to charge you but humor me. Do you have the funds to pay for the cut?"

"I'd have to take it from my gas money to get back to campus. So, no."

"And that's why I'm not in college. I like having money. If you're trying to sell me on paying thousands of dollars to read books that I can buy for like 15 or 20 dollars, only to become a barber which is exactly what I am now, I'll pass. I'll do the reading myself and keep making money, thanks."

"Damn, son! Look at her!" Rashad was looking out the window barely listening to the conversation when he saw a tall redbone walking towards the shop.

"Oh, that's Stacie, son. Told you she was a banger. She's coming to meet you clowns and then she has to go. So, behave yourselves and don't embarrass me."

"She got any friends?"

"Seriously, Preach? What would you do with her friends? Convert them to over to Christianity? Just sit down and chill, clown. 'Does she have any friends?' Carrie would beat you down."

"Hey, fellas."

"Shad, Jujuan, Nehi, this is Stacie. Stacie this is my crew. Jujuan is over by the window, I promise I usually have Jujaun looking better he just hasn't been in town for a few weeks, dealing with school and all that in Iowa. This clown in the chair is Nehi, aka DJ Neo. Got his name from the character in the movie, The Matrix, he's the one. In all seriousness, he's a beast on the Ones and Twos. The quiet one over there is Rashad. It's just today that he's quiet though. Like the rest of these fools, he's having women problems."

"Shut up, clown! I'm Rashad and we've heard a lot about you, shorty. You got my boy on some new type shit lately. He's not much of a, 'let me talk about my girl type of dude' so the fact that he's constantly talking about you is different, but I can see what he's talking about. Nice to meet you."

"You too. Rashad, right?"

"Yep."

"So we've heard a lot about you from Ra, but why don't you tell us a little about yourself!" Preach was being nosy. For some reason when he saw Stacie, the first thing he thought was, 'what would Chris do with this?' "I just got back in town and since I've gotten here, you've been the talk of it. 'Stacie that. Stacie this' I mean you gotta tell us something. What does Stacie do to get this kind of attention from this kind of dude?"

"Stacie is short for Estacia. I work a lot, but I make time for your friend here." Rashi had stepped away from the chair and was holding her by the waist. His crew had never seen him giving out PDA, it was weird for them.

"Esta- what? You mean Ester?" Nehi was tripping because he'd never heard anyone make Stacie short for Ester, or whatever she said. "Stacie" wasn't doing it for him.

"Oh, it's spelled E-S-T-A-C-I-A. When it's written down or you see my signature, it's usually pronounced wrong, so I go by Stacie for short."

"Right, I gotta see some ID cause that sounds like your model name. I'm sure your real name is Mable or Avis, something like that woman." Rashad liked her so far. She was cool and she looked pretty good, too. "Ester, right. Maybe your name is like Dorothy or one of them old names, so you hit us with the Stacy joint. I'm seriously going to need to see some ID, woman."

Everyone was laughing and having a good time. Stacie stayed for about 30 minutes before having to rush off.

"So, what you idiots think?"

"I like her, son. I mean, when you said she was a model, I don't know. I immediately assumed she would have a snobby type attitude and be kind of a ditz, but she seems cool as hell." Rashad was impressed. "Looks like you'll be having those, 'my girl is stressing me out,' days too now, son. In all seriousness, she was on point B. Tall, cute as hell, and she's funny, bro."

"She's aiight, B. I mean don't get me wrong, I like her and she's a fun girl, but like I said, I don't trust her. We have fun together and she is funny. But dude, she stays on that phone, texting and all of that. The funny thing about it is when I get on my phone, she's not so nice and funny anymore. She feels like I got groupies and exes. I tried to tell her. I don't have any exes. I ain't never had a girlfriend. She just assumes I'm lying or making that up."

"Well like I said B, I like her. If you don't, you don't. I ain't going to tell you what you should or shouldn't do. If you don't trust her though, what are you going to do?" Jujuan couldn't help but think to himself, 'Damn!!! Stop Jujuan! You really are the mature one.' Jujuan was starting to sound like a mom talking to her son. "I mean, what's different about Stacie from the rest of the random chicks you give the pipe to? Is it the three movies thing or is she really something different?"

"I don't know, son. I nabbed a model and I guess I wanted to keep her. I like spending time with her, B. You saw that she's fun and funny. I just can't get over that feeling, and y'all know I really don't do feelings at all. I mean, I ain't really dealt with anyone else since I met her. That's unlike me. At the same time, I do text a chick or two every now and again." Kionna came into mind because he'd been not only texting, but talking to her as well. As much as he'd been telling himself not to find her attractive or to even think about her in that way, the conversation had been becoming more and more intimate. Recently, the conversation had started out about Nehi and worked it's way around to them. Somehow their new conversation was about what if they were a couple and laughing about Nehi's reaction to that. Rashi shook that thought off. "And as far as-"

"What the hell were you thinking about, clown?" Rashad saw Rashi shake his head. Like he was shaking off a thought and decided to say something without even thinking. "I don't know what was on your mind, but if Stacie got you like that, then I think you should rethink this whole situation with her. She's a dime I'll give you that. But you looked crazy just now."

"Oh, I was just thinking about something we were talking about yesterday. She's going to Vancouver next week and she invited me. Everything paid for, son. On top of that, she wants to know if I'll cut the heads at the shoot. You know, make some dough."

"Sounds like a keeper to me, son. She's a model and she's looking out for you as well." Nehi dug Stacie and thought Ra could use a girlfriend instead of another damn fling.

"Shut up, clown! Aria sounds like a keeper to you! Cool out, I'm joking. Anyhow, you're done. Preach, come sit yo ass down. My clippers are screaming to cut that off. Dude, the season's coming up. Please if you ever need a cut this bad, hit my cell, son. I'll drive down there and make sure you're good. You can't rep Chicago with this nappy shit. I mean, I know Carrie got you cuffed up, but damn, B. This is a terrible look, son. Seriously preach, you look like a slave."

"I might look like a slave, but your girl likes it. She models for me. I don't know if that makes her a professional cause I usually pay her for what she does after the modeling session. I mean don't get me wrong. She's tall and cute, but I love looking at the top of her head. It's nice, too. I'm sure you know what I'm talking about"

Nehi and Rashi were cracking up. It wasn't often that Preach was bringing the jokes like this. Rashad, on the other hand, was still sitting in the front of the shop kind of dejected. He wasn't really paying too much attention to the jokes and all of that. Rashad was deep in thought, and although the season was approaching fast, that wasn't what was on his mind.

"I see Iowa made you funny, clown. So, what are we doing today, sir? Taper as usual or you need something else for the season?"

"Well, Stacie likes fades so I'm going to go with the drop fade, my guy. I need three parts on the left side though and then something different. Since I am bringing the fade back, I think I want three parts in my left eyebrow, too." As soon as Jujuan said it, he knew that this was Chris' look and it was totally different from the look Jujuan was known for. Chris was real and would be around for a while. Being "Preach" was tiring, and if need be, Jujuan could do the Preach thing for the rest of his life. He was young, smart, and good looking. No need to act like he was 30 or 40 years old. "This is my year in Iowa, son. I plan on averaging 24 and ten. All with a drop top fade, wavy as hell, B. Today's drop fade is the jump off point."

"I should put a bible in the back. 'The top of her head,' that was funny, clown. But then you came and sat in my chair, huh? That'll be 25 bucks. Seriously though, y'all clowns like Stacie? I mean I really don't care, but if we going to be chillin, I need y'all to be honest with me about what y'all think about her, gentlemen. I ain't trying to have no awkward situations when she's around y'all like Nehi and Aria. I mean Aria's not comfortable around us to this day. Stacie ain't getting the business from none of y'all, so of course that's a whole different situation, but I need to know. What? Too soon?"

Nehi didn't like that last so-called joke. "Nope, it's cool with me. Your girl seems cool. Does she know you don't trust her? Or that you slept with your best friend's girl? I mean, she should know what she's getting into right? You don't trust her, but should she really trust you?"

"That's what's up, Nehi?"

"I'm kidding, son. Cool out. Or let me guess, that was too soon?"

Jujuan felt like he had to step in because apparently Rashad wasn't going to. "Whatever, B. Just don't mess up my fade, Ra. I ain't got time for you and this idiot Neo, or this lame argument. Finish me up first, son. I ain't trying to head back to school with a bad fade cause one of y'all got your periods."

"I'm just saying, he doesn't trust her? Of all the dudes walking around, you seriously telling me that this one right here doesn't trust someone? Seriously? Think about the trip. Think about the last year of high school. Think about how no one wanted to leave their girl around him. I'm just saying, you not trusting her is foul, bro. Is her track record like yours? Or do you not even know? Like you said, she's a model and

I'm sure she has a very busy life and what not. You're a barber Ra. A much less hectic life and I rarely see you without that phone in hand texting. Don't get me wrong, I ain't saying she's this or that. I'm just saying your reasons for not trusting her aren't good reasons. You not trusting her because of her phone is like Ike Turner not trusting Chris Brown because he heard he's violent."

"I feel you on that, Nehi. I don't know. I'm a really good judge of character. I thought that I have a good reason not to trust her, but when you're right you're right. In all honesty I don't know who she's texting when we're together. I am most likely being a little judgmental, but ain't nothing wrong with going into a situation with your guard up. Actually, you should take what I just said and apply it to your current situation. I understand you think you love this girl and that you trust her, but get your guard up. She might be perfect for you, kid, but think about it. What's wrong with looking out for yourself? That's why the police carry guns and not sling shots. They aren't looking to shoot you, but they ain't trying to get caught out there either. So, like I said sir, I just don't trust Stacie. I should and I'll try harder. Yeah, I have my phone all the time, but when I'm with Stacie, I ignore it. She doesn't know me well enough to know that me ignoring my phone is a big deal, but at the same time, she does hear it going off all the time." Rashi still didn't like Aria, but he wasn't dating her. His number one priority as far as Aria was concerned was to support his friend and build from there.

"Well, like I said, she seems cool enough to me. She leads a busy life, son. I just think you aren't used to dating someone as busy as you. I'd trust her, Ra." Nehi was serious and to him Rashi with a girl was a plus for everyone on earth with a girl. Dude was a snake in Nehi's eyes and Nehi doubted that would ever change.

What Rashi wanted to say was, 'Yeah, you dating a girl who slept with your friend and your dumb ass took her back.' What he actually said was, "Yeah, I feel you, son. I'll take that into consideration. She is busy and she is from a totally different world than us. I guess we'll see."

JuJaun could tell by the way they were talking that they were still walking on eggshells around each other. In the past he might have said something, but now he was focused on his return to Iowa. The new look was all Chris, but how would he explain it to Carrie? She was used to Jujuan a certain way and this wasn't it. College. That would be the excuse. She'd known him all of his high school life. He'd just say he wanted to try something new now that he was in college. What could she say? It was his head, and on top of that, she'd changed a lot of things about herself since they started dating. Even when he'd gotten back from the trip, she had a new look going. He was cool with that so he wasn't expecting anything different from her as far his new look was concerned.

"So, what else is good in the Chi, y'all? I know I miss home, no home cooking, you clowns don't know how to call, and when I left this piece for school I was worried about who would break you two clowns up when y'all finally fought. This dude was talking about breaking your hands. It was funny as hell though. 'He's a barber, Preach! I gotta break his hands. Put an end to his happiness like he's trying to do mine. That makes two girls he snaked me with.' You should have heard him, Ra."

Rashi hadn't heard this before. This was new. Had he heard it before now, he was pretty sure Nehi would be sporting an MC Hammer type cut. "Damn, son! He was talking about breaking my hands? Seriously?"

"Dude shut up! You were the same way, in this very shop trying to put some base in your voice, 'Let me find out you got me in trouble with my momma, I'm gonna beat yo ass!' Both of y'all are clowns. Friends for all these years, about to fight over a girl. Nehi you can look like that, but you were scared to bring Kionna around him, too. And Ra, when was the last time you smashed a grape? You talking about beating somebody down? I'm going to keep it real with you, Ra. Nobody here believed you. I know I didn't. Me and Rashad was standing there cracking up cause you a clown sometimes. ***You*** slept with ***his girl***, Ra. And then you threatened him? How does that work? Just like this idiot said he was going to break your hands. When he said that to me, I couldn't help but laugh. Nehi, look at your hairline, son. Aside from Ra, who can do anything with that? You break his hands, I'm sure Aria would leave you cause all of your haircuts would be terrible until he healed. Plus, after that, I doubt he'd cut your hair anyway. Anyhow, what we on tonight? I gotta be on I-80 tomorrow night and I'm trying to have enough fun to last me at least a month just in case I can't get back. Iowa ain't as fun as you would think, clown."

"Oh, I forgot to tell you clowns, cause all you lames have girls, but tonight we're partying with models. Stacie has something going on downtown so we on it, kid. I mean, y'all already know I got y'all covered so everything tonight is free. Whatever y'all want. If you clowns, especially you Nehi, were single it would be a model free-for-all. Stacie says it's an exclusive joint. We're all on the VIP, so get ready. We're doin it real big tonight."

Nehi was excited. Aria was a good look for now, but a model? A model was an entirely different story. "I told you I liked Stacie, son. You don't trust her? She's looking out for you for real. Got you a gig in Vancouver-"

"All expense paid, too. Did I mention that? So that trip is all profit."

"Like I was saying, she's looking out for you, kid and you're questioning her? She's a good look, Ra. Don't mess this up. I ain't even been to the party yet and I know this is something I won't get tired of. Partying with models, being on the VIP, yeah I want to look up in a few years and say, 'I'm sick of this luxurious shit!' I don't know about y'all. She's a real one." Nehi was looking forward to this for real. Maybe he needed an upgrade, and a model chick would be an upgrade to the nth degree.

"And I told her you were a DJ, so she might be able to put you on downtown, too. I mean, I know you like rocking the college parties. That's a good crowd, but from what she says, you can meet some connects and network this way, Nehi. Get your name out there even more than it is. I know you ain't feeling being a broke college student, son. How would you have paid for cuts had you broken my hands dude?"

"I ain't going, bro." Rashad finally said something.

Chapter 7

Of course, they tried to talk Rashad into going out, but after his haircut, he had some things he needed to do. The jokes and all of that in the shop were one thing, but this was another. He had to talk to a couple people and planned on doing it that night, the sooner the better. Hanging out with models was sure to be the opposite of what needed to be done. It would only complicate things at that point. Throughout his whole haircut and until he left, the topic of the conversation was him and why he wasn't going. He wasn't feeling good. He was sure Rashi knew what was going on because he didn't push the issue as much as Jujuan and Nehi.

Rashad went back to campus to shower before he headed out to pick up Caryl. He called her and told her that he'd just gotten a fade so showering was the first priority. She was okay with that. They hadn't really been out in a while and had it not been for her busy school schedule, this would have been a bigger deal. He was coming to take her out, so she was cool for now. Maybe he was finally coming around and was getting over the comment she made the last time she was in the dorms with him. Rashad knew he should have missed her more, but spending time with Jackie was making it easier to not see her as much.

When Rashad got back on campus, he headed right for his dorm. Jackie was in the hallway in front of his door waiting for him when he got there, crying.

"What's wrong, kid? You good?"

"Rashad, he hit me. I didn't want to go home, and I didn't want to be around my roommate, so I came here. I'm sorry."

"Jackie, you know it's cool, woman. You okay? How long you been out here waiting on me to get home?"

"Almost three hours, where were you?"

"I was with my guys at the barbershop. Why didn't you at least call me woman? You know I would have come right back. I can't have you in the hallway just crying."

"He took my phone, Rashad. He saw some texts from you and just flipped. The thing is Rashad, I told him we're just friends. I'm not even with him, so I don't even know why he was so concerned, but he flipped out. He slapped me, Rashad. And when that didn't make me cry, he punched me. All I could think about was you and getting out of there. Sorry I came here, but I couldn't go home, and I couldn't head back to my dorm. Sorry."

"Woman, you have no reason to be apologizing. Come on in. We can talk and figure out what we're going to do about this clown. My guys just went out, so we aren't going get them involved … yet. I need you to tell me everything that happened, and you can stay here for however long you need to. I'll talk to your professors Monday and what not. I got you, shorty. I promise you, Jackie. I'll take care of this and make sure you're good. My guys and I will handle your boy, but I need all of his information from you, kid."

"I don't want you and your friends getting in trouble over him. He's a lame and it's my fault." Jackie started to cry again.

"What? Your fault? Are you serious?" Rashad's pops, Flip, was abusive and he just wasn't feeling this at all. "Jackie, ain't nothing you could have done to make what dude did even remotely acceptable. He put his hands on a woman, and as far as that goes, any man that puts his hands on a woman deserves at least one ass whuppin. So yeah, you might not want me and my guys to get at him, but like I said, he crossed a line and has something coming his way. I don't really do the 'hit the girl you love to show her how much you love her thing.' So, yeah, he's about to feel it. I need his information, woman."

"Can we not do this tonight? I just want to rest and not think about this for a while, Rashad. Can we please just chill? I promise I'll get you all the information you need tomorrow. I've been through a lot tonight and I just want it to be over with. I can't believe he actually hit me! I just want this night to be over."

Rashad was thinking about cancelling with Caryl, but if Jackie didn't really want to talk and just wanted to rest, she could have his bed for the night. He'd either stay with Caryl, or crash on his Love Sac until the morning. "Well, this is what's up, woman, I'll let you rest and get today over with. You can sleep in my bed, and I'll just crash on the Love Sac. I have to shower and then go out for a little while. When I get back, I'll be quiet and let you rest. Okay?" She made a face. That's why he said 'okay' more like a question than a statement.

"Rashad, can I ask you something?"

"Of course, Jackie. What's up? You know you can ask me anything. What you need? Like I said, I got you."

"I won't ask you not to go out and kick it, Rashad, but when you get back. I don't want you on the Love Sac. I came here cause I just wanted to be close to you and when you get back, that's what I want. Even if I'm asleep, I want you to climb in with me."

"I snore, Jackie. I don't want to wake you up." Rashad wasn't sure sleeping in the same bed was a good idea, especially after seeing Caryl. "Plus, I don't know how late it's going to be or if you have practice tomorrow morning. You feel me?"

"Please?"

Damn, those eyes, son!!!! "Yeah, I guess shorty. I have to shower, but I'll let you know when I'm leaving out. You get some rest lady."

Rashad showered and headed out the door. He texted Caryl to let her know that he was on his way. He was thinking about Jackie but trying his best to get her out of his head just for the time being. He'd cross that bridge when he came to it. Finding parking downtown was always hard, so Rashad parked near the hospital and hopped on the El. Caryl was at the Cheesecake Factory waiting outside when Rashad got there.

"Did you think I wasn't coming or something, woman?"

"Nope. I was just excited to see you, boy." Caryl was dressed to impress. "I was just out here thinking about you and how nice it is tonight. After this we should do the lake or something, Shad."

"I feel ya, kid. It is a hell of a night. I guess we could do something after we leave here. I'm hungry as hell right now though. Let's do one thing at a time."

"I've missed you, Shad."

"And I've missed you too, Caryl, but we do need to talk. I've been thinking about this all day and we really just need to talk about us … about everything, kid. I mean as much as I like you, woman, I know that if we didn't talk today, it would have been deuces. I know I said we were fine, but it's been on my mind all day, Caryl. We really need to discuss where this is going and what we're doing. I know we just got here but as much as I've been thinking about it, we need to talk now. I could be out with my guys. Preach is in town for a change, but I'm here because this is serious, kid."

"Is this about the Jennifer thing, Rashad?"

"Yeah. You know that ever since I told you about all of that, we haven't really been vibing. I mean, look at what you're wearing. If that ain't a 'eff him dress,' I don't know what is. I have a crazy situation going on at my dorm right now. As important as that situation is, I still put it on the back burner to come and talk to you, Caryl. I need to know the absolute truth, woman. What do you think will happen with us? Cause I ain't trying to waste my time."

"I don't know, Rashad. I was really just trippin cause I was looking at you and your friends, and I let that get the best of me. I mean, Rashi, Nehi, and the girl had some kind of triangle going. Then I hear about you and a pair of sisters, and I'm just not trying to deal with any drama right now, Rashad. The only one who wasn't in some type of craziness was Preach. What would you do if you found out I was with a dude and his brother, Rashad?"

"I'd think whatever I was going to think, but I wouldn't judge you now. I'd know it was your past though and leave it at that. Kid, you can say what you want, but I've been an exemplary boyfriend. We talk. We chill. We laugh. And then you come at me like that over some hearsay? Shorty, aside from what you've heard, and by the way that happened like two years ago, you don't really know anything about me and what I do in relationships. The only reason you know about that is because it was so out of character for me. I'm sure you've made mistakes and all of that, and you know what I'm going to make them from time to time, kid. I don't know who you dealt with in the past, but if they weren't making mistakes, why are you not with them now? I ain't perfect, woman, but at the same time neither are you. The difference is, no matter what your mistakes are, I don't make them bigger than what they are. Also, just so you know, and I'm telling you this cause I want you to know exactly how I feel about it. I don't regret a damn thing, Caryl. I did it. I don't act like I didn't. I don't make it seem as if I'm ashamed of what I did do. I'm a grown ass man, Caryl and I think excuses are for kids, I did it and take the full responsibility. If I were supposed to be with Jennifer, I don't suppose I would have cheated on her, huh? I like you. You're a cutie, but even for a cutie, as shady as you are, I'd be willing to shoot you the deuces."

"Rashad-"

"Let me finish this. I got friends, and I know a ton of females. At the end of the day, if you're my girl, you're my girl. If you feel like this or that and you thinking I'm going to step out, I think that means you need to find you somebody else. If I didn't want to be with you, Caryl, I wouldn't be with you. I got choices. I picked you cause I felt you and I was digging you."

"I know that, Shad, I don't know why I was trippin. I talked to my roommate about it and she asked me if I wanted to lose you over some trash I heard. I knew I was overdoing it then. Rashad, my roommate very rarely makes sense, so when she was right about this, imagine how I felt. I apologize. I just want to make things right. Tonight, dinner is on me."

They sat and ate as planned, talked trash, caught up. Rashad caught her up with what was going on with the crew. He told her how Rashi and Nehi made up, but every now and again you could sense the beef was still there somewhere. It just wasn't as pronounced as it once was. He told her about how Rashi was taking Stacie seriously, and how she was a model. He said how Rashi, of all people, didn't trust her because she does exactly what he does on his phone. He even told her how they went partying that night with models and how Rashi was supposed to be going to Vancouver with Stacie.

The one thing that was absent from their conversation was who Rashad had lying in his bed in his dorm room. She was just now starting to trust him like she should. No need to shake things up the same night. Plus, what she didn't know wouldn't hurt her, especially with Jackie. She was just a friend.

After dinner, Rashad wasn't in a rush to get back to the dorm. Football was tomorrow, but that didn't start until like noon. Plus, he had Jackie there and climbing into bed with her didn't seem like a very good idea after the long speech he gave Caryl. He looked to hang out a while longer, "So what about the lake, woman? I mean dinner was good and I know your roommate is at the dorm with her lame ass." Caryl's roommate Tenesha was a bit of a square. She was kind of churchy, and this made alone time at Caryl's dorm boring. Tencsha liked Nehi, but Nehi thought she was crazy. When they met, Nehi jokingly talked about going to church with her and laughed about it later. Rashad knew that on a given night like tonight she was probably reading her bible.

"I wish we could go to my dorm, but you know Tenesha is there and I really don't want to hear her mouth. She does go home next weekend, and to church tomorrow morning, so I could stand a visit both in the morning and all next weekend."

"Okay, so what about the lake for a little while tonight?"

"If you're coming in the morning, then I need my rest tonight. You know it's been a while."

"True indeed, although the lake tonight was your idea. So, what time then woman?"

"I'm thinking nine. She usually doesn't get back until later in the day anyway, like seven or eight. She usually has dinner and all that with her family on Sundays. You can come any time after nine and we can just chill all day in the dorm making up for these last couple weeks. Wait, why not head to your dorm Shad?"

"Oh, we can't. Ever since we started practicing, coach has been really strict with the dorms and company at night." That was a lie, and a pretty good one seeing as to how he'd thought of it just then. He didn't want to say, 'Can't, shorty, I have another broad at the crib, in my bed waiting on me.' "So what I'll do then is go back to my place and just head your way first thing in the morning. You didn't drive, did you?"

"Drive what?"

"My bad, woman. You know it's been a while. You could have gotten a car and what not. Anyhow, lady, I'll get you home safely."

After dropping Caryl off, and hanging out there until Tenesha was basically complaining about his presence, Rashad finally left and headed back to his dorm. He decided to call his guys and see if they were even answering their phones. Rashi picked up.

"What up, clown? You need to get your ass here, B. All kinds of women here, Shad. Tall, short, extra pretty, obvious model chicks all that and it's like 50 women for every six dudes, B. I mean, women to the left and right, son. You need to get here. Where are you now?"

"Leaving Caryl's on 94. I was going to head that way, but nowhere to park. Plus, I ain't trying to be hanging at the door until one of you clowns comes to get me."

"Dude, I know why you didn't come. I mean, don't say anything, but I kind of have the same situation, son. I know you had to talk to Caryl and most likely Jackie as well. At least you had a good cut while doing it. In all seriousness though, take care of business, son. Hit me tomorrow. I'll tell you what's going on over here. It's crazy. I mean, it's more than just the Stacie thing, bro. Way more. And when I tell you what's poppin over here, you might lose it. I even know it's wrong, but you know how it is. So yeah, we're going to finish partying and what not, but tomorrow, bro, whenever you get a chance, just hit me. That's if you want to talk about it."

"Aiight then, Ra. I'll get at you later. Let me head to the dorms. I still have a long night ahead of me."

"What?"

"I'll tell you when I call you tomorrow, bro. So like noon, I'll get at you. One Hundred."

"Deuces."

The rest of the ride home was quiet. Rashad was hoping that Jackie was asleep. It had been four hours since he left her at the dorm. This clown hitting her. Her staying in his room overnight. Her coming to him about it, and not telling anyone else. This was a lot to deal with, especially for a college freshman with problems of his own. This was a little too much.

So much for hoping and wishing in the car on the way home. When he got to his dorm, Jackie was awake watching TV. She was eating leftovers he'd made a couple days earlier when they chilled after practice.

"What you doing up, woman?" Shad had eaten a while ago and it was smelling great in his dorm room. He decided to grab a little bit for himself as well if they were going to talk. He put some of the leftovers in the microwave and pulled up a spot by Jackie.

"Waiting on you. I got bored and something told me that if I fell asleep, you would end up sleeping in here. Probably try to send me off talking about you were too tired to make it into the bedroom or something. Plus, I slept about an hour and a half and now I'm not very tired. How was your night?"

"It was cool. I chilled with my guys, partied it up a little bit. Thought about you a bunch. I'm trying to figure out what we're going to do about this lame. I can't believe this dude hit you, Jackie. I'm for real pissed"

"You didn't think about me tonight, you're looking good and smelling all good, I'm sure you were thinking about random chicks you can have here instead of me."

"Shut up, woman! I got some dessert for us if you want, cheesecake from the Cheesecake Factory."

"You and your guys went to the Cheesecake Factory? Or did you have a date, dude?"

"Whatever, woman. Rashi and his new girl treated us. Oh, I forgot to tell you, she's a model and she's taking him to Vancouver with her. It was a celebration, I suppose. The worst part is, he doesn't even trust her like that. She's a model, and apparently her using her phone to text is ruffling dude's skirt." Jackie was laughing. After the night she was had, that was all Rashad wanted her to do. Seeing her cry like that earlier was a little bit much for him. "She's a hottie, though. Tall as hell, but cute in the face. So, to celebrate, we kicked it at the Cheesecake Factory then hit the lake. I would have invited you, but I figured you were in here knocked out. Plus, you got a black eye." She laughed at that too. She didn't have a black eye, but Rashad was just trying to keep the subject light.

"Whatever! So when will I meet your guys?"

"Seeing as to how we have to beat this dude up … I mean they're going to want to meet you before the give your boy Chris Brown the biz."

"Whatever, dude. Anyhow, it's late. How long you plan on being up? I'm tired now and since you're finally here I can probably get some sleep."

"Well, I need to shower." He was sure Caryl's perfume was all over him. "Then I'm hitting the sack as well. I can sleep comfortably right there on the Love Sac when I get out."

"Shad, you said- and you promised- that you'd sleep with me. Of all nights Rashad, I just don't want to sleep alone."

"Jackie, I was kidding, woman. I'll be there. Just let me shower real quick and we can watch some Sportscenter or something. Okay?"

"Okay. I'll be there."

In the shower, Rashad kept repeating in his head, 'Shad don't smash her. Shad don't smash her … 'After a longer than normal shower and hopes of Jackie being asleep, Rashad headed into the bedroom.

"Took long enough, didn't you?"

"My bad, lady. I like to be clean. Anyhow, why are you still up? You just had a professional wrestling match, and you're up watching Sportscenter with me. Something ain't right with you woman."

"Whatever, Shad. Come lay down."

Rashad laid down and they talked about what happened that night. Rashad talked about Rashi and Stacie, and his thoughts on the situation. Jackie talked about her date. It started off shaky and she knew by the time they got to lunch that it was going to be a long night. Her ex-boyfriends name was Josh. From jump he seemed to have an attitude. She didn't know if it was her talking about Rashad, or how much time she'd been spending with one of the male hoopers, but Josh was giving off bad vibes the whole night. According to Jackie, as everything went down, all she could think about was Rashad and how close they had gotten. How she would have rather been with Rashad than with this clown and how as soon as she was hit, she knew what she needed to do. That was when they started kissing …

Chapter 8

Things with Rashi were happening so fast that he really hadn't been able to tell anyone. Yeah his guys knew about Stacie. And yeah his guys knew how he felt about her and the no trust thing. What they didn't know was what he was calling the ex-factor. Kionna was the ex-factor to him. She was Nehi's ex, and he'd taken her to lunch to get her closer to Nehi. But since Nehi made his "dumb ass decision" to take Aria over Kionna, she'd been staying in touch with Rashi pretty regularly.

In their last conversation, they'd talked for nearly three hours about nothing. She called because she was sad and thinking about Nehi. Next thing you know they're talking about Jay-Z, Diddy, Gym Class Heroes, and just hip-hop in general. When he looked up, it was two in the AM. Rashi wasn't trying to get at Kionna, and Nehi being his friend was a major part of it. She was cool, but kind of flirty. She also kind of copped an attitude when he mentioned Stacie to her. It was another occasion where there were talking and laughing. She actually asked him what was new, so thinking that she was genuinely interested in what was new, he mentioned that he'd been seeing this one girl and was trying to take her seriously. He said that she was a model, and all of a sudden it was time to go.

The fact that Stacie was a problem for Kionna was weird to him. Rashi had done little talking to Kionna, and even less talking to the guys since the party. Sure, he talked to Rashad the next day, but he'd been kind of distant. He was trying to wake Caryl or something. Rashi wasn't the "I need someone to talk to" dude, but at this point in time, it kind of seemed that one of his best friend's exes was trying to throw the panties at him, so maybe he did need to talk to someone. Smashing Kionna wasn't an option, was it? He was thinking about this when he decided to go to his sister's and kick it with the family for a bit. He ended up talking to his youngest sister Danai because he knew she wouldn't understand what he was talking about anyway.

When he got to his mom's house, he was immediately in a better mode. His mom was cooking and old 70's music was blaring through the house. Rashi kissed his mom and headed upstairs to see Danai. She was doing some kiddy puzzle, 'man kids are idiots' he jokingly thought as he picked her up and took her downstairs to the couch.

"So Danai, should I smash Ki?"

"I say, umm, yeah you should smash Ki! Who is Ki, Rashi?'

"Danai, I need you to keep up. Remember Stacie? The girl you met last week who took us to Chuck E. Cheeses?"

"Yeah."

"Well, she ain't Ki."

"Why would you smash Ki? Is Ki a girl? What did she do to you to make you want to smash her? She must be evil. Want me to smash her for you? You know I don't like bad girls, especially when they mess with my brother. You know what? Let's smash her ass."

Rashi was cracking up at this point. Danai was seven and it was hilarious to Rashi when she cursed. "Danai, watch your mouth. Now that you mention it thought, I might go ahead and smash her. Some bad girls need smashing. Here's the thing, Danai. Stacie is coming over later, so we'll keep our smashing plans to ourselves, okay? Anyhow little lady, how's school?"

"School's good. D,Angelo, he's in my class, he's a jerk. He thought he could beat me in basketball, but I just did like you told me. Pump fake and take it to the rack."

"So, you beat him?"

"Rashi, I smashed D'Angelo!"

"Danai, you did not smash D'Angelo. You beat him down, woman. Oh, guess who else might stop by later? Uncle Rashad, little lady. He's been talking about seeing you for a while. You and all the girls."

"Yayyy! I haven't seen Uncle Shad in so long. Is he in college now?"

"Yeah, he's in college. He's on the hoop team. He's probably coming to see you today, but we're going to see him play ball next week. Just me, you, and Stacie."

"Why aren't you playing, too? I loved seeing you and Rashad play basketball together. And Nehi, and Preacher."

"Danai, it's Preach. And college means that he's on another team. He's in another school, and you know I'm finished with school."

"Why?"

"Because I don't really need college, I have the job I want already."

"But don't you want to play ball with Uncle Shad and them?"

"Yeah, but college would mean no time to chill with you, Angie, and Nae. It would just be us chilling like this every once in a while instead of all the time, like we do now."

"Why is that?"

Rashi knew this conversation was coming to an end. When Danai got into the "why's" of everything, it was time to start looking for an escape route. One came just in time though. The doorbell rang. Rashi was hoping that it was Stacie, but it was Rashad. "What up, clown. You're early son. Who is this, Shad?"

"Oh, this is Jackie, clown. Jackie, this is Rashi, my guy and my barber. These are the girls."

"Rashad, is this your girlfriend?" Danai was still in question mode. "Oh, and guess what? We're smashing Ki"

"What?"

Rashi decided now was a good time to interject. "I'll tell you all about that later, dog. So, Jackie, tell us a little about you. I mean, I've heard about you, but my sisters haven't, of course. We weren't expecting you either, so hook us up, woman."

Jackie was a little uncomfortable, but she was forewarned by Rashad about Rashi and his millions upon millions of sisters. She decided to entertain the girls with her story. "Well, I go to school with Rashad and I play on the women's team. I'm the starting point guard…" As soon as she started, she saw Rashad whisper something to Rashi and they left the room.

"Yeah, B. We got a problem son."

"Dude, she's seven years old Shad. You can't take what she says seriously. I mean she don't even know Ki."

"What the hell are you talking about?"

"What are you talking about?"

"I'm talking about Jackie, bro, and what happened with her the other night. What keys you talking about?"

"You know what? Don't even worry about it, son. What happened with Jackie?"

"We are going to have to give her ex a beat down, Ra. When I left the shop, I had a lot on my mind, son. I was planning on changing clothes and what not, going to talk to Caryl, and hitting up Jackie the next day. When I got to my dorm, she was in the hallway looking beat to shit, bro. I mean, as soon as I saw her, I knew something wasn't right. So, we have to beat this dude down, son." Rashad wasn't asking because he already knew. If he was down, his guys were down. He was surprised when Rashi said no.

"Naw, dude. *We* can't beat nobody down, not even this clown that beat up your girl, B."

"What!"

"Calm yo ass down, Shad. I ain't saying he ain't going to get beat down, but *we* can't do it. Meaning you, Preach, and Nehi gotta sit this one out, B. I mean look at y'all, college students with stuff to lose, clown. I'll take this one for the team and if something happens, it's just me. I mean if I get in trouble, I'm in trouble. I ain't never been in trouble before and I just plan on beating the dude up, not killing him. So, what's the worst that can happen?"

"Nope, kid. We in this together, like always. You don't even know Jackie and you talking about getting into real trouble over her?"

"You vouch for her, so I know she's good people. Plus, she was a topic at the shop, so it's like she's family."

"Dude, I can't let you do this, Ra. You're about to head to Canada and what not. You get in trouble, bro, they will definitely take your passport."

"You really think I care about going to Vancouver with Stacie, huh? I'm going cause she asked me. I don't need Canadian clients, clown. I have plenty of clients here. I'm going to Canada cause she invited me. I mean, I like to travel, but if dude has to be dealt with, I guess he has to be dealt with. So, what am I dealing with here?"

"Shut up Ra. We ain't letting you do this by yourself and you know that. You get in trouble and it's going to be on all of our heads. Like I said, you don't even know the girl and you talking about doing this for all of us? You're a clown, son."

"Am I? Cause it seems to me that you are in college, but not using your brains, Shad. You'd rather four people get in trouble than one? You'd rather make it so that we all lose our passports and y'all possibly lose y'all scholarships? What if you or Jujuan don't make it to the league and you have to play overseas? You can't cause you beat up this clown. Who is he anyway? We know him?

"Nope, he's her ex and his name is Big Josh. He's a bouncer at a club or something, B. That's why it has to be all of us clown. They don't call him Big Josh cause he was a big baby. I mean I ain't trying to have to you go trying to beat this big ass dude up and get hurt cause you didn't know what to expect. Plus, you don't even know Jackie like that, son."

"This is the thing, Shad. You'd go into battle for her, so you automatically know I would. In this case, I got this. I mean just cause he's a bouncer doesn't mean he can throw hands. I'm going to give the kid a south side PHD, a pumpkin head deluxe, then we're going to just keep it moving like nothing ever even happened. You tell Jackie that we're chillin and we're staying on our square. I mean you're going to have to get information on the low, as far as where he chills and where I can catch him slipping, but don't be obvious about it."

"I still don't think you should do this, man. I mean we are a crew, son. If one goes down, we all go down."

"Nope. We're a crew, but this is a situation where looking out for the rest of the crew is more important than that all for one, one for all attitude we had in high school. With this, it can't be a 'we' situation. I got this. Think it about it, bro. We all get caught jumping this clown, there will be real charges. It'll get all of us in trouble and we're looking at real time in jail cause of the whole premeditated thing that will come along with it. If only one of us does it, we run a lower chance of getting caught. We do it like a sneak attack PHD, he'll never know who did it. If it turns into a fight, it's just two dudes fighting so there is no premeditated jumping an innocent individual thing there. Just think about it. I know you care about this girl. If you didn't, she wouldn't be here, and I know you want to be involved, but we still have to approach this intelligently son. As far as him being 'Big Josh,' whatever doesn't kill me only makes me stronger. That's my way of approaching everything. So, if we box and I lose, then that's it we box and I lose, but I won't be losing again."

"Dude, you quoting 'Ye."

"No, clown! Kanye made a song, but Nietzsche said that first. You in college, Shad, open up a damn book!" This was enough to lighten up the mood of the conversation. They were both laughing. "Let's get out there before my sisters eat her alive."

"What was Danai talking about when we came in, son?"

"I have no idea."

"Whatever, son. I think you do. She's talking about smashing. What the hell is that about?"

As if on cue, as soon as Rashad and Rashi stepped out of the back room, there was Danai being Danai. "Rashad, are you smashing Jackie?"

"What?" Rashad was shocked. Not that she asked if he was smashing Jackie; he was sure she had no idea what that meant. He was shocked cause through the whole conversation with Rashi, this clown didn't ask. It wasn't a matter of if he actually did or didn't, but he had been spending a lot of time with her and was expecting questions. Even had a speech prepared for when someone did ask, and he didn't want to give his prepare speech to a seven-year old.

"I'm just saying Uncle Shad, her face looks like you smashed her. It's not that bad, but she does have a mark right here." Danai was touching her cheek.

Rashi decided to step in. He'd put smashing in her head anyway. "Nope, she fell down, woman, but you're nosy as hell, though. So, tell me what were you up here talking to Jackie about anyway?"

"She's like you and Uncle Shad. She plays ball. She won a dollar from me though. I bet her that she couldn't spin the ball on her finger like you, and she did. Can I have a dollar?"

"Oh, you want my dollar cause you lost yours, huh? I got you, but you gotta do something for me. You gotta stop talking about smashing. I mean that was wrong. If you fell and hurt yourself, would you want me to ask someone if you were smashed?" She was shaking her head no. "Exactly, woman. That hurts people's feelings. You didn't say anything to Jackie, did you?" She shook her head no again. "Okay, woman. So, chill with that. Here's two bucks. Go be nice." Rashi turned to Rashad. "He left marks her face? You sure she ain't dating Chris Brown?"

"That's what I said. So, we're getting out of here. I'll bring her by the shop this weekend so that everybody can formally meet her. Tell your moms next time I'll stay for dinner."

"Aiight, clown. Deuces, Jackie, I know we didn't chat much, but it's nice to meet you, lady. I'll see you later this week at the shop, minus the sisters, and we can get better acquainted."

"Okay, it was nice meeting you Rashi. And ladies, don't forget y'all promised to come to one of my games, so I'm holding y'all to that."

"I'll get at you later, Shad. And it was nice meeting you, number 23. I'll have my sisters at a few games this year, woman. Look for us, and watch out, cause young Danai gone have game. She's a hooper, ain't you, Danai?"

"I'll smash you!"

Jackie turned to Rashad as they were walking towards his car, "I like Rashi's sisters. Danai is hilarious and it seems like Rashi is pretty cool too."

After Rashad and Jackie left, Rashi had somewhere to be. He said his goodbyes to the girls and left. He'd told Stacie he'd meet her at Macy's downtown on State, so he left his car there and took the Red Line downtown. Although he loved driving, Rashi loved the El train. Something happened every day on the El, and if you're driving, you missed it. On the train that day, the sock man and the cigarette man got into it, which was hilarious and of course there were a couple cuties in tow. He got a number and although he didn't plan on using it, he still felt good about getting it. Nothing like a Chi-town girl, cute in the face, thick in the waist, and that Chicago attitude. Can't beat that.

When he got to Macy's, Stacie wasn't there yet. Rashi went up to the second floor and did a little looking around. He was in the sportswear section when his phone rang. Of course, it was Stacie. She was coming into the store and thought he was late. She came up to meet him. She was looking quite good today.

"Rashi, I think you should get that shirt. It's cute and I can see you in Vancouver all over the place with me. Oh, and that reminds me. I was talking to my agent and she was saying that we might be able to take some pictures of you. Maybe see what you're like in the life."

"I'm a barber, not a model. My guys would clown me if they heard I was on some modeling stuff, lady. I'm a south side kid, just a dude with some clippers. Nothing sweet here, so me being a model is one of the things we both know ain't happening. Thanks for the offer, though. That's funny, me … a model."

"I'm just saying, Rashi, you have to weigh your options sometimes, all of them. I'm just thinking about you and us and maybe presenting you with more options than what's in front of you. I mean, I know you like being a barber, but do you want to cut hair forever?"

"Stacie, I do want to cut hair forever. I mean I had quite a few chances to go to college. I ***chose*** not to because it wasn't in the cards for me. I've been cutting hair since I was a shorty. I mean I feel you on the options thing, but I try to do me. I know to a suburban little female like yourself, you'd think that being a barber is my job. But being a barber is my life. I love three things at this point in my life, cutting hair, Hip-Hop, and of course basketball. You probably look at me and see a barber and that's it, but I'll surprise you, woman."

"Will you? How would you do that? I'm all ears, Rashi." They were heading downstairs to eat. "I know you're smart, Rashi, and I know you played ball in high school. Rashi, you can't surprise me, dude."

"Okay, lady, keep thinking that. Anyhow, what we doing today? I mean this is cool and all that, but I took the train down here so I'm thinking Michigan Ave for a while and maybe the movies? Then we can hit Giordano's or something like that. Sound good? Or we can head to the south side and you can meet my peeps." Rashi thought about Danai and her big mouth. "Actually, I was there earlier. Let's just chill here and I will pick you up sometime and bring you to the house."

"You don't think I can ride the train?"

Rashi knew she couldn't handle the Red Line. Maybe the Yellow Line out to the suburbs or the Purple, but the Red Line, the Blue Line, and the Green Line were the heart of the Chi. "I'm sure you can, but let me ask you this. How you get here today?"

"What?"

"You heard me, woman. I know you can ride the train, but how you get here today?"

She just started laughing cause she'd taken an Uber. "Does that even matter? I can handle the El."

"So my question, you answering it or you going to keep on dodging the question?" He knew how she got there, she took Ubers everywhere or the Metra, but definitely not the El. It was funny watching her dodge the question, and she was cute as hell when she was squirming. "Stacie, the question is still out there, but I also have another one, but I need them answered in order. I know you can handle the train and we might ride on it after we hit Giordano's and all that. So, the second question is, would you be scared to ride the train at night?"

"Why?"

"Seriously? Is answering the questions that tough? Two questions, how you get here? And are you scared of the El at night?" Rashi was enjoying this, not just Stacie and her obvious avoidance of the questions, but the whole having a girlfriend thing seemed like it may actually be pretty fun. He was having fun with Stacie and although he did like "chillin" with different girls and what not, he was enjoying this. "So, answer the question for me, Estacia'?"

"I got here in a Uber, but I can ride the train whenever. Just cause I grew up in the suburbs doesn't mean I'm scared of the city, Ra." Rashi was laughing and getting into the conversation when it happened like it always does with Stacie. "Can you excuse me for a minute, Ra? I have to answer this text."

"Okay." Rashi acted like he didn't care, but this was the part about maybe having a girlfriend that he hated. When he was with Stacie, he silenced his phone and ignored any calls from anybody but his guys. He'd heard it a million times about him and his texting. Rashi this and Rashi that, and now he kind of saw what they were talking about. He wasn't really feeling being on the other side. He was debating saying something to her about it, but was he really trying to look like the jealous type? Should he start taking his texts right in front of her? Kionna usually seemed like she knew when he was with Stacie cause she seemed to text whenever they were together. Then there was Dayna, this female he met in Old Navy a few weeks ago, right downtown across the street from where they were now. She was cute and he thought about smashing, but she was kind of hood. She was always texting, trying to come by and Netflix and chill or what not.

Rashi thought if he had chicks texting him all the time seemingly wanting to smash, Stacie had to be getting the same type of texts. He was thinking about asking her to come to his place tonight, which was the reason for the 'can you handle the El at night' question, but at this point he, was second guessing it. This just felt different and weird to Rashi; him on the jealous side of things sucked. He always felt jealousy was a female trait. Trying to trust Stacie and her constant step away texts was tough.

Maybe that was it. She always seemed to want to walk away or hide in a closet to answer her texts. If it wasn't another dude, then answer the text right there. He was trying to make it seem like whatever to him, but he was ignoring smashing texts. Was she? Going through her phone to see wasn't an option though. You have to draw the line somewhere and for him that was it. He hated people in his phone and he really felt like as long as he didn't go into your phone there was no reason for you to go into his. His theory until now was either you trust me, or you don't. He knew that he gave women a reason not to and since he wasn't emotionally attached, he was okay with the deuces. Not so much now. He was really feeling her, and his thing was, she was a model and deuces weren't really an option in his opinion.

He was going to have to bring this up at the shop this week. Would telling her how he felt make him to look like a clown in this situation? If he brought it up, would he look like he was being jealous? And would they say he wasn't giving her a fair shot? He knew he stayed on his phone in the past, but he was trying something new for her. Why not expect the same thing? Why not chill smashing these other broads? He did bring up smashing Kionna to his sister though and he had given it some real thought here and there. Was he even ready to chill on smashing and giving this girl 100 percent? He was having a good time until that text came through. Rashi was in a very unfamiliar territory. Stacie was coming back so it was time to act like he didn't care again. "Everything good, woman?"

"Yeah, it was just a friend of mine from the party trying to make sure everything is square as far as Vancouver. He's on the same flight as us, so he just wanted to make sure everything was good. Anyhow, what were we talking about ?"

"Nothing, woman. You answered the questions. You done yet? I mean if we're hitting Michigan Ave, we have some walking to do. Plus, I want to go up to men's in here and have another look at some stuff up there." Rashi had decided in his head that for the time being, he wasn't inviting her over. He'd see what happened toward the end of the date before he did all of that. She didn't seem to be taking this seriously. Why should he? 'I'll chill tonight and text with Kionna for a while. I don't need the headache.' Rashi thought, lying to himself. He was trying to convince himself that he was good and that he did trust Stacie. Being on this side of things was a lot to handle.

"Yea, but can we hit Michigan Ave first? I saw a jacket at the Macy's in the Water Tower that I want to get you. It's hot. I can't wait to get you in Vancouver, Ra. There are so many places there I want you to see, and so many people I want you to meet. Plus, I can't wait to see my friends in your cuts. Can you put the cuts in your portfolio?"

"We'll see. If we get there and the cuts are hot, I'll put some of them in. I have to talk to you about something though, as far as the trip goes. Something came up that put me in a position where I will or won't be able to go. Stop laughing, woman. I'm going to tell you what happened this morning and then we'll decide what I should do from there, kay?"

"What happened, Ra?" Staci was laughing because the 'I will or won't be able to go' comment was funny to her.

"Well, Rashad came over this morning right before I came to meet you. He was with his friend from school. Little chick named Jackie. They have been chillin lately and what not."

"I thought Rashad had a girlfriend."

"How bout you let me finish the story? Anyhow, Rashad and Jackie come over this morning. Jackie is on the female hoop team, so her and Rashad have been chillin because they're friends and what not. Over the last few weeks, they have gotten really close. They hoop together, eat together, crack jokes and what not, but they both have significant others. Well, did have significant others, Jackie apparently went out with her guy last week and I guess because she has been getting close to Rashad, her ex dude took offense to that. He's a big dude, a bouncer, and he hit her. From what I understand, he beat her down pretty damn bad. I mean she didn't have broken bones and all of that, but my sisters noticed some bruising on her face or whatever. I didn't really notice it, but I was only around her for a little while. I was in the back of my mom's house talking to Shad. The thing is, Big Josh, that's the boyfriend, hit her and that really ain't standing well with Shad. He wanted us to roll on him and I had to tell him that we couldn't."

"So, what does that have to do with you not going to Vancouver, Ra?"

"Well, what I told him was that I'd do it on my own. I mean we are a crew, Stacie. So, the thing is I'm a barber and all my guys are in college. I can't put them at risk of getting in trouble. Scholarships and all of that in jeopardy over this woman beater? I can't let that happen. I'm proud of them clowns and I know they are all going to do well. I can't let it go down like that. You feel me?"

"What does that have to do with you going to Vancouver?"

"Well if I get caught Shad say they'll take my passport away. So that is what would keep me from going."

"So why not get him after you get back? I mean, I'm supporting you in this, so I agree you should beat him up, but is there a timeline on beating him up? You could do it when we got back: kind of like an element of surprise. You go have fun with me, get out of the country, and when you get back you can get right back to doing whatever you need to do to Joshua."

"Get out of the country?" Rashi took offense to that statement. She knew about the trip that he and his guys took, So, he really couldn't understand why it sounded like she was assuming he'd never left American soil. "I hadn't thought of doing that, but just so you know, lady, I've left the country a few times. When we met in France, it wasn't my first time traveling. I ain't a model, so I probably ain't jet-setting like you, but I know more than you think as far as international travel goes, woman." Yeah, she really wasn't coming over tonight. It's one thing to be all on your phone texting some clown, but to just assume something like that, that's like another strike against her.

"Ra, it ain't like you tell me all of this. Whenever I get stuff out of you it's always a surprise. Like, you have traveled internationally. How would I know that? We met in France, but all you talk about is the south side. I honestly thought you were there on like a class trip or something. You might not be able to go? When would you have told me that had I not brought it up today? So, dude, don't make it seem like I'm saying you're a loser. I didn't know."

"Whatever, clown, that actually was a good idea though. The element of surprise, huh? I can roll on dude and he'd never know why. From the time we hit Vancouver to the time I get back, I'm sure he'll get into it with somebody. From what I heard, he's a jerk anyway so I'm thinking that would be on point, lady. You are real smart to be a model, you know?" Rashi was teasing her, so he was glad she was laughing at the last joke. "Let's get out of here Stacie."

After the movie, eating, and shopping, Rashi and Stacie ended up at a Cold Stone Creamery for ice cream. He was thinking about asking her over for the night, but there were a few 'excuse me while I check my texts' moments, so he decided against it. He did invite her to come over in the morning to head over to the house to meet his sisters and his mom. He went with her back to the Metra station to drop her off and make sure she got there safetly. When he was on his way to the south side, he decided to text Kionna, and see what was good with her.

Message to Kionna:

Wassup woman, how u doing tonight?

Message from Kionna:

Heyyy Ra. I'm gud just got in had a long day with the family.

Message to Kionna:

You think about me today woman? I thought about u from the time got up.

Message from Kionna:

Yeah, wat about me?

Message to Kionna:

When will it be cool to chill w/ u and not have to worry about Neo trippin. I mean don't get me wrong woman I can chill w/ u now, but I ain't trying to have dude crying.

Message from Kionna:

He chose the Big A remember. It shouldn't matter to him who I mess with.

Message to Kionna:

Whatevs woman. Anybody but me. Remember that. We cool and like brothers and what not but he ain't trying to c u with me. Why am I talking about nehi anyway woman. U think about me today?

Message from Kionna:

U know I did.

Message to Kionna:

What about me cutie?

Message from Kionna:

Just getting to c u and hoping I finally get to chill with u. y didn't you call me earlier 2day we cud have chilled. I was with my family, but I always chill w/ the fam. I wanna chill with u ra.

Message to Kionna:

I was w/ shad today and he wuz w/ one of the chicks from the girls hoop team. She had a little situation and we had to talk about that and what not. I thought about calling u when they left, but I ended up taking gretch and danai downtown. They talked about u all day woman.

Message from Kionna:

Y?

Message to Kionna:

Cause I talked about u all day woman. They're only 7 & 8 but they are 2 of my fav sisters. They listen and are quite inquisitive.

Message from Kionna:

Yeah, so wat u on 2nite?

Rashi dug Kionna and actually liked the texting back and forth, but as much trash as he talked, he was trying when it came to Stacie. So, the coming over thing really wasn't happening. He was all for entertaining the conversation, but he wasn't trying to find himself in a compromising situation with Kionna just yet. She was cute, smart, and funny, but he also knew that she was trouble. Getting with her would cause a rift, not just with him and his guys, but with Stacie, too. If something happened between him and Kionna it would have to be after a long while. Nothing now.

Message to Kionna:

Y cutie?

Message from Kionna:

Cause I wanna c u

Message to Kionna:

Damn im here @ my moms for the nite

Message from Kionna:

U should go home

Message to Kionna:

Should I?

Message from Kionna:

Ra ... u don't wanna c me 2night?

Message to Kionna:

Shorty, u know I do. I'm here w/ the girls though and I cant just leave. Moms is working late 2nite.

Message from Kionna:

Ra, I want to c u now. Guess what I'm doin.

This was the part of the texting that Rashi really liked. Kionna was kind of a freak, in text. These were the kind of females Rashi usually dealt with on the regular. Aside from the dirty texts that were about to start. Rashi knew there was something else to Kionna; something more than just this. For the time being he could deal with just this.

Message to Kionna:

IDK shorty, what a u doin?

Message from Kionna:

I'm rubbing on my kitty kat ...

Chapter 9

Why in hell am I with Aria? Nehi asked himself as he got ready for a party he was spinning. It had been over a month and a half, and from what he could tell, he probably should have stayed with Ki. He called her a few times here and there. She said she was single but talking to somebody. Plus, every time he called or texted, she'd find a way to bring up Aria. Nehi was feeling it now, Aria and her attitude. Since she'd been in college a little longer, damn she thought she knew everything. Every time he was going to class or coming back, she had some bull to say.

Kionna, on the other hand, she was smart as hell, funny, and he liked chilling with her. Aria never shut up and it seemed like the only time she was trying to kick it was after he did his thing. She had complained about him partying and then all of sudden wanted to chill when the party was over. The sex was okay, but was it worth leaving Kionna? Probably not. It was his decision though, and he was sticking with it. Nehi now knew what it meant when people said misery loves company because he was seriously thinking about telling Stacie what kind of dude Rashi was. He knew it would be hating, but every time he saw Rashi lately, this clown was smiling and happy and what not.

Rashi was his guy though, and on top of that Stacie was actually getting him high paying DJing gigs downtown. For some reason, he just wasn't happy seeing Rashi happy. He'd been playing it cool and was even scheduled to head to the shop that day to meet up with the guys and Jackie too. Rashi had been really cool lately, which was a huge reason as to why he hadn't told Stacie anything, but this "happy with one girl Rashi" was the Rashi he'd been waiting for since high school. He'd been thinking of numerous ways to get at Rashi. He just didn't want to jeopardize his lifetime of free haircuts. What if Stacie didn't like what she heard? Would it effect his gigs? What if he already told her about him being a dog? She'd tell Rashi what he told her and next thing you know, no cuts or no gigs for him. Broke and looking bummy with no haircut, that's not really an option. So, at that point, saying something wasn't an option either.

There was also the whole, "this was his first girlfriend" thing. Made it sound like he was virginal, which everyone knew he was not. And look at his first girlfriend. Who in the hell gets her for a first girlfriend? A model? A model who takes him out of the country, all expenses paid! Nehi had Aria who was damn near worse than having a nagging wife, and this fucking guy, who has messed with so many women and broke so many hearts, he gets a model? He gets the opposite of a gold digger his first time out? Talk about life not being fair.

Nehi's phone started to ring. Of course, it was Aria and her boring conversation. "What's up, Ms. Aria? What you up to?"

"Nothing, called to see if you had any plans for today."

"Aria, you already know I do. I'm heading to the shop and then after that I have to be downtown. I Have to set up and all of that. I'm working tonight. We've talked about this maybe ten times."

"Oh, I was hoping that had maybe changed. Wanted to see if you wanted to go to the Lincoln Park Zoo or something."

Seriously? Had it come to this? Was she asking him to come to the zoo knowing he had things to do? Was she just super bored or super jealous? "I wish I could, woman. I really do, but I told you more than two weeks ago that I had these plans. Why don't you come out to the party tonight?"

"Ha, I'll pass. I have studying to do and I'm sure you do, too. You need to be studying."

"Do I? A minute ago, you wanted me to go to the zoo, now I need to be at home studying. If you won't come to the party, why not come to the shop with me. Carrie, Jackie, and Stacie will be there."

"Who is Jackie and who is Stacie? Why isn't Caryl going to be there?"

"I don't know why Caryl won't be there, but Stacie is Ra's girl and-"

"What? Rashi has a girlfriend? Who the hell would date him?"

"Some chick named Stacie. She's a model and she's cute as hell, too. She's actually taking him to Canada next week, so we're meeting at the shop and I'm sure Rashi is fine with you coming."

"And who is Jackie? I thought Rashad was so in love with Caryl. He's moved on already? Or is he cheating like the rest of your so called crew? I bet Jujuan is probably cheating too, ain't he?"

"What are you talking about woman? This ain't a cheating party. Jackie is a friend of Rashad's from school. She had a bad situation and they've been hanging out a lot since. Him and Caryl are still together, woman. Why are you even trippin?"

"Whatever, Nehi. And the answer is no. I don't want to be anywhere near your stupid ass friend Rashi. I don't even see how you're cool with him. He's a snake and a liar and you should beat his ass."

"Is that what I should do? Why is this even an issue right now? Aria, he's my friend. We're past what happened in high school, why aren't you? What is your deal, Aria? You talked to his mom. You seem upset cause he's obviously maturing a little and got a girlfriend. I mean what the hell, Aria? He doesn't give a damn about you, what's going on with you, who you're chillin with, what your grades are like, none of that. And somehow here you are, still somehow worried about Rashi and what he's doing. What's up?"

"Nothing. I just thought you'd be more upset like me. He's the reason we weren't together for more than a year, Nehi."

"So, I should hold this grudge forever? This dude has had my back for years. He's cut my hair for years, too. I say you need to let it go, woman. I don't have any beef with the man. He's a friend of mine and he's going to be a friend of mine. If that's going to be a problem for you, then you need to let it be known. I can't put you ahead of my friends. I did that before and slept with one." As soon as the words left his lips, Nehi knew something was about to go down. Before he had a chance to apologize, Aria was already worked up and from what he could tell crying.

"Forget you, Nehi. I told you he took advantage of me. I thought we were past this, but apparently we aren't."

"It's not like that, Aria, but you seem like you just don't want dude to be happy." He was one to talk. He was just thinking before she called about blatantly hating on the kid. "I said he had a girl and you almost lost your mind, woman. Should he just be single? As a matter of fact, in a perfect world, ***your*** perfect world, where would Rashi be right now? Dead? In jail? What? I mean you can be the judge and jury of what happens to that man. What do you do to him? Don't forget the fact that you slept with him knowing full well that he is one of my best friends. I mean, I think whatever happens to him should happen to you, too. Why not, right? There were two wrong individuals that night. Don't you find it kind of funny how you always want to make it seem like Ra is the devil, but we tend to forget that he had a partner in crime right? He had someone else there with him, Aria. This wasn't a rape, woman. We are talking consensual sex. So like I said, you're the judge and the jury. What happens to Ra, for basically doing nothing? He didn't betray you. He betrayed me and apologized more than you, but somehow you're the one keeping the beef up. So yeah, tell me cause I feel like the only one losing here is me. The shop is going to be fun today cause there are going to be females there. We are making it a whole night together, but not me and from the sounds of it, forever. Whenever we do things together, I'll be fifth wheeling it cause my girl apparently thinks that Rashi was more wrong than her when they both back stabbed me." Nehi wasn't really trying to take up for Rashi, but they were both wrong and she'd been acting like it was only Ra from the moment he found out. When Ra told him, cause in his mind, she wouldn't have.

"I don't know."

"Of course, you don't. According to you, Rashi was wrong as two left shoes, and I'm guessing you were the victim, right?"

"I ain't saying that Nehi-"

"Yeah, I gotta go. I'm heading to the shop and to be real with you, I plan on having fun. This conversation is actually the opposite of that right now, so I'm going to go ahead and get ready. You can text me if you want, but I'm shooting you the deuces now. Deuces." Nehi hung up the phone feeling better than he felt when he got on it. Aria called right back, but he decided to ignore it. He said what was on his mind and he was feeling too good about it to let her bring him down. It was about time I started weighing other options, meet someone new, or even give getting back with Kionna a real shot. Yeah, she was talking to some lame, but she knew what was up. All I have to do was give it real shot. Let her know what was up. At this point he decided to invite her to the shop. Why not? They were still cool, and he wasn't trying to be the only one there by himself. She wasn't his girl but was still his friend.

The phone call to Kionna was kind of weird. When she answered, she seemed like she didn't want to bothered by him at all. As the conversation went on, and she found out he was inviting her to the shop and that all the guys would be there, she started to loosen up. She even asked why Aria wasn't going to be there. He told her that she wasn't invited. She seemed to be in good mood by the end of the conversation and had even agreed to come to the shop and the party. Why had he picked Aria over her was still a mystery to him. She was almost perfect. Supportive, cute, funny, fun to be around, he did make a mistake, but maybe this could be the first step in fixing it and Nehi was seriously thinking about fixing it. He then called the shop. Rashi was there with Stacie, Jujuan, and Carrie. Rashad and Jackie were in route. They were riding together. Nehi wanted a new and different because his guest was going to be a little late, but he still wanted to impress her.

"Who is it?" Rashi was asking because he was sure when plans were made that the Big A definitely wasn't coming. So, this special guest business had him thinking otherwise.

"Oh, you'll see, son. And believe me, you aren't expecting her. I mean this would probably be the last person any of y'all would expect to see in the shop with us."

"Oh." It was official in Rashi's head that a long night of being uncomfortable was in front of him cause apparently Aria was coming the shop. "Okay, well we'll be here, clown. I'll see you when you get here. Deuces."

Nehi liked the idea of having Ki come to the shop. No nagging, no constant Rashi talk, no school and homework talk. Plus, this could be the beginning of a reconciliation. That was the plan now. Do what he had to do to get Kionna back, not take no for an answer.

When Nehi got to the shop, it looked exactly how he expected it to. Everybody was there laughing, and Rashi was in his chair holding the page in a Greek mythology book, talking trash.

"Carrie, yo momma so fat, every time she turns around, we throw her a welcome back party! Oh, Nehi, what's good, clown? I see you brought your date with you, your right hand!"

Rashi was clowning as usual, but it seemed like everybody else was, too. "Shut up, clown. Sup Shad, Preach, Carrie, Stacie, and I'm assuming you're Jackie? Sup, woman? I'm Nehi, the DJ." Jackie was kind of cute. If he didn't know any better, he'd say Rashad was smashing her on the side. He knew better though, and knew Shad was feeling Caryl way too hard. Although she was absent from the shop today. "So, what's good, people?"

Rashad was first to answer him. "We chillin, getting cuts, just really letting the girls, aside from Carrie, get acquainted. I heard Aria is coming, this should be fun."

Nehi thought it was funny that they had just assumed Aria was coming. He'd talked to Ra, so he was sure Ra broke the 'bad news' to them. This was a good surprise. The crew would be on his side because they really couldn't stand Aria anyway, and Ki would have to at least know he was serious. Inviting her to chill with the crew and their girls, except for Jackie, but this would almost be like the trip. He didn't even bother to say too much, just sat down and waited on Ki and laughed at these clowns making yo momma jokes and clowning. He was next in the chair when Rashi came over to the window and talked to him before his cut.

"Nehi, can I get a minute, son?"

"Wassup, B? Another yo momma joke?"

"Nope, I have to talk to you, B. Step outside the shop with me for a minute, okay? It won't be long, and I'll hook you up for tonight. I just have something to say to you, bro."

"What?" They walked outside and Nehi had no idea what Rashi was all of a sudden serious about. "I know I wasn't making a bunch of jokes, but I was just waiting on my guest to get here is all."

"It's not about that. I was just about to say once again, B, I'm sorry about all that stuff with me and Aria, son. I wouldn't lie to you about it, but since our stories obviously differ, I'll take the blame. I mean, I just want you to know that when she gets here, no matter how she acts towards me, son, I'm going to keep it one hundred. She won't feel like an outsider. I promise, B. I mean, I know I can be a jerk sometimes, but on my momma, I'm sorry. I know what went down was wrong and I'm just saying, B, when she gets here, it will be like nothing ever went down, son. So, I was just bringing you out here to let you know that. Again. We boys, Nehi, and I wouldn't do anything to mess that up, son."

"I feel ya, B. All is good, Rashi. Plus, when my girl gets here, you won't have to act like anything." It was funny to Nehi, apologies and everybody tense about Aria, and she wasn't even coming. That meant when Kionna got there, everything would be perfect. Rashi walked back into the shop and Nehi saw Kionna parking her father's car on the corner. He went to meet her. He wasn't one hundred percent sure, but it looked like she rolled her eyes when he got to the corner. When she got out the car, she seemed fine. It could have just been a trick from the sun or something.

"What's up, girl? You're looking good as hell today. That dress is a beast. Well, everyone is here, and they aren't expecting you, so this should be good."

"Yeah? Who's all there?"

"You'll just have to see when you get in there. I don't even know everybody like that. Let's just get in here and have fun."

When Nehi and Ki came through the door of the shop, Rashi looked like he'd seen a ghost. Everyone seemed to be happy to see Kionna. It had been a while. But Rashi just got up and headed to the restroom in the back of the shop. Nehi noticed this but guessed that Rashi was just shocked because he was expecting Aria.

"Ra, stay calm. You ain't did nothing wrong. A text or two ain't never hurt anyone. Keep it together, son!" Rashi was in the restroom throwing water on his face and talking to himself. "What the hell is she doing here? Did she tell Nehi about the texts and all that? What the hell am I going to do?" Rashi decided to head out and just try to keep it one hundred. Hopefully, she wouldn't say anything cause at that very moment he was sure she was being introduced to Stacie. Rashi decided to go out and face the music.

"What are you doing, bro?" Nehi was the first person that said something to Rashi. It looked like the girls were just getting to know each other over his shoulder.

"Nothing, B. Had to run to the washroom. My stomach hurt all of a sudden. You ready for that cut?"

Rashi seemed kind of anxious to Nehi, but he didn't know why. It couldn't be Ki. So, what the hell was it? "Yeah, Ra. You feeling up to it though?"

"I'm good, bro. What's up, Ki? Long time, no see, lady. How you been?" He'd actually seen a lot of her yesterday on his phone. The texts had started turning into pics and videos and things like that. This was kind of awkward. "Man, it's actually pretty good to see you. You and Ne back together?" He asked because it was something he NEEDED to know. He couldn't have another Aria situation on his hands, especially after that embarrassing ass speech he just gave. "Did you tell him to keep you coming a surprise or something?" That seemed like something a female would do, but she knew the situation. She told him a ton of times over texts that she wouldn't deal with him if Nehi was anywhere in the picture. He was saying that when 'his girl' got there this and 'his girl' that. Damn, son! Not again.

"Nope, he invited me out because everyone was going to be here and I miss y'all. So, what's new with you? Ra Ra?" She'd started calling him Ra Ra for some crazy reason, kind of their own little thing, and she was putting it out there for the world to know.

"Nothing at all, woman. Going to Canada next week, and then beating some dude name Josh down when I get back. What's new with you, lady? You're looking good. Nehi must be doing you right." Yep, he said that. Rashi wasn't very good at backing down or being humble, so this was about to be one of those situations where either one of them would chill for the time being, or the whole night would be a disaster. "He told us his girl was coming. I was expecting one liar but got you … another."

The whole shop got quiet and looked over at Rashi and Kionna. "What?" Yeah, he said that. "What did you say to me?" Kionna was getting loud.

"Why's is everybody looking over here? I was joking. I said I was expecting lying ass Aria, and we got you. You know, expecting one chick, got another. An upgrade, right? Anyhow, woman, welcome to the shop. Ne, you ready for your cut?" All that without taking his eyes off Kionna once. "Oh, you meet my girl, Stacie?"

"Oh yeah, this guy went and got a girlfriend. I forgot you ain't talked to the crew in a minute." Nehi decided to step in. It was starting to seem like the conversation with Ra and Kionna was getting a little personal for some reason. "Can you believe this clown? A girlfriend for this dude. I was almost a shocked as you. You look way shocked woman."

"I am."

Stacie heard and came over because she wanted to know what was up too. "Why are you shocked?" This was Nehi's girl, but it seemed to her like something just wasn't right.

"The trip." Ki was trying to get herself composed and look like she didn't really care.

Rashi finally jumped in to change the subject. "She went on the trip with us, babe. It was fun. She and Nehi were like the couple of all couples, then they ended it, or so they say. Anyhow Nehi, you're the DJ, get in the chair so we can get you to the party and we can shake our asses. I mean you can DJ like that if you want, but I doubt your girl will like that, son."

"Whatever, B. Let's get this going, son."

Rashi started to cut his hair, taper fade two parts on the right, right above the ear. Every now and again, he'd look up and every time sure enough, Kionna was staring at him. Not in an obvious way that Stacie and Nehi would notice, but there it was every time. She took out her phone and put it away. A couple seconds later, Rashi got a text. "Stay here, son. I'm just about done. Gotta run to the washroom real quick." When Rashi got there, he knew who the text was from.

Message from Kionna:

LIAR!!!!!!!!!!!!!!!

Message to Kionna:

Me? I never said I didn't have a girl, and you're here with Nehi. Let me finish Ki, we'll talk later!

Rashi came back out of the restroom. Nehi was talking to Stacie about the party and of course Kionna was looking at him crazy. She must have gotten the text. Nehi was still in the chair. He was texting on his phone as well. Rashi came up to finish his cut. He could see that Nehi was texting Aria about something, but that wasn't his concern. Kionna was really in here acting like she was upset with him, and she was here with Nehi.

Nehi, on the other hand, was trying to dodge a bullet. Aria was texting him, talking about how she could come by. After that whole thing earlier, she was really trippin. Did Rashi text her from the bathroom and tell her that Kionna was here? All of a sudden, she seemed real interested in coming. From what he could tell, Kionna really couldn't keep her eyes off of him though. She looked mad, but she was watching him like a hawk. She was most likely upset that he was calling her his girl. By the end of the night though, they would be closer. He'd talk to her later about another chance. At least that was his plan until she came over.

"Damn, Nehi … Did I tell you how good you looking? I mean before the haircut you were fine, but now, I mean I could eat you up." She said it to Nehi, but it was obvious to Rashi that she was on something else. Her lying ass, son! It seemed like she was trying to make him jealous.

"Man, get a room!" Preach was joking, but from what he saw, everything was cool. "Ki, you and this clown, Nehi, how long y'all been back together? I'm glad to see it. Look at Nehi. He looks happier, too."

"Oh, not long at all. Right, Nehi?"

"Nope, but we're working on it. You know what I say. We do it one day at a time, so tonight, we chillin. I mean, I was going to say something later, but after the party Ki, I want you to stick around and kick it with me."

"Of course, baby." She was looking directly at Rashi. "What you want to do after the party?" She wasn't expecting it, but she wasn't trying to look like a fool in front of Rashi.

"Not in front of these clowns, woman! We'll talk later so whatever we say is between me and my girl. I'm not talking about anything between me and you in front of them. We talked earlier and we talked a few times over the last couple weeks." He didn't seem to notice, but Rashi had stopped cutting at this point and was watching this interaction. "We already know what we have to talk about."

Apparently, everyone else was listening because Carrie whispered to Rashad, Jackie, and Preach, "Is she pregnant?" They all started laughing, and Nehi noticed then that the whole shop was watching. He must really dig her. They were damn near having a full private conversation with an audience.

"Like I said, woman … We'll talk later."

Rashi finished the cut and they all went back to talking and laughing. Nehi noticed a couple things in the shop. Ki wasn't really talking to Rashi, or Stacie, which was a plus to him. And Rashi kind of seemed distracted. His girl was there, but he was usually extra comfortable at the shop like he was at home. It seemed like he was expecting a call or something. He kept checking his phone. He didn't care that much though. After a few feeble attempts the last couple of weeks, it seemed that all it really took to get at Ki was her to actually see him. He didn't blame her. Over the phone was different than in person. They were in the shop for about another hour when Shad, Preach, Jackie, and Carrie decided to leave to get dressed. Nehi had to leave too. He wanted Ki to go with him, but she seemed to be more interested in her phone right then.

Message to Rashi:

We can talk at the party cause it's not what it looks like Rashi. I know from there it looks like I lied, but I didn't.

Message from Rashi:

Yeah? Whatever woman, if we talk we talk, if not then we don't. MY GIRL is with me tonight woman. Plus your man is DJaying. Show him some damn respect!

Message to Rashi:

Rashi I'm serious, it's not what it looks like. You don't agree to talk to me I promise yesterdays text will be all over this shop. Your girl know you a liar? She know you trying to get with me? I'm sure she don't.

Message from Rashi:

You think I give a damn? Your man know you sending out pictures of your goods? To me? His best friend? Like his last girl Aria? Shorty you don't scare me, Stacie is my girl, but if you decide to do what you're talking about doing, I can give a damn.

Message to Rashi:

Lets just talk later please.

Message from Rashi:

Whatever.

"I have to grab my stuff and get ready for the party, woman. You want to come to the crib with me? I mean we can chill for a bit, but I have to be there before the rest of them."

"Yeah. Let's go, Nehi."

"We out of here, people. Y'all be good. See y'all later and Stacie, thanks again for the gig. I appreciate it."

The party was off the chain. Nehi was doing his thing. Feeling good, looking good, and he had his favorite girl back. He was going to have to break the news to Aria, but he could do that tomorrow. Tonight, was all about him and Ki. Deuces, Aria. You had your second chance. Who knew you went and aged like a granny, forever talking that trash? While Nehi was doing his one-two thing, he saw Rashi and Kionna dancing. He was cool though. Rashi apologized and maybe this would kill some of that barbershop stress they seemed to have.

Rashi was chillin. He didn't really dance much at these parties, but of course Stacie was off somewhere texting. When Kionna asked him to dance, he originally said no. But she said they needed to talk, and since she was going to be there all night, texting was out of the picture.

"What you want, Aria … I mean Ki. What you need, Ki?" He did that on purpose. She ignored it.

"Rashi we need to talk. Nehi see us over here arguing or whatever, it's gone raise a bunch of questions. So, can we please talk? Like on the dance floor"

"Shorty, I ain't got nothing to say. Just today I told Nehi I'd never do him dirty again. Then you show up at the shop. Keep it moving."

"Me and Nehi ain't together!"

"What?"

"Come dance with me and I'll tell you, Rashi."

Rashi reluctantly went to the dance floor. He passed Preach and Carrie dancing on the way. "If you see Stacie, just let her know I'm on the dance floor. She can come and cut in anytime. Ki didn't have anyone to dance with since Nehi is doing his thing right now." They got on the dance floor, and although it was loud, he was able to talk to her a little bit. "Shorty, we don't need to talk at all. We both know I have a girl, you have a guy, and that's it. You do you, and chill with texts."

"Ra, it ain't like that at all. He called me today and the only reason I came was to see you."

"Okay, and you saw me, Ki. I have a girl and there's nothing else to it." Rashi was keeping his cool. If someone else was looking, which he suspected they most likely were, it would just look like some guy and some girl on the dance floor talking. "I gotta give it to you, kid. You played me, but it's nothing. You do you kid and you don't need to worry about hearing from me again."

"What? What about you, Rashi? You have a girlfriend. This tall, funny looking chick comes from out of nowhere, and you of all people decide to make her your girl? More importantly, you didn't even bother to tell me. We're texting and all of that. I'm sending you pictures of me, and you have a girl. You played me, Rashi."

"Did I? Let's be real, kid. You ain't even ask me if I had a girl, not once. You think I'm going to pass on pictures of you? Had I known you were messing with my guy, I would have. But what can I say? You lie like a rug."

"I told you. I came to see you. I wanted to see you all this week, last week, and the week before that. In all honesty, Ra, I want you. I came cause Nehi mentioned you. I wanted to see where my future man worked. I wanted to see where you were when you were thinking about me. Rashi, you are sexy as hell when you're cutting hair."

"Chill, woman. My girl is here. Plus, you think I'm going to stand here and listen to you talk about my guy? Dude, even if you're telling the truth, you think it's cool to play my guy like this? You hurt him with this shit. It's going to come back to me cause you on that bullshit. You need to tell him something and not what you just told me. If he calling you his girl, and you aren't his girl, that still makes you off limits. Kionna, I'm involved."

"Are you? Rashi, I saw how you were in Europe. You aren't taken. I mean you might be involved, but this whole girlfriend thing is dead. She ain't cute, for one. For two, she's way to tall, and three, she's probably hood as hell, too."

"Yeah, you think? Kionna, she's a model. Not a Kmart catalogue model, not a hand model, or no bull like that. She's a runway model, that real model shit. So, all that trash you talking, you might as well kill it. Ki, I need you to hear this. You're a clown, Kionna. You got dumped by this dude then you come back to him cause you trying to play games. Nehi should drop your lying ass. And you gotta know, girl or no girl, after this, I definitely ain't smashing you. Damn! Nehi, what the hell?"

Nehi took a break to come down and dance with his girl, and of course he walked in on the conversation. "What you talking about, Ra?" He heard him loud and clear, but was hoping he misheard.

"Man, nothing, B. Get your girl though. Me and Stacie are leaving, son. I gotta get up early, son. Deuces." Rashi found Stacie after looking for what felt like forever, and they left.

Nehi was a little pissed. He walked up on what seemed to be Rashi telling Kionna that he wasn't going to smash her. He had to keep his cool because he was working. He told Kionna that if she wanted to leave, she could. She said she would stay because they needed to talk, and she had to clarify some things. At that point, he kind of felt like whatever, and went back to the DJ booth. He finished up and bid Shad, Preach,

Jackie, and Carrie goodbye. He didn't tell them what was going on, but they could see that he was upset. He told them not to worry and they would talk the next day. He was getting his things together to leave when Kionna came out of nowhere.

"What you hear, Nehi?"

"You tell me, woman."

"I don't know. I was talking to Rashi about us. He asked and I told him. He wanted to know why I was here. I told him why. You invited me."

"So, the smashing was what? Let me guess, a joke? Kionna, what the hell is going on?"

"Nehi, you shot me the deuces. While you were playing house with Aria and all of that, Rashi was the one calling me and checking up on me. I mean, yeah lately you call. But before that, Rashi was calling to check up on me, bring me things I needed, and keep me company, over the phone of course. I would ask about you and all of that, and every time he'd make sure I was good. You had someone and your situation was like a happy family. You picked some girl who cheated on you; some fat girl who slept with your friend. You knew her longer, and that was the reason you chose her? Yeah Nehi, I'm attracted to Rashi, but it's because I see that he's a good guy. Yeah, he may have done some dirty stuff to you, but you tend to ignore all the other stuff, Nehi. He talked me into fighting for you. He apologized for the Aria thing, and he checked on me after you dropped me. He still cuts your hair to this day. I came cause I wanted to see him, Nehi. I'll never give you another chance with me. You're a lame. You and that fat bitch!"

"Then deuces, woman. You stayed here for that? You could have just texted." Nehi's mind was made up. He would do what he had to do to get back at Rashi. Stacie, he would either smash her or let her know what Rashi really was. Big Josh, he would warn him about Rashi and his dumb ass plan. Forget Rashi and his 'captain save a hoe' ass. That lame ass apology, once again this dude was playing him behind his back.

Chapter 10

Going to Chicago those couple of times made things a little easier for Chris. Chris had been dealing with an older lady named Cierra for a few weeks. It was getting a little too comfortable. She cooked, cleaned, and didn't ask too many questions about anything. When he left town, she was cool with it. She knew Chris was a student from New York, so she let him do his thing. What Chris or Jujuan didn't know about Ms. CiCi was that she was a die-hard college basketball fan. She was a season ticket holder for the Iowa men's basketball team and she liked the fact that Chris's roommate was on the team. She hadn't really questioned Chris too much about who it was. She knew eventually that Chris would introduce them.

Practice was going well, and they had won their exhibition games. To Jujuan, Chris was providing him with a break from school and Carrie. She'd been trippin lately, so when he took her to Chicago out to party and spend quality time, she felt better about the situation. The trip back home let her see everyone she was missing, so some of her homesickness would go away. It also made her back off Jujuan a little, giving Chris a little room to operate.

Chris was at a Barnes and Noble's bookstore, when he met Ms. CiCi. She was sitting on one of those comfy chairs reading a Tony Morrison book. He didn't plan on even talking to her, but as he was walking past her, he accidentally knocked her book over. He picked it up, and of course apologized. The next thing you know, they were having a conversation. Originally, he was going to introduce himself as Jujuan, but he decided that Chris would be a better man for this one. She was a cutie, five foot four, stacked, and her conversation was good. In that first talk, he found out she was 41, no kids, and a nurse at the hospital across town, nowhere near the university. That was a definite plus. She grew up in the area, so the campus wasn't appealing to her at all. She was an older local whose life didn't revolve around what was going on at the University. To Chris, she was older and had so much more to think about than him. Chris found himself a cougar and planned on having a blast with her. They had a good conversation at the bookstore. She gave him her number, he called the next day, and they had another good conversation.

The following weekend, they hung out, Chris tried to impress her as much as he could, he opened doors and pulled out chairs. The only bad thing was that sometimes he called her ma'am. He wasn't trying to make her feel old, he was just being respectful. Where in the hell did he get these Southern manners? They'd spent a few weekends together, Sundays mostly, watching football and eating whatever she cooked. She was fun, and he always tried to make her feel young when they were together. The sex was good as well, so no complaints there. He'd been out of town twice in the last month, but when he got back, he'd had some good stories about his friends back home and what had been happening in his life outside of school.

Jujuan loved living as Chris. Everything Jujuan didn't want to do or wouldn't normally do, he made sure Chris did. Cheating, check. Lying, check. Crazy haircuts, Check. Sleeping with old ladies, Check. Chris loved this old lady thing cause once a week was good enough for her, and any time more than that, she treasured. If he stopped through on a Wednesday, she'd get up and cook for him. She'd stay up late and watch TV or DVDs with him. To Chris, she was just another girl; an old one, but just another girl all the same. She was doing the things these other females weren't doing. Being on campus for all these months and being able to get a steak, now that was a plus.

She was a mature kind of sexy to Chris. It was obvious that she worked out, and that she was very conscience about how she looked. All these girls on campus in sweats weren't really what he was looking for. Plus, he was known on campus. He was the freshman guard from Chicago so a chick there would definitely reach out to Carrie. Or Carrie would find out on her own, and what Chris did wasn't Jujuan's business. Chris wouldn't get Jujuan in trouble and vice versa. Cici wasn't Fresh or Tia, so this would be easy. Tia the clinger, all she wanted to do was hang out and have sex, which was pretty much all Fresh wanted to do as well. The biggest thing was that Ms. CiCi wasn't pulling Preach away from Carrie.

Carrie didn't like football, so on Sundays, Chris got to be Chris, and during the week Preach got to spend time studying and hanging out with his girl. Jujuan still felt like he and Chris were the same person. He loved living this double life he had. All week he was boring Preach, weekends and every so often during the week, he got to be Chris. Practice during the week as Preach, chill with Ms. CiCi and be Chris on Sundays. Chris provided a break from the boring Preach thing cause outside of practice, school was starting to get to Jujuan. He didn't like his professors, and the reading was too much. With practice and all of that, Chris was therapeutic for Jujuan. On the other side of it, Jujuan got Chris away from this old lady. Since Chris didn't have to make everyday appearances, chill, and watch "her stories," he was fine. The food was good, but the time away was better.

Chris was at Ms. CiCi's house eating, when he let her know that he'd be leaving early. He had to go because Jujuan had a basketball game the next day. This was the real season, so he had to be serious. She would never know it, but Sundays this season were pretty much open so aside from a few games on those odd Sunday's he'd be at her house happy. Chris wasn't expecting Ms. CiCi to make it the whole season as his woman though. She didn't know, and Chris liked it like that. Chris would give it a few weeks if it was bad and a couple months if it was good. Maybe it would be an accident, or he would pick a fight, but it would end. Those were the "Gotit Rules."

These were the Gotit rules, Jujuan spent a whole night writing them:

1. No girl for over three months - Three months start to look and feel like a real relationship, and since Chris wasn't a real person, being in a real relationship wasn't an option.
2. No matter how good the sex or conversation was, no tw- day sleepovers. This rule was there for Jujuan. Two days off campus meant no Carrie, and if Jujuan wasn't in his dorm that long, questions started to arise.
3. No bringing girls to the dorms - even a dog can remember how to get home if you show her where you live. He would hate for some chick to just pop up looking for Chris and get Preach.
4. Chris could use Jujuan as a friend to get rid of a girl, but that was it. No mention of Jujuan or anything like that. Jujuan was there for breaking thc 'bad news' about Chris's accidents, and that was all.
5. No backtracking. Any girl that was a girl of Chris's once, wouldn't have that pleasure again. Chris was only moving forward. If he moved backwards, he took the chance of putting Jujuan in jeopardy.
6. If a girl recognized Chris in public, ignore. In character or not, the past is the past and if she recognized Chris, she was a girl from the past. No speaking, smiling, no head nods, nothing. Chris didn't answer to Chris, and neither did Jujuan.

Dinner with Ms. CiCi was cool. When he left, Chris was feeling good. Jujuan would get to play his season in peace. No Chris stuff, no Ms. CiCi stuff. When Chris wanted to see Ms. CiCi, he would. And when he wanted to be Jujuan, he could just chill and be Jujuan. After all of this, he was feeling good. But his lack of foresight was Jujuan's Achilles heel in this matter. He was nineteen. Looking at life like a chess game wasn't his thing. Thinking five moves ahead instead of one was something that Jujuan wasn't ready to do. You live in a small town and you're the new star of the basketball team, you will be in the newspaper. Both faces in one picture, Chris and Jujuan. So, when Ms. CiCi saw the article on Jujuan, of course she paid attention. She thought it was Chris at first sight.

Freshman From Chicago Shines in Iowa Opener

Freshman from Chicago, Jujuan West, looked sharp last night as he lead Iowa past Ball State University in the season opener. Going 9 – 14 from the field including 3 for 4 from the three-point line and making all 11 of his free throws. The freshman from Chicago had 30 points, 4 assists and 5 rebounds. A shining moment came late in the second half when Iowa was down by 7 with just 6 minutes to go. West made two 3-pointers and the go ahead lay up for Iowa. Listed at only 6 foot one inches, don't let his size fool you. This kid, if he keeps it up, could make sure Iowa is playing deep into March.

She stopped reading after the first paragraph. Ms. CiCi wouldn't say anything until she actually saw this Jujuan in person. When Chris got there, Ms. Had a feast waiting for him. Baked chicken, homemade macaroni and cheese from scratch, biscuits, green beans, and for dessert, peach cobbler and vanilla ice cream. This is what he loved about this whole older lady thing. These young chicks can't cook. These young chicks don't rub your shoulder and legs. Ms. CiCi was a win.

"Damn! It smells good as hell in here, woman! Is there a special occasion or something?" Jujuan, while being Chris, loved going over there. It always smelled like something was coming fresh out of the oven. It reminded him of his granny's, which was hilarious. His girl was old enough to be a granny. Rashi would love that little fact, jokes for days.

"Nope, I just missed you baby. It's been a few days and you know I get lonely when you're not here. I mean, I love you studying and doing you. When I know you're coming, especially in the middle of the week like this, I like to make sure when you go back to campus, you're fully satisfied."

"I missed you too, woman. I've wanted to come out here and kick it with you all week. My English 101 class is killing me. I'm working hard to get at least a B though. I wanted to come yesterday, but I was in the library until about 1 am. I'm tired, but I had to get out here and see you. I was missing your touch, lady."

"Were you?"

"Yes ma'am. I mean I was out of town last weekend, then the following week was all work, no play. This weekend, I was busy with an English paper, but I'm good now. I'm here with you." Chris had missed the cooking, but she was old. She was built nicely, but she had this old ass way of laughing and talking. A nice ass, but it'd been walking around for like 50 years. How many more years of nice would it have left? Chris didn't know and didn't plan on sticking around to see it.

"Chris, you know you are sexy as hell. How did an old girl like me get a sexy young'n like yourself?"

Seriously? Did she say young'n? Damn, she was like slavery old. "I don't know, ma'am. I just know that from the first time we talked, I had to have you no matter what. I don't know. You're right to me, and I'm sure there are a gang of guys out there wishing they were in my place. With you, right here, right now, no matter how class is going, I got you, so life is good."

"Yeah. So dinner is just about ready, baby. You hungry?"

"Hell yeah. I've had trash all week. I'm ready to eat whatever you put in front of me, woman."

"Chris, you stay here and get comfortable. Let mama get your food. Put your feet up. Here's the remote. Find us something to watch and I'll be right back with your food, baby."

"Okay, shorty." Damn, she was making this hard. 'Let mama get your food for you?' Come on, old ass! Sometimes, when he was over there, it felt like he was dating a golden girl. Chris felt like he shouldn't be there. Something just didn't feel right. She was always this nice with her old ass, but it just seemed like she was either hiding something, she was being too nice today. "Oh, and can you grab me a Hawaiian Punch too?"

Dinner was good and chillin with Ms. CiCi was cool as well. They ate dinner, watched a couple DVDs, and when she was ready for bed, he laid down with her for a bit. Chris smashed and when she started snoring he knew it was time for him to leave. Chris could have stayed the night, but he made his mind up that night. She was too nice for the Chris stuff, so this was going to be his last time seeing Ms. CiCi. Her old ass was going to have to find another young dude to spend her time with. What he didn't think would happen, was her old ass getting back at him and Jujuan. It all started at the first home game of the season.

Sure enough, this new guard from Chicago had another big game. Jujuan scored 22 points, had 9 assists, and 4 rebounds in an Iowa win. After the game he went to Carrie and told her where to wait for him.

Ms. CiCi was at the game saw all of this.

During the week, talking to Ms. CiCi was hard. He wanted to let her down easily and get it over with, but pieces of Preach were still in Chris. Breaking those young girls hearts were a breeze, but she cooked for him and made him feel good. This was going to be tough as hell. No ghosting her and no ending it over texts like a jerk. Chris planned on the other night being the last time seeing her, but he was going see MS. CiCi just one last time. Do the break-up right.

They talked a few times during the week and decided that they'd see one another on Sunday. It was really getting to Chris because she was super excited to see him and had big plans. Chris on the other hand, knew what was about to happen. Her heart was going to be broken, but he wanted to do it in a dignified way. Just in case she had a heart attack. Sunday finally came and he got there just in time for football.

"Welcome, sir."

"How are you today woman? Looking good I see, are you ready for some football? I'm feeling this look today, I'm glad we decided to stay in." She was in a nighty and Chris wasn't expecting that. He liked surprises though, especially this kind.

"Yeah, I had a surprise for you and although I'd love to see your face if you got your surprise in public, but it's all about your reaction tonight baby." She pulled him in and took off his coat. He sat on the couch, she went back into the kitchen where dinner was already ready.

"Damn it smells good in here woman, what you make?" Chris was over here for one reason, to shoot this old lady the deuces. He was going to tell her that he was dropping out of school and since she's never on campus that would have been enough. No more her Ms. CiCi and unfortunately no more of that home cooking.

She came back carrying a plate of food in one hand a drink for him in the other. "Here you go Jujuan, your favorite, friend chicken." He didn't even notice that she called him by his real name. The smell of fried chicken did that to him.

"Thanks woman." He immediately started to dig in, but a few forkfuls in, he thought to himself, 'I'm trippin son, I could swear she just called me Jujuan. Nah.' So he just continued to eat up. "We need to talk, but it can wait a few I guess."

"What's do we need to talk about baby? You okay?"

"I can't make it next Sunday woman, and probably no Sunday's after that." He seemed sad and sincere about it, but he was just tired of her old ass and her old ass ways.

"Why is that? Did I do something wrong? Do you need space? Are your classes too much? If they are you can come here whenever."

"Yeah, I might be dropping out. I thought I could cope, being so far away from family and all, but I can't. I mean you're the only bright spot here in this town. When I'm not with you, I'm usually miserable. The thing is, I'm here for school, not for a love connection, and to be honest classes are kicking my butt. I'm just going to have to head back to New York and maybe do community college." Chris practiced this speech in his mirror like ten times before he came, he had to admit that his acting today was almost Oscar worthy. "Sorry shorty, I'm not the giving up type, but with this it just feels like I'm all alone out here. I don't have family and all of that here and to be honest you were the closest thing I had, and we barely know each other. So you're the first to know, I'm leaving. Sorry."

"It's okay, I understand when it's hard, sometimes you just run out of options. And you're saying you're totally out of options?"

"Nope, been trying and looking, but it all comes down to this, if I don't get the grades, I'm just wasting my family's money being here, and I'm not getting the grades."

"Oh is that so? Why not just learn how to play basketball and get a full scholarship?" She wasn't playing this game anymore with him.

"Excuse me?" Chris was shocked she said that. What the hell? She was just buying everything coming out of his mouth now she was coming from way left field talking about why doesn't he get a scholarship. Damn, the jig was up wasn't it? It was over though, what the hell could she do?

"I mean, from what I saw at the game the other day, you seem to be the best thing since sliced bread in this town. Now you're about to leave? Or are you giving me more shit? Chris- Jujuan whoever the hell you are, you're a liar, and now you're going to have to pay. You think it's okay to hurt women and be a player or whatever? You think that's cool? It's not."

"What?"

"Don't play Jujuan West, star guard, 25 point a game. I'm a season ticket holder. I saw every shot and rebound Jujuan. I saw that birth mark on your left leg. I saw that face you make when you're frustrated and you want to know the best part of all, I saw her. The girl you kissed after the game. So, my question to you is, who is she?"

Jujuan tried one last time to play Chris and get out of this. "What woman? What are you talking about? I'm roommates with dude, and people say we look alike, but you're trippin for real. Basketball ain't even my thing."

"Really, can I see your school ID then?"

"Nope, you don't believe me, then you just don't believe me Cierra, but I ain't gotta prove shit to your old ass!"

"Is that so? So next game, can I walk up to the girl and tell her about you and I? Can I show up and Jujuan West not know who I am? Can I go into detail about our sex in front of 'him' and her and nothing happens? Is that what you want Chris? Since you say you aren't Jujuan."

"Okay, so now what? I am Jujuan, and yeah, I have been playing with your emotions and all of that. I was wrong, so what do we do now?" Damn, Jujuan knew that eventually this Chris stuff would catch up with him. Right about now he was feeling the nervousness in his stomach, all could think about was Carrie. This stupid plate on his lap he felt like was making him sick. "Look, I apologize Cierra. Lets just call it what is and we both move on."

"Ha! You think that's even an option? Let me ask you something Jujuan. What do you care about more, that girl or that scholarship?"

"Why?"

"Cause today, you're going to have to choose which one you want to keep and which one you want to lose. See I got bills and I can save, but I can also bet. I can bet on Iowa and let you play well, and still lose, but I can also bet against Iowa and have an ace in the hole. A terrible Jujuan West."

"What?" Jujuan definitely didn't like where this was going. What did she mean a terrible Jujuan West? "If you're telling me I have to throw games, I can't. It's illegal and I'd lose my scholarship like that. College is important to me Cierra, I mean, I know I was a jerk, and I took advantage of you, but I can't lose this."

"That's something you should have thought about a long time ago Jujuan or should I say Chris. If you really wanted to keep that scholarship, you'd have done what you needed to do to keep it. You wanted to play games on and off the court, so now you have to pay for that."

Jujuan was damn near in tears. He didn't see things going in this direction. He acted like he didn't care and did things the way Rashi would have done them. Now, at 19, his whole future was in Jeopardy over having some fun. "Look, I was being something that I'm not. You got me. I've never done anything like this before. Can this just be over, please? Cierra, please? I was stupid for doing any of this to you."

"Oh, you're mad? How in the hell do you think I felt the other night? You playing ball under some other name? Kissing some girl after your game. I bet you felt like you were on top of the world, didn't you? Well I felt like you stepped all over me, used and abused me."

"I apologize for that Cierra."

"Chris, I've told you not to call me that. You know what to call me and on top of that an apology isn't going to cut it. Like I said it's either one or the other with you. Either you're breaking it off with the girl, or you're breaking it off with the team. I can tell from the way you kissed her and how you interacted with you that she wasn't just some little skank you met on campus. She means something, you know like I thought I did. So, which is it going to be? You going to play for the team, or play for the girl?"

"Ms. CiCi, please, don't do this. I mean I only did the Chris thing because of how sheltered my life has been. I mean I didn't plan on hurting you and I know now that I did. I keep apologizing because I know I was wrong, but I can't put my scholarship in jeopardy. I have a lot of people depending on me Ms. CiCi. I mean I don't plan on taking hoop to the next level, but I do plan on graduating and I understand that I have to perform on the court and in the classroom to get that done. If I slack up on the court what I do in class doesn't matter and vice versa. If I throw a game for you and the press or anyone finds out, I'm back in the hood in Chicago. I know I don't deserve any sympathy from you and normally I wouldn't ask, but this is my life in the balance."

"I don't give a damn sir. You played with my heart, and now you have to deal with the consequences of your decision. So, make up your mind, you decide to play well believe me, you will be losing your little girlfriend. You play like shit and win me a couple of bets a couple thousand bucks and you're free to live it up with your girl, oh and you will be making it here on Sundays. I liked the sex, I don't plan on losing that in this deal."

"Damn, come on CiCi. This isn't a joke and as far as that goes, why can't we just call it okay at the sex?" Jujuan knew as soon as that left his mouth that it was a stupid idea. He basically just asked her to forget he tricked her into thinking he was someone else, basically came over only for the cooking, and had sex with her for almost two months, and continue to just have sex with him.

"What? Did you just ask me to have sex with me, while having a girlfriend on the side and I get nothing? You played me Jujuan. This is what's up, I got tickets to every home game and I promise you won't be having any games like you had the other night. What was it, 20 something points, like 10 assist and what not. Well, I guess that was your last good game huh? You're a jerk, I actually thought you were going to come over here and tell the truth. I would have actually respected that, but of course you tried to lie. That's not you, it's your roommate? Come on Jujuan, what do I look like?"

He wanted to say an old ass lady, but instead was still trying to get her to chill on all of this she was talking about doing. "Seriously, is there nothing I can do to change your mind about this? I'm willing to do anything CiCi. I mean I know I was wrong, and I know I was a jerk to do that to you, but like I said, this can't go down like this. My mom, my pops, everyone is counting on me to do this and not mess this up. My whole community is counting on me. You can't really let this happen. I mean I know was wrong Ms. CiCi, there has to be another way around this."

"Chris, Jujuan, whoever you are, I have to do what I have to do, and I have to come out on top in this. I mean I love the fact that you do your thing, but you have to stop. I have to make something from this situation. I lost Chris, what did you lose? See you have no idea where I was going with this or how I felt about Chris, you were selfish and an asshole. I was there and willing to do whatever it took to make you or your alter ego happy. You were coming here at 11 at night and I was getting up to make sure you were taken care of. Cooking, cleaning, laundry all that, and if you wanted, I'd have come to the dorms and everything to do the same thing for you. You played games and now you're trying to make it seem like you can't handle when games are played with you? I was really liking being with you and you didn't appreciate it. I knew when I got involved with you, a baby, that there was something about you. Too good to be true, well now you're playing by my rules, so this may be the last time you hear it here in Iowa, but good game Jujuan, good game. Now I need you to leave and I'll see you Thursday night before you and the team leave for Michigan."

"I usually spend the night before a road trip or a game with my girl." Jujuan was a defeated man. What could he do? If he were to tell Carrie, he'd lose her, if he were to score or play like he should be playing, she's tell Carrie and he'd lose her. Even if he played like shit and she got what she wanted what would stop her from telling people that he was shaving points. He loved Carrie to death and losing her just wasn't an option. Why did he create Chris in the first place? Now Chris was the reason that his whole life was in disarray. "So what about Wednesday?"

"No. You'll be here Thursday night. You lie a lot, think of a lie to get you away from her, and be here. I'm not cooking, you're coming over, you know what for, and then you're leaving. Jujuan, I'm going to need some before every game, home or away and also every Sunday. So, get used to it."

"How do I know that you won't get mad at me one day and let it slip that I'm performing bad on purpose? How do I know that you won't just come out and just put all my dirty laundry out there? How do I know that after all this bad play and embarrassing myself that you won't decide to embarrass me even more?"

"I guess like I trusted Chris, you're going to have to trust me. Goodbye Jujuan West. It was nice to actually meet you, and just so you know, before the season I didn't know who you were, but I'd heard of you. Kind of crazy you'd think you could be the star of a major college team and people would not know what you look like. You have a Genius IQ on the court, but I'm guessing someone else took your SAT test for you to get into college because that was just dumb. Goodbye."

Jujuan left not knowing what to do or what to think. He'd just put his college life in the hands of an angry old woman. She was smart though, he had to admit that, and she had him. "Deuces Ms. Cici and once again I'm sorry." Jujuan went back to the university, didn't want to be alone, so he headed right to Carrie's for the night. He stayed with her and although he didn't tell her what was wrong, she could tell that something wasn't right.

Three weeks later, Ms. CiCi was walking past the Barnes and Noble bookstore where she met Chris at when she brought a newspaper, there was an interesting story leading the sports section:

Freshman Guard To Be Benched After A Hot Start

Freshman Guard out of Chicago to be benched after starting the first three games of the season on fire. After the first three regular season games of the year, Iowa freshman Jujuan West was averaging 26 points per game, 7 assist and 5 rebounds. In the following 6 games, West, has been terrible from the floor. Averaging a measly 5 points, 3 assist and 3 rebounds since. In the latest game, West, was visibly frustrated as he only scored 2 points going 0 – 12 from the field and turning the ball over 5 times. When West was asked about his being benched, he didn't seem to be surprised saying, "It's the best decision for the team. I haven't played my best ball lately and if me being on the bench presents us with our best opportunity to win ball games then I can't argue with that. I'm just disappointed that I haven't showed the fans and supporters of this team that I am better than this. Hopefully my game will be back where it was at the beginning of the season and I'll be able to produce for the team." West's stats for the season to this point are 12 points, four assist, and three assist. Story continued on page 7.

She called Jujuan after reading the article, "I see you're being benched, it's okay, you've done fabulously for me. Your performances at my house have been MVP like. Just from your terrible play on the court, I've won almost $10,000. Mr. West, I have to say, since I found out what kind of liar you are, I've been extremely happy. Thank you, sir.

He didn't get a single word in, she just hung up talking about how happy she was. Jujuan on the other hand was feeling the complete opposite. When this first happened Jujuan blamed Chris like Chris really was a different person. Over the three weeks in which he lost his starting position he started to realize that Ms. CiCi was right. How did he plan on doing all of that and not expect to get caught? His first bad game he was all over the newpaper, even had he pulled of the Chris wanted to drop out thing, all she had to do was pull see a newspaper and she'd be able to find him. Preach understood now that Chris was a brilliant idea, he just executed terribly. He'd been thinking about this and going over this over and over again, is Chris still alive? Should he kill the whole thing? Over the three weeks, Chris was dead about 50 different times, and alive but on a sabbatical about 50 times as well. At this point he just didn't know. The first time going to Ms. CiCi's as Jujuan was uncomfortable, but the more he went the more he thought about bringing Chris back out. In Jujuan's head, this wasn't him going to see Ms. CiCi and doing all of this ungodly stuff, it was Chris. Yeah, he loved Carrie, but he liked the fact that he was having sex on the regular, and not just his same old high school sex he was having with Carrie for the last almost four years. Right now though, Chris was the last thing on Jujuan's mind. He was experiencing something he'd never experienced in his life before, he was riding the pine. Damn!!!

Chapter 11

While Preach was being benched, over the same amount of time, Rashad had been doing his thing on the court as well. Sometimes your friends are your closest competition and that's how Rashad felt. Those first three games Preach had were huge and trying to top those were hard. Preach had the numbers that first couple weeks, but his numbers started to drop. This was bittersweet for Rashad, although he saw Preach as his main competition, his drop was ridiculous. His last game he had like two points in yet another loss, which was their fifth in a row. Rashad could count on one hand how many bad games Preach had in four years in high school. He's had like six in row recently, what was going on? Keeping up with Preach was important to Rashad because this was his guy and he was sure Preach was doing the same.

Aside from that though, he and Jackie had gotten very close. They were almost inseparable. Over the last six weeks from the time of the Big Josh situation until now, they had lunch together almost every day and when he wasn't out with Caryl, he was with her. She was like part of the crew now, to a point. Things in the crew weren't really going well. Nehi was on this crazy trip about Kionna. Wouldn't tell him or Rashi what the problem was, but he was back with Aria for some reason. Rashad had been trying to call and keep up with everyone, but it just wasn't really happening. Rashi was out of the country for a few weeks, wasn't answering his joint, and Nehi had been so busy lately with school, Aria, and working that getting in touch with him for anything was basically impossible.

Rashad hadn't told Caryl about all the time he was spending with Jackie. The one game that Caryl made it to, Jackie wasn't even there, she had an away game the same day so they missed each other. Hanging out with Jackie was fun and if he didn't have a girlfriend, he'd have gotten with her a while ago. After his last game it almost happened. They won and he had 37 points, he was on fire and Caryl was nowhere to be found. Jackie was of course at the game, and after the game, they decided to celebrate. After scoring 37, you feel good and the good almost got him in trouble.

They never actually discussed the kiss that happened the night Jackie got into it with Josh. They let it go and although it was unspoken, being friends was a better bet. She was just getting out of a seriously stressful relationship. Rashad on the other hand was in a relationship, and actually trying to do right in that relationship. Caryl trusted him and he wanted to be able to look her in the eye. So on this particular night, he doesn't know if it was the high of scoring thirty-seven, or if it was a full moon, or if it was just that Jackie was looking really good, but for one reason or another things got a little too close.

After leaving the café, Jackie and Rashad went downtown Chicago to celebrate. It was kind of late, and not too much was open, but they wanted to do something, and downtown Chicago always gave you something fun or funny. They decided that walking downtown would be fun enough. It was, they went to Giordano's and had deep dish pizza. They had the waiter put ESPN on the TV and watched as ESPN reported on his game. This was a great night. At the end of the night they ended up in a very compromising situation.

"We should head back to the dorms Shad. It's late and I have practice in the morning. I ain't trying to be all tired and worn out, I want to score thirty-seven points the next time we play."

"Whatever woman. Anyhow, you off to bed or do you want to come over and watch movies and what not. I have a couple new joints on blueray and Hulu has some new movies I want to see"

"How do y'all get all that stuff? I hate the men's basketball team. Every time I look up, y'all got it easy. Classes, do y'all ever go? Test, please I know you aren't taking them. How do you get it so easy?"

"Hey big head, I go to class, I take test, and my mama bought my TV. I brought my stuff here with me, don't hate. Especially after I have a game like Bron. And I know you saw the game, so don't start dodging me on that one-on-one we have planned." For weeks they'd been talking trash about playing ball against each other one on one. It hadn't happened yet since they were both pretty busy, and it was getting cold in Chicago. "Stop with the hate crimes Jackie. The kid was on fire tonight. Did you see when I hit dude with the Iverson crossover? Made his knees buckle, if you didn't when we get back, turn to ESPN, they'll show it again!"

"Whatever Shad, what are we watching tonight? I don't want to see How High again or 300, lets watch something different. Oh, and that doesn't mean Stepbrothers.".

Rashad loved talking to Jackie, it was almost like talking to Rashi. She knew hoop and liked a bunch of the same things he liked. She was cool as hell too, when he had dates or anything like that with Caryl, she didn't get mad or let it bother her. By the time they got to the Fullerton stop on the EL, and were heading towards the dorms, she'd already turned down the new movies he's suggested.

"Then you pick woman."

"I don't know, let me see what you got." She finally picked a movie, and they ended up both on the lovesac. It was like a race how they ended up there together, who wants to give up the most comfy spot in the house? "Move over dude, you know I was here first."

"Whatever, this is my dorm, so that clearly trumps your seven year-old 'I was here first' logic. So here are your options, you can get off, or you can scoot over. And don't be trying to put your big ole butt on me woman."

"Shut up Shad."

They watched the movie together, laughing and just pretty much enjoying being there on the lovesac. Fifty-five minutes into the movie and Rashad's back started to hurt. He didn't say anything, but she could tell something was wrong. She asked him what was wrong, but he was comfortable on the lovesac with her and although it was hurting his back, he said nothing was wrong cause he wasn't trying to get up. He couldn't stay still though, so he just came out and said it.

"Jackie, you feel like giving me a massage?" Yeah, every dude on earth knows where the whole 'can I get a massage' thing is trying to get you. Rashad really needed one though and getting one from Jackie was almost the same as getting one from like one of his guys, nothing would happen.

She must have knew what it meant as well cause the first thing out of her mouth was, "don't be trying nothing either."

"Shut up woman, it's this lovesac. I don't want to get up or miss the rest of the movie Jackie, but I have to get up. I mean you don't have to give me a massage, but I have to lie flat."

They got up and headed to his room. From what he could tell, she didn't mind pausing the movie for this. Yea, she said not to try any thing and he wasn't going to anyway. Still, it seemed to him that she was more than willing to head into the bedroom and give him a massage.

When they got into the bedroom, Rashad took off his shirt and jeans leaving him in his gym shorts and a tank top. He then laid out on his bed and handed her some oil to rub on his back. To say that she gave the worst massage ever would be wrong because he was comparing this massage to maybe being shot. Her massage was like being man handled by Mario from the Mario Brothers games. He breaks bricks with his hands, so you just know he couldn't give anything a light touch. Rashad basically started kissing her to stop those strong ass fingers from further injuring his back.

They were deep into the kissing, Rashad's tank had come off, Jackie's shirt was off with her jeans unfastened, and Rashad was working on her bra hooks when his phone rang. Of course, right now it would be Caryl. The funny thing is, he knew she was calling, she calls after every game to see how he did. He didn't want to stop kissing Jackie, and if it was anyone else on earth he wouldn't have, but maybe this was a sign that he was in the wrong right now. He didn't know, but he took the call.

"Sup woman?"

"Hey Shad. I heard you had a good game dude. They're saying that you scored like 40."

"Who told you that woman?" Rashad had just gotten the thirty-seven points but didn't mind hearing about it from other people. He played his ass off tonight. She usually had to ask, and of course act like she understood basketball. This time she was calling him with the facts.

"I heard these two guys talking about it. They were like, 'that freshman should be here, blah, blah, blah. He scored forty points, blah, blah, blah.' They were all over you dude. I wanted to say something like, whatever he's a scrub, but I didn't."

"Whatever woman, sounds like you're hating." Jackie started to get dressed. "Hey, let me hit you back Kid. I gotta do something real quick. Deuces." He didn't even hear if she said okay, or said goodbye, he just hung up. "What are you doing, Jackie?"

"Shad, the moment is gone dude, but that doesn't mean it won't happen sir. I already know it will, it's just a matter of time Shad. So, don't take this as like strike two, let's just say that the timing once again wasn't right. We don't do too happy or too sad. I got hit by Josh last time and you stopped it because you said you didn't want to take advantage of me. Too sad, I was crying and all of that, you were upset, that just wasn't the right time. This time, you had damn near forty points. You had a monster game tonight, so of course your phone is going to be blowing up tonight. Just too happy of a time. So, this isn't a dead issue, and just because I'm dressed right now and about to head to my dorm doesn't mean things will be different tomorrow. I didn't let things get weird when we kissed a couple months ago, and I won't now. Oh, and by the way, Rashi was at the game. He's actually been at like the last three. I gotta get to my dorm Shad, you have a good night. Deuces."

"First of all, when did you start saying deuces? Secondly, what do you mean Ra was there? No, he wasn't. and Thirdly, you don't want me to walk you?"

"I'm a big girl Shad, plus what's going to happen between here and my dorms? Its like three steps away. Also, you're on the court playing, the two games before this he brought Stacie and tonight, he was with I think Gretchen and Danai. We waived, but he was talking to some chick, so I didn't go over. It looked like the Kionna chick from the shop that day, but I don't know. Anyhow, I'll call you when I get to the dorm. Call your girlfriend back. DEUCES."

"Aiight woman, one hundred." Rashad knew he'd have to call Rashi. He was sure that Ra was in Canada somewhere. Although, if anyone were to show up to one his games and slide out before he knew about it, it would be Ra. Ra was a standup dude when he wanted to be. He was going to call Caryl, but he also wanted to get a critique from his guy. "Jackie, do me a huge favor please, can you call me when you make it? Your fine ass out here alone, makes a dude worry."

When Jackie left, Carol wasn't the first person he called, hearing that Rashi was at the game made him think of something he'd heard a few months ago. So he called Rashi, "Dude, is that what Gretch was talking about when I came by before the season started? She said you were smashing Ki. Please don't tell me you're smashing Ki."

"What? What are you talking about?"

"Come on now man, I saw you at the game B, and I saw you with Ki." Shad lied, but Jackie knew Rashi well enough to know what he looked like in person. "Dude, you bringing Ki out to games with you? What happened to Stacie? I guess that's dead, huh?

"Dude, first of all, good game. You're doing your thing B. Secondly, I wasn't there with Ki. I was there with a girl named Dayna, but that's beside the point. Bro, you're balling."

"Ra, you came to the last three games and ain't called or talked to me about them".

"I was going cause I needed to see what was up with you. I went to Iowa last week and dude, Preach ain't hooping. I don't know what he's doing, but he ain't hooping. He's out there shooting air balls and shit. Missing wide open lay ups. I mean I still wouldn't want him guarding me ninety-four feet, but he's not balling. We need to get him here and find out what's good. You had to see him son. I was thinking it must be college and the pressure, but the last three games you had bro, you're killin em. Stacie liked coming out, she couldn't make it tonight, and I know she's going to be mad she missed it, but she's liking seeing you play. I told her I'm better, but she doesn't believe me."

"That's cause you're lying clown. Anyhow, let me hit you back son, and next time you're at a game make sure you say something or at least come and hang out a bit. I gotta call Caryl son. One Hundred"

"Deuces bro, and just for the record, I ain't smashing Ki."

After they hung up he called Caryl and invited her over. He planned on getting some tonight and his first option fell through. She got there with an overnight bag and a toothbrush. It was good seeing her, He'd been hanging out with Jackie so much more. Not because he liked Jackie more or anything like that, it was basically because Jackie was closer. They went to the same school, had a class together, and both played ball. Jackie was a constant, he could barely get Caryl on weekends. He doubted she'd have been there had he not had such a good game tonight. Caryl was just walking in the door when Jackie called. All he could think to himself was, did she see Caryl come over? "Hello?"

"DUDE YOU'RE ON SPORTSCENTER!!!! TURN TO ESPN RIGHT NOW SHAD, YOU'RE ON SPORTSCENTER!!!" Then she just hung up.

"Who was that?" All Caryl heard was yelling into the phone and then a click. It sounded like a stalker or something calling him.

"Girl that was just Jackie, she was calling cause I'm on ESPN." Rashad walked up to the TV and turned to ESPN. Sure, enough there he was scoring, passing, and sticking defense. Dick Vitale was calling him a PTPer (Prime Time Player). He was on ESPN earlier when he was Giordano's, but not like this. This was a full story on him, not the team, him. The coach had even given him some huge praise in an interview. He was giving his moment on ESPN his full attention. Maybe that was why he didn't hear Caryl ask him who Jackie was.

"SHAD!"

"Wassup?" She finally got him to look away from the TV for a second. He wasn't trying to be rude, but he'd been talking about being on sportscenter probably since the first time he picked up a basketball. "Whatever it is woman, I'm sure it can wait until after this."

She got up and turned off the TV. "You playing Rashad, answer the question! Who the hell is Jackie?"

Rashad hopped up as soon as the TV went black. "What the hell you doing Caryl? I'm on ESPN and you playing. What are you doing?" He couldn't believe she really turned off the TV like that. Was she nuts? He wasn't thinking about it then, but it'll most likely be on all morning on the reruns, but this was his first time on ESPN so that wasn't even going through his head. He was steaming mad at this point, but trying to keep his composure. "What? What you want? What's so important that you just turned off the TV? What? Please tell me what?" He was really upset.

"I asked you a question and you're stalling Shad. Who is Jackie?" She was starting to realize from Rashad's demeanor that he probably really didn't hear her.

Rashad had forgotten that Jackie knew who she was, but he'd kind of neglected telling Caryl who Jackie was. "Seriously? Okay, well my moment on ESPN is over now, so I guess I'll tell you. She's my girlfriend."

"What? What you mean your girlfriend Rashad?" She was about to cry, then she looked, and he started smiling.

"Woman, she's a friend. She's on the women's hoop team. She was at the game, she plays here and comes to the games as well. I go to their games too. She's in a few of my classes and she obviously has my back, she called me when I was on Sportscenter. She was more excited than me, so way more excited than you. I can't believe you turned off the TV Caryl. Let's head to my room."

The night with Caryl was okay, they talked and chilled for a while, but when they finally did get physical, all he could think about was Jackie. The way she felt, the way she tasted, he just couldn't get Jackie out of his mind. He wasn't trying to not think about her, so when he accidently moaned, "damn, Jackie" he just froze like a dear in the headlights.

"What did you call me? Rashad did you just call me another bitch's name? Are you serious?"

Rashad tried to play it off as best he could. "Ha, that's for turning off the TV. Now you know how I felt. That was my first time on ESPN, ever and you played me. So, I decided to play you back, don't like the way it felt huh?" He was hoping she would go for that. It sounded like maybe that would work, he could tell that she was thinking about it. He felt a whole lot better when she finally said …

"Okay, you got me. I'm sorry I turned you off, I really thought you were ignoring me Shad. My bad, but the next time you decide to play a joke like that, just know that it won't be like this. I might cut you."

The next day when he saw Jackie, he had to tell her what went down. She said that they would eventually have their time, he was ready for that. She was leaking into his thoughts when he was getting intimate with his girl. He had to have Jackie. When he saw Jackie, of course she was looking her worse. She was in sweats and a jacket, but the reason she was looking so bad made him want her even more.

"You're looking beat the hell up woman. Late night?" Rashad was joking and the good thing about Jackie is she knew it. She didn't take it personal or make it a big deal out of it.

"Whatever, clown, let me guess you score thirty-seven and now you wear a tux to class. Let us all bow down to the thirty-seven man. You need change he has thirty-seven cents, you need the time it's thirty-seven after one, you need an essay, he'll give you thirty-seven words." Jackie was laughing hard at her own joke, while Rashad was just standing there looking at her like she was crazy.

"How was class Morris?"

"Class was long, I kept falling asleep."

"Why were you up so late?" Granted she left his house at midnight, but she usually didn't leave until later, if at all, and still managed to look better than this. "Did you have Big Josh come over?"

"Shut up clown. I stayed up late for you. I know you didn't get to tape yourself on Sportscenter right? I stayed up until the 2am episode to hook you up." She started reaching into her backpack to give him the DVD she recorded his Sportscenter episode on. "So now what you gotta say about how I'm looking this morning?"

"Thanks Jackie." He gave her a big hug, he was impressed, plus he missed it. This was yet another reason why he was feeling Jackie. She was a cutie, and she did little things like this. She could have just gone to bed after she left, but she saw him on Sportscenter and called him.

Then even put them on DVD so he can show his crew and family. "So, when you left I talked to Rashi-" As he was talking his phone began to ring. It was Rashi. "Hold on woman, this is him right here. Sup clown?"

"Chillin B. You saw me at the game, right?"

"Yeah why?"

"Well, remember that thing we talked about at my house son? I took care of that last night. Anybody ask or say anything B, I was at the game. I'm going to be honest I don't think anyone is going to ask, but if they do, I was at the game last night."

"What happened?" Rashad put his phone on speaker because he wanted Jackie to hear. She had given him Josh's address a couple weeks before and told him where he hung. He asked and promised he would not do anything to him, so she told him. Rashi wasn't Rashad, so if he did something to him, oh well.

"Oh, well after the game I had to take Dayna home or whatever, she lives out west near Harlem and Lake, and since I was near where Josh stays I decided to swing by and see if I could get lucky. I don't know where he was going or what he was doing, but I decided to give that PHD I promised you. So, I'd been keeping this roll of quarters in my car for when I do see him."

Rashad knew what the quarters we for but couldn't help the joke. "So you gave him ten dollars?"

"Yeah, he got Jackie to shut up, he deserved ten dollars."

"Yeah? I got Jackie right here son. You're on speaker clown."

"What you do with the quarters?" Jackie wasn't trying to hear the jokes she wanted to know what happened. Josh hit her and she knew he had it coming.

"What up Jackie. I saw you at the game yesterday woman, you the reason this clown went off like that? Damn near forty huh? He had the whole gym rocking."

"I saw you too, were you with that Kionna girl?"

"Nope, one of my cousins. Anyhow the quarters." Rashi was trying to change the subject, he forgot that if Jackie saw him, she definitely saw Dayna. "So what I did woman was basically grab the quarters and-"

"You threw them at him?"

"Yeah Jackie, I took the quarters out one at a time and tossed them to Josh. Now, can you listen woman?"

Rashad was cracking up, Jackie was too though. She knew that was not what happened. "Okay, just finish the story Ra. You and Rashad are just alike. Always joking and clowning around."

"So y'all gonna let me finish or what? Anyhow, I just put the quarters in my hand, and made a fist around them. Just took them in my palm and cracked your boy. I maybe got him seven or eight times. When he started bleeding from the nose and mouth, I stopped and then I said. 'Next time you'll let me in the club bitch!" Then I took off running the opposite way. I didn't go towards my car I maybe ran like 3 blocks out of the way, then doubled back around. When I was pulling off there were police and everything there, but nobody knows it was me and I'm sure your boy thinks it was some clown from the club. So all is well kid. I wore a ski mask, so I tossed that in some random alley."

"Good looking out B. I gotta get to class, but I'll be at the shop this weekend. Thanks for doing that for me Ra."

"Me too." Jackie was happy that Josh finally got his. "Rashi I owe you one, I appreciate you looking out for me."

"Woman you're part of the crew now, so it's nothing. Y'all do the college thing, just remember, if anything happens or you hear anything, just remember I was at the game last night."

"Aiight kid. One Hundred."

"See woman, told you I'd take care of the Big Josh thing."

"Didn't you say you talked to him last night, didn't he tell you then?"

"He must have done it after we talked. He was talking about Preach and all of that. He said he went to one of his games in Iowa and that the pressure seems to be getting to him. I don't know Morris. Preach pretty much keeps it together, I mean I was the leading scorer in high school when we played, but he's a beast. I mean I didn't lead the team in scoring every game. He used to have spurts where he'd look like he could go for forty or fifty. I mean he goes hard."

"So, you think it's the pressure?"

"Or the fact that he is far from home. I mean I don't even know if he's going to church or what not out there."

"That's crazy."

"I know woman. You want to hit the café?"

"You know I do." Jackie thought for a second and turned to Rashad. "You know what, let's not go to the café." Jackie grabbed his hand and started heading towards his the dorms. "Is your roommate home?"

"I doubt it, why?" Rashad wasn't expecting this, he didn't even know what she would want there right now.

"Want one of my famous massages?"

Was this a test? Was he being punk'd? When she said that all he could think about was her Donkey Kong hands. "Ummmmm, how about I do the massaging. I mean yesterday I got a hell of a massage from you and I'm feeling so relaxed today that I think I should just go ahead and return the favor. I mean I'm feeling good and on top of that, you were up all night for me. Taping ESPN just for me. Who deserves a massage right now? I mean you might not think it's a big deal, but I missed it yesterday woman, my cable was acting up, so you got to see me on Sportscenter and I didn't." Rashad hoped she bought that cause there wasn't anything remotely seductive about a massage coming from her. It was more like a punishment. Maybe she should try massaging Preach, he was the one only scoring like two points a game.

"That's could work for me. Before we head back, I want to make some things clear. First off, I appreciate what your guy did to Josh and all of that, but I want it to be known, I'm not too happy, and I'm not too sad either."

Rashad got the hint right away. "I feel ya woman, and I'm not too happy or sad myself." They went back to Rashad's dorm and as soon as they got through the door, they were right at each other. It was sort of like déjà vu, she was out of her shirt and her jeans were unfastened when Rashad's phone rang. It was Caryl.

"It's your girlfriend huh?" Jackie was a little annoyed.

"Nope that's my old girlfriend, I think right now, I'm with my girl." He pushed his ignore button and decided to tell her what was on his mind since yesterday. "Jackie I want this to happen and not just this time. I want this to be a regular thing. Us hanging out us chilling, I enjoy it. I mean basketball is my reason for being here and school, but

I promise woman, if you weren't here with me, I'd probably be gone. I keep trying to figure out what's keeping me with Caryl and my thing is, the reason just doesn't seem to make since to me these days. I honestly feel like I'm with her to show her that I'm a good dude. At one point I was sure she was a great one, I was sure that she was what I wanted. I was wrong though Morris, I don't know if you feel our vibe and how natural we get along, I want you. Jackie, I'm sure you're a great one, and believe me, it's not just your famous massages that make me feel like that. It's everything about you. So, I gotta admit, I lied to you. When I said I wasn't too happy or too sad, I didn't mean it. I'm too happy you're here with me. I can score one point and if you still want to kick it after the game, then you know what, I'm having a hell of a day. So, yeah, my old girl just called cause right now in the middle of the day, on a Friday, I'm about to smash my new girl. My great one from the west side. Who would have thought it was even possible-"

Jackie just started kissing him. "You're a clown Rashad, but I'll take you I guess. Just so you know though, you made the right choice. I love being around you and your friends."

Yep, Rashad had sex with Jackie, at least she wasn't Caryl's sister though. Now there was the whole getting rid of Caryl. He asked Jackie first how he should do it, she said in person, a real man breaks up with a girl in person not over a text and not over the phone. When he called Rashi, dude knew as soon as he answered the phone, 'you smashed Jackie didn't you?' Rashi said just to shoot her the deuces over a text and let her deal with it. Nehi didn't answer when he called him. Rashad just wasn't trying to call Preach right now. He just got benched for the first time in his life, he was sure dude wasn't trying to hear about breaking up and little things like that. He even talked to Stacie, who had a totally opposite opinion from Rashi's and Rashad was sure that their opposite opinion had somehow started and argument between them. Rashi even suggested talking to Gretch about it, but he passed on that, and just decided to take Jackie and Stacie's advice. He called Caryl and asked her can he come to her dorm and talk. Of course, she said yeah, expecting a good surprise.

When he got there, she was looking good, like she'd just gotten her hair done and was wearing skinny jeans, heeled boots, and very low-cut shirt. "Are you going out woman?"

"Nope, I was waiting on you?"

Shit, this was going to be harder than expected. Why couldn't she look like Jackie was looking this morning. She was looking sexy as hell, that definitely wasn't a getting dumped outfit, but he was all the way out here and Jackie knew where he was, so he had to stick to the game plan. "Oh, well you are looking good kid. We really need to talk though."

"Wassup"

Why in the hell was she so damn chipper? This was going to suck she was in a good mood and looking all good. "What's up with you woman? You seem awfully happy to see me."

"That's cause I was waiting to hear from you all day. I thought you'd forgotten, so when you asked to come all the way out here, I knew that you remembered. So I got dressed and ready. What we doing tonight?"

Rashad had no idea what she was talking about. What did he forget? "I'm not here for that though Caryl."

"Whatever Rashad, anyhow, let me grab what I got you." She walked out of the dorm and came back a couple seconds later with a gift-wrapped box. "It's been a bumpy four months Rashad, but I wouldn't trade them. You're like the best guy I've ever dated. I mean that Rashad, I was so sure that I was going to be mad at you, especially when I called you earlier and you didn't answer. I was like 100% sure that you forgot. Look at you though, you remembered baby."

"Of course, woman, I didn't get you like a big gift though, I was just thinking a nice dinner and movie, then a walk or something. Maybe talk about our four months and about what's to come." Rashad wasn't going to dump her today. Who in the hell would do that? Who dumps a girl on her four month whatever this was. Rashad didn't call it an anniversary, those were yearly, but apparently, she did. "So what do you think of that? A fancy dinner, a movie and a long walk?"

"Can I change shoes after dinner and the movie? I don't know if I can walk in these Shad. We can do whatever you like though, but open your gift though before we go, it took me forever to pick it out."

Rashad opened the box. He couldn't believe it, she got him a pair of diamond earrings. They had to cost a ton, and here he was here to dump her. Of course she made it worse by saying, "I know I turned you off on the sports channel, but I know you'll look good in these the next time you're on. You know for interviews and all of that. And once again, I'm sorry for turning it off. All my friends saw it and I was just so proud of you baby. Happy anniversary."

When Rashad got back on campus it was almost two in the morning. When he went into his room, Jackie was asleep on his bed. He felt bad, he had to wake her up. He had to tell her that he didn't dump her. "Jackie. Jackie, wake up. Morris." She finally started to wake up. "Wake up woman, we need to talk."

"You didn't dump her did you?" Jackie could tell by how sad he looked that he didn't accomplish his mission. "You didn't have sex with her did you?"

"Nope, but I couldn't dump her."

"Why not?"

"Well, when I got there, she was all happy and chipper. I couldn't figure out why, I thought she was going out and I don't know I just wasn't expecting that."

"You didn't dump her cause she was happy?"

"No, it's worse than that. She was all happy and chipper cause she thought I came all the way out there to celebrate out four month 'anniversary' with her. She was all dressed up and ready to go because she thought that was my reason for being there. She even got me diamond earrings woman. So with the intention of going out there to shoot her the deuces I end up taking her on our four month anniversary dinner. She was mad I couldn't stay the night with her, but she let me leave finally at like 1 o'clock."

Jackie started laughing. "So, what did you get her?" She managed to get that out in between laughs.

"Shut up Morris, what am I going to do? I ain't trying to have her thinking it's one thing and it's another. She was happy as hell to see me and all I could do was sit there and act like I remembered. She happy and smiling, I'm sitting across from her like, 'should I do it now?' She's over there talking about four months and all the months ahead."

"Yeah, so now what? Are you giving her the earrings back dude?" Jackie couldn't help it, this was funny to her. Not the fact that Caryl was going to be dumped, but this clown went out there to do it and ends up taking her to dinner. "I hate to tell you this Shad, but it looks like you're going to have to dump this chick via text. I know I said it was wrong, but you took the earrings and I'm going to be honest with you, I'm thinking she's going to take a swing at you if you do it in person."

"Damn son, I should have just did it earlier."

"Well, you can text her tomorrow Shad. Right now, just come lie down with me and tomorrow we can fix this."

"I guess."

Chapter 12

Rashi's favorite time of the year was coming fast and he'd had a huge surprise for his guys. Christmas was right around the corner and he went all out this year for the crew. They'd have to drive, but it didn't even matter, he knew they wouldn't mind a road trip. He got four tickets to All -Star weekend, NBA All-Star weekend. Three-point contest, dunk contest, celebrity game, and the game itself, they would be seeing it all. He was excited because he took care of his sisters too. Rashi was a give gifts type of dude, didn't really care about getting things, but as long as his people were happy, he was good. Since he'd gotten back from Vancouver he hadn't been in the shop as much as he would have liked, but his guys were playing college ball now, so it would have to wait some things are more important.

The Vancouver trip was more fun than expected though, from the time he landed until the time he left it was just fun. When they got there of course Stacie immediately needed to walk away and use her phone, but it was cool this time, his phone was going off too. It was Dayna, she knew he was leaving the country and for some reason she seemed really concerned about his safety. He'd just met her a couple weeks before and she was asking him to make sure he texted when he got there, to keep her posted on what he was doing, and to send plenty of pictures. It seemed a little crazy, but he was cool with that, it was better than the texts coming from Kionna.

When they got to Vancouver, they met Stacie's manager, he was a funny little guy. It was obvious to Rashi that he wanted to get with Stacie, but she really didn't see it, so he didn't say anything. They headed to the hotel and things were busy from that point on. She took him to the photo shoot, he met all the models, but for the most part he'd met most of them already. There were a bunch of male models there he had never met though. There was a photo shoot and a few shows in the days that followed. He found out he was going to be there and a big part of it. He had heads to cut and they paid him a large sum to do that. $5000 for ten heads, that was crazy to him, but he didn't turn it down either.

He was sure that Stacie had the photographer ask him about being a part of the photo shoot, so when he asked, of course Rashi declined. That, and the fact they wanted him in skinny jeans. When he asked Stacie about it, she said she didn't know anything about it, but he didn't believe her. He enjoyed being there more than he thought he would and the fact that they gave him creative control over the heads he cut and let him freestyle made it even better. When they weren't there they were out in Vancouver and in British Colombia (which was a short ferry ride from the island to the mainland) just sight-seeing and shopping. It was there that he met a guy with a hookup on the tickets to the All-Star game so he made sure to get his number and use it when he got back into the states. Rashi was making sure that every second they spent outside the hotel and work, Stacie was having fun. He took her bowling in British Columbia, out to a few movies, and out to eat everywhere. She had a small frame, but Rashi knew first hand that Stacie could eat. He loved that because he loved to get his grub on as well. He even found a court to hoop at, not a great run, but it was keeping him busy and active,

While in British Colombia they went and got tattoos. She got a butterfly on her ankle and he got a bigger tattoo on his chest. It said Hip-Hop is Life. He even took her curling, he was shocked when he found out that she was twenty years old and never even heard of curling. They had fun.

While at the shows Rashi found out who certain clothing designers were, the history of some clothing lines, and for some the reason clothing design was even something they did. Talking to these people he found old designers with the same passion he has for being a barber. All he could think was 'I hope I still have the passion for what I do when I get that old.' When it was time to go, he didn't even want to leave. Chicago was home though, so reluctantly he headed back, ready to tell his guys what was up and that they should hit Vancouver soon.

When he got home though, things weren't right. His sisters were good, but when he looked up Jujuan on the internet to see how he was doing, it was in the middle of his six-game terrible streak. He'd read that Preach had been terrible since his so called 'coming out party' he'd had the first few games of the season. Bloggers were writing how he was good against terrible teams and how as soon as some moderate competition got on the court with him, he was choking. When he looked up Rashad's, at least the reports were better. His reports were about how he was doing good and every game was looking like he just might break out. Rashad had made a buzzer beater in a game to win, then the game after that he'd had 26 points. Nehi wasn't answering his phone, so he figured he's talk to him later.

Preach had a game the day after they got back, so he invited Stacie to go to Iowa with him and see Jujuan play. When they got there, he'd wished that he hadn't brought her at all. Preach was terrible. Missing shots he made in high school with his eyes closed, missing the open man, turning the ball over. She thought he was ashamed and that was why they didn't say anything to him after the game. She would have been embarrassed too had she drove that far and her friend who was supposed to be good was that bad. So, when they left without saying anything, she was cool with that. What do you say to a guy who just fouled out and had like 5 point and 5 turnovers? Nothing, you leave his game and go home.

When he invited her to Rashad's game, he had to promise that Rashad was going to do better. She had fun at this game, Rashad scored like 20 something points and was all over the place. She didn't know why they left this time without saying something, but they did. The next game too, they went, Rashad had a good game and they left. She saw Jackie and they talked for a while, but as usual, they left right after. She wanted to ask why, but she was sure he had a reason.

Rashi did have a reason though. He was going to say something, but after the Preach game decided to not to, he wasn't trying to put any more pressure on them than what was already there. Rashi wasn't there for a prize, he was supporting his guys. Nehi for some reason still wasn't answering his phone though, whatever he'd go to dudes next party and talk to him then. The funny thing was that nobody had even called him to see how his trip was. He was gone for almost three weeks and when he first left, he was getting texts from Rashad, but that stopped after a couple days. He used that though as an excuse when Dayna was texting. Just told Stacie it was Rashad and she left it alone.

Rashi and Stacie had been getting along very well, he still wasn't feeling her walking away to text, so that was something that was making it hard for him to trust her. The trip did a lot though in that department because being with her, he could tell that she was feeling him a lot, it was just that phone though. She was here with most of the people that she said texted her and here she was again walking away to text. He didn't want to, but when he got back, he decided to not shut Dayna down. She was a cutie and although she was from the west side, he was willing to take a chance.

With Dayna, he was pretty much just talking to her when he had the time. When Stacie wasn't around, when he was at the shop after it closed. He'd sit in his chair spinning, talking to her. She was smart, a student at Loyola and she had a job. Full time at school and full time on her job, so that was a good look. They were texting like every day when he was gone, but it was just friendly. She didn't start making it known that she wanted to go out until he got back. When they decided to actually do something, he'd just found out that Stacie wouldn't be in town, so he decided to take her to the game. She had a blast too, he was going to take her and let her meet Rashad because he had a monster game that night, but he saw Jackie. Didn't need her telling Stacie about this, so he decided to leave, call Rashad about his game in the morning. So that's when he decided to take her home though. She wanted to go to his place, but he felt like if they did get physical, it would have to wait. He already knew that if she let him smash, he's be shooting her the deuces the next day. So he took her home, she was excited about the game though and actually asked when they were going to another one. "I'll keep you posted woman. Just text me or whatever and we'll definitely do it again." Then he was on his way, on that's when he saw Big Josh.

After the Big Josh thing went down, he was on his way home nervous as ever, but he got a text that he wasn't expecting, it was from Kionna. What in the world could she want?

Message from Kionna:
So who were you at the game with?
Message to Kionna:
What?
Message from Kionna:
I know who you weren't at the at the game with Playa.

Rashi knew that 'Playa' comment was on purpose, and he knew that she saw him with a girl who wasn't Stacie. He thought about ignoring her, but knew if he did, she'd still keep texting. She thought she had him now, he knew that in a way, she kind of did. Somehow this crazy chick saw him at a basketball game without Stacie. Unlike Preach though, he did think five moves ahead. Rashi actually played chess, so that's how he approached a lot of things.

Message to Kionna:
What are you talking about lady?
Message from Kionna:
Who was the girl that wasn't your little model?
Message to Kionna:
Lol, oh you mean my sister Angie?
Message from Kionna:
Didn't look like ur sister
Message to Kionna:
Dude you don't even know what my sister looks like. u should probably just stop texting me
Message from Kionna:
Rashi I know that wasn't ur sister
Message to Kionna:

Do u? Is this what you texted me for woman? How bout you keep it moving? U thought u saw something u didn't see lady. Nice try.
Message from Kionna:
So I guess I didn't see u beat some dude up either huh? Wait let me guess, that was ur 2 sister right?

This stalking ass chick. She had him. What could he do about that? She saw him and Josh. Rashi's stomach started to hurt at this point. He didn't know what to say to that. No? That wouldn't work, she followed him, she knew his car and most likely his plates. What was it going to take her to not mention this to anybody?

Message to Kionna:
What the hell you want Kionna?
Message from Kionna:
I'm on my way over!!!!

Rashi wasn't worried about Stacie finding out about Dayna, he didn't do anything with her except bring her to a basketball game. He wasn't worried about Kionna trying to hold that over his head, she was a joke and she was Nehi's girl, he'd just call Nehi and have him take care of his crazy ass girl. He was worried about her going to the police, or even Big Josh. Dude probably just took it as some clown who couldn't get into the club taking it out on him. What was she going to do? What did she want?

As soon as his bell rang he knew who it was, but he asked anyway, "Who is it?"

"It's Ki. I want to come up"

Rashi buzzed the door and unlocked his apartment door. When she knocked, he told her to come in. He was sitting in his living room watching TV when she came in. "Kionna, I don't have all night, what do you want?"

"First of all I want to clear a few things up Ra. Ne and I aren't a couple. You know he picked Aria over me. Second Ra, is that you say she's a model and all of that, but she's not that hot. I mean I can see you with someone better, me of course. And third, I saw what happened, but I wouldn't tell anyone. You know I wouldn't Ra."

"Then what do you want Kionna? Why are you here? I'm going to be honest with you woman, I can care less if you are with Nehi or not woman, that has nothing to do with me. I have a girl Kionna. So, no you and Nehi doesn't mean anything to me, I have a girl, a model chick. There is no Ra and Ki. Can't be. And quite frankly I don't care Ki, there was a point in time where I wanted to get at you, but I'm over it, and just so you know, seeing you with Nehi was a huge part of it. That's my guy woman, so you might as well just go ahead and dead that idea of you and me. Nehi's is where you should be, he's not over you."

"Rashi, why are you acting like this? A couple months ago you and I were talking about hooking up Ra. All night texting and all of that, how can we go from that to where we are now. All of that Nehi was stupid for not picking me, now you aren't picking me?"

"Yeah, well he downgraded when he chose Aria, I definitely made an upgrade. You're cool and what not, but I need you to know that ten times out of ten I'd pick Stacie over you. See Aria is a liar and she's using Nehi, when it comes to that, yeah, you're a better pick. To me though, I see you as a liar just from that day at the shop-"

"I JUST TOLD YOU I DIDN'T LIE!"

"Yeah maybe not to me, but to Nehi you did. Did you tell him you were coming to see me? Did you tell him you and I were texting and all of that? Damn, you really thought that? These last couple months you thought I was mad cause you lied to me?" Rashi started to laugh at this point. "All this time you never thought that you lying to my friend, getting his hopes all up was okay with me? All this time you've been worried about lying to me? Kionna I have a chick. I have a good chick, took me out of town, spends time with me, and makes sure I'm good. Nehi doesn't have that. You led him on. Did he deserve that?. Yeah, he made the wrong choice, maybe. What you did though was hurt a good dude cause you're selfish."

"Rashi you can't say that nothing is there. Between us, you can't look me in the eyes and tell me that these two months haven't been hard for you, I know you got a girlfriend, but you don't miss texting me? You don't miss talking to me and getting pictures of me? These two months have been a hard two months for me Ra."

"Yeah? You think they been easy for Ne? You're a liar and he has feelings for you."

"Dude you ain't going to keep calling me a liar."

"I just call them like I see them and with you, that's what I see."

"Well I guess you need to get over it then huh?"

"What?"

"Well you say your girl is a model, right? Let's not put her career in jeopardy then Ra. I mean she don't really look like much to me, but I can make it so that she doesn't look like much to anyone else either. I mean wouldn't you hate for something to happen to her like what happened to dude?" She was talking about Josh and from the look on Rashi's face she was certain of two things. He knew who she was talking about and that she had him.

"Don't play woman." Damn, how did some texting with an ex of one of his friends become this? Stacie was now in jeopardy because of some lame texts to this crazy. "She ain't got nothing to do with this. You and I aren't a couple because Nehi was wrong when he hurt you and I should have left it at that. I supported you because he was wrong for what he did, but when you use me, use him, and then do the same thing. Well you were wrong then, and Nehi is still my dog. I don't have a reason to stay friends or whatever with you. Anybody do any of my guys wrong, I shoot them the deuces, flat out. You can't threaten my girl over this."

"Oh, you think this is a threat? Well I'm going to tell you, so that you don't go almost three months thinking the wrong thing. This ain't a threat Ra. You don't even have to dump her, yet. You just need to open our lines of communication again?"

"And you're saying that if I don't start talking and texting you again, you're going to do something to Stacie? What because she's a model and you're like a seven out of ten? Leave her out of this woman. She's- you know what? What if I just go to the police?"

Kionna couldn't help but laugh at this point. "After what I saw today, I doubt you will. You beating some guy up, did you even know him? I mean I'd say that wasn't something you'd do, but I don't know like that, and you did it. That's interesting Rashi. You of all people going to the police?"

"Kionna, is this seriously what you want? You're basically begging me to be with you. When did that become acceptable? Ki, you're better than this, I mean look at you right now, you're putting yourself in a position where either we start talking again or you hurt my girl. That's not a good look and on top of that, do you really think that I'd start liking you now? You're a catch woman, you shouldn't have to force yourself onto anyone. I mean yeah, we almost worked, but we didn't. You should be looking at it like, 'then it's his lost.' Kionna, you can't make me want to get with you woman." Rashi was hoping this was working. This whole you should feel better speech was like his last hope.

"Ra, the funny thing is you think she's so great or think she's this and that. I was on the trip. I watched you with all those women and I heard you. I watched you closely and I knew then that I wanted you. It ain't about her either, you got a girl Ra. I've watched you do you constantly and not have a girl. I was here and I was in position to be your girl, your first girlfriend. I don't even know where she came from. With this agreement Ra, you don't even have to stop dealing with your little 'model.' Two months ago, you could see us up here doing way more than talking, now look at us, this is easily fixable Ra. Easy."

"You know what lady, I'll just have to make sure I'm with Stacie all the time then." Rashi knew he wasn't doing that, but this chick was obviously crazy, maybe she'd believe him and back off. "You want to play this game, I can play it, but know this kid, anything happens to Stacie, talking to me will be the least of your worries."

"What?"

"The thing is woman, you really think 'you got me'. You don't, the whole Josh thing, yeah that's your word against mine and you're just a jealous girl trying to get me in trouble. I don't even know dude and I have no reason to do anything to him, he wouldn't recognize me if I did it again tomorrow. Kionna just know that if anything happens to her, I won't be going to the police, not a chance at that. Now get the hell out!" Rashi had enough of her, she pretty much ruined his night. It was his fault, and he wasn't in denial about that, he was just tired of this with her. She had to go, and he had to call Stacie and tell her the whole story with Kionna, if she decided it wasn't worth it and left him, then that's just what might happen. There was only one way to find out.

It took a little more than 'get the hell out' to actually get Kionna to leave. She was determined to get under his skin. She tried a few different ways, but Rashi just wasn't having it at this point. Threats really weren't the way to get to Rashi and her threat pretty much closed his ears to whatever she was saying. She tried but he wasn't trying to hear her now. She can do what she wanted, but he meant what he said, if anything happened to Stacie, there would be hell to pay. He couldn't walk around with something happening to her on his conscience and Kionna being the reason why it happened. After he finally got Kionna to leave, the first person he called was Stacie. He'd planned on calling the whole crew including Nehi, but he had to call Stacie first.

She didn't answer when he called, so he left a message and told her he'd just see her the next day when he picked her up at O'Hare International. He then called Rashad and told him about what was going down with Kionna. Rashad said he was just about to call him with a funnier story, but he'll tell him next time this was much more serious. After Rashad he called Preach who seemed like he really didn't care. He was on the bench now, so Rashi could understand him not caring. Finally, he called Nehi, who of course didn't answer again. He left a message for him though, "Ne, what's up this is Rashi. Hit me when you can B, it's important and it's about Kionna. So, I know that you haven't been answering lately and nobody knows you're alive except for Stacie cause she's getting you gigs or what not. Well if you can when you get this, hit me back. Deuces Nehi." Right now, he couldn't worry about Nehi and his issues, dude wasn't answering on purpose because he was emailing back and forth with Stacie. So, he was alive he was just either upset about something or his phone was broken. Rashi would have to worry about that later he had to tell Stacie what was good and be truthful.

When Rashi picked Stacie up from the airport two days later they'd talked, but Rashi hadn't given her the whole story yet. She just knew that they had to talk and in person was the way Rashi wanted to do it. So, the last couple days were a bit stressful, talking on the phone, but not addressing the pink elephant in the room. It was stressful to Rashi as well, trying to talk to Stacie about this and not give too much away and at the same time take calls from Dayna.

When he got there, she didn't have much to say, she wanted to get right down to business. "So, Ra, you said you wanted to talk to me, I'm listening."

"It's a long story woman, and at the end, you might not even want to be with me. I mean I've done some dirt." Her face changed and it was clear that he had to fix this right away. "Nothing recently, but in my past. I've done some dirt and it's not catching up, I wouldn't say that, but it has made a situation."

"What's this about Ra?"

"Well, Stacie, you know I wouldn't do anything to you and as far as you and I go, this is something I want to last for a while kid. I mean I think this is something strong and something that can last, so with that being said let me start from the beginning. First of all, you're my first girlfriend. I mean my very first, so before I met you, I wasn't into having a girlfriend at all. I was that dude- you know, the strictly smashing dude. I didn't care what people said, and especially didn't care what people thought either. Still don't care now to be honest. I do care what you think though. I want you to know everything and from what you hear, I'm okay with whatever you decide as far as we go lady."

"Rashi I want this, I love the time we spend together and what we do when we're together. I doubt there is anything is your past that could change the way I feel."

"We'll see." As they pulled off Rashi started the long story. "It starts in high school woman. As you know me, and the crew have been tight since we were kids. I mean really tight, we planned on being like the Fab Five from Michigan. That was five freshmen who started for Michigan in the nineties and kind of changed the way college ball was played. There were only four of us, but we had goals woman. Anyhow, We were tight all the way through grade school and all picked the same high school just so that we could stay together. It was cool and everything was fun. Now

Aria, whom you haven't met but heard a ton about was Nehi's girl. They grew up together, so it was like they were damn near married woman. I mean you didn't see Nehi without her. Just like Carrie and Preach, they were the same way. For a while Rashad even had a high school marriage going with a girl named Jennifer or whatnot. Anyhow, Shad and Jennifer broke up, and at the same time Aria was on some cheating stuff. Nehi didn't know, or he did and didn't believe it, but she was letting just about anybody smash. I mean anybody woman, and we were telling this dude left and right and he just wouldn't believe us. His boys, he was taking her word over ours. So, I smashed."

"Rashi, seriously? I mean isn't there some kind of unspoken rule or something between friends where you don't do that? I mean even to prove a point you don't sleep with your friend's girlfriend. That is dirty Ra."

"There's more lady." She was taking it pretty well so far, so he decided to keep going and see what she thought. "So, like I said, I as doing what I had to do so that dude could know that she was dirty. I smashed, but I went right to Nehi like, 'son Aria is dirty as hell B, she let me smash, here are the details and blah, blah, blah' of course this clown doesn't want to believe me. He's like 'Ra we know all you do is go girl to girl and you're scared to get a girlfriend, so now you're jealous of me and mine.' I couldn't believe he went there, woman. I'm like dude we all been telling you this, now all of a sudden, I'm jealous? It was like he forgot about Preach and Shad telling him the same thing."

"Yeah Rashi, but they didn't sleep with his girl to prove it. That was dirty and I don't think he was wrong for siding with her so far. What kind of best friend sleeps with you girlfriend? No matter what the rumor is, you don't cross that line, I mean that makes you just as bad if not worse that her."

Now this was more like he was expecting, and he had so much more to go. "So anyhow, I tell Aria flat out. 'You dirty and Nehi will find out. I didn't want you and the fact that this happened just strengthens my case' or whatever. She gets all nervous cause she didn't know that I'd already told him, goes to him and says that I took advantage of her and damn near made it sound like I raped her or something. I couldn't believe it. Anyhow once again he takes on her side like he's trying to save her. By this time, the whole school knows about it, and with me smashing Nehi's girl and Rashad smashing Jennifer's sister, the whole school is thinking we're about to break off into two different crews, me and Shad on one side and Nehi and Preach on the other."

"Wait, Rashad slept with his girlfriend's sister? I mean not even his girlfriend, his high school wife? He slept with her sister? Damn y'all are all dirty, no wonder he's always with Jackie."

"Lady, I need you to focus because the story isn't about Rashad. He can tell you his story when he sees you. There is a lot more to this and is this how you're reacting this early into the story, then the rest only gets worse. Also, Rashad is a good dude, he made a mistake. You have a million male friends, Jackie is his female friend." She made another face at this. "Yeah, and like I was saying, it gets worse. So, where was I?"

"She told Nehi."

"Yeah, so I'm getting all the blame now. I mean I don't really care what people in the school are thinking or saying about me, I'm trying to get this clown Nehi to understand that I'm sorry and that I wouldn't do that, I had to this time though so that he could know that we weren't lying to him. I know that was a terrible way to do it now, but that's the way I did it then. So, what happens is, he basically dumps both of us. I mean he wasn't talking to me and he wasn't talking to her either. She took it hard even though she was cheating on dude, me, I knew he'd come around. So, I was patient or whatnot. I chilled and let him cool down a bit. We all graduated the year before last, but we took a trip to Europe last year, the crew. I was single of course, Rashad was too, Preach was still with Carrie, but he went for the historic part of Europe rather than the fun. Then Nehi, met the chick you met at the shop Kionna. She comes from money, so she came along. I'm not going to lie I went to see how many European women I could smash while I was there and that was about it. French chicks, English chicks, Roman chicks, whatever son, I was on a mission. I met you and then I wasn't on said mission anymore. Anyhow, he's there and he gets really close to this girl Kionna. I mean we were supposed to be there like a few months, but Kionna's pops had us taken care of so we made it an expanded trip. Anyhow, we get back and everything is good. Nehi and I are on speaking terms and everything, but apparently, he was still talking to Aria. Which is cool with me, they were friends for ages and as long as he wasn't being cheated on by her I was cool with that. He somehow was discussing me with her though and that was bogus to me. She decides that she's going to relay all this information about me to my mom."

"She did what? How does she even know your mom?"

"Why wouldn't she? She's known us all for years, he and Nehi just were the closest. It wasn't like he only knew her. She went to the same grade school and high school as well. We don't really have middle schools in the city, so we all went from school to school together. Anyhow lady, my mom gets on me about Europe, and I've already told you how rocky me and my mom's relationship is, so this didn't really help." Rashi had actually told her about how his mom wanted him to go to college and how he decided being a barber was a better choice for him. "So, this puts Nehi and I back at square one. At each other's throats and Aria is the reason for it yet again. I'm so angry by it though, I threaten him. I know, I was wrong, but she was in my business for one and for two she was telling my mom? Who in the hell does that?"

"Maybe she had feelings for you, I mean y'all did sleep together Rashi."

"She was my guy's girl, so she shouldn't have feelings for me, it would never happen with us." As soon as Rashi said that statement, he knew that the end of this story was about to suck. He just said the one thing that should have kept him away from Kionna. "So, while he's all buddy, buddy with Aria when he gets back, he starts to neglect Kionna. Who steps in to fix things though? Me. I took her to lunch and pretty much told her to step her game up. Let her know that dudes just aren't that smart, including Nehi and Myself. We just aren't the smartest and that she should say something to Nehi. This is like a 5 months ago that I'm telling her this. The next month this clown shoots her the deuces for Aria."

"Seriously? Why? Is Aria prettier? I mean that Kionna girl was good looking so Aria must be a dime huh?"

"That's the thing Stace, no. Aria is what we call, the Big A. Dude, she's far from cute lady. Like when I smashed, she had on these leopard panties and all I could think was, how do you get an elephant in leopard spots. That's how big she is. Anyhow, he dumps Kionna and just leaves her out to dry. She begins to call me because she's really hurt. He doesn't seem to care, but in Europe he was extra protective. He thinks I didn't notice, but she couldn't be in the same room with me alone without him running in like he was saving her life. Now all of a sudden, she wasn't worth his time. So, her and I started talking."

"Started talking like what?"

"Not like that woman, we started talking like, about Nehi. He left her out to dry and I was more like moral support. So, I guess it got to a point where we'd be texting and Nehi wasn't the subject. Ki and I became friends and over the next couple months from the time he dumped her we got close. Now she didn't know I had a girlfriend though. I didn't tell her cause although we were friends we weren't hanging out and all of that, she was just some chick that I texted. Nothing else, just a girl I was texting, I considered her a friend, but she was a friend I kept at arm's length. So, this brings us to that night at the shop. I was expecting Aria cause Nehi kept talking about his girl and all of that. I was shocked when she showed up. From what she'd told me her and Nehi didn't talk or any of that."

"It did seem like there was something going on there. Ra, I wanted to say something at the time, but she was staring you down when you were cutting his hair. At first, I thought she was staring at Nehi, but I noticed it was you when every now and again you'd look up and y'all would catch eyes. It was obvious to me that she wanted you, now I know why."

"There's more Estacia." Rashi usually never calls her that, so this got her attention. "So, since that day I told her not to text or call me to keep things from getting all crazy between me and Nehi again. I mean before she got there I was out there apologizing and all of that to him for the Aria situation, wasn't trying to have another one. She didn't like that, but for like a whole month I hadn't heard from her at all. No text, no calls, nothing. So, I was good and happy. You and I were good, and I thought I had everything in the bag. So, you left town last week and I take my sister to a game. I drop her off and guess who I see that night walking alone?

"Who, Kionna?"

"No, Big Josh. So, I take my quarters and I give him the PHD we talked about. I mean I got him good woman. He was hurt, and bloody. As I leave, I yell something like 'next time you'll let me in fat boy' or something like that and I take off. I get home I'm chillin, feeling good. I told Rashad and Jackie, I mean it's done so everyone is happy. So, a couple nights ago I'm chillin and of course Kionna texts me. She wants to know who I was at the game with, like I was with another chick or whatever. I tell her it was my sister and she doesn't believe it. All she knows is that it wasn't you. I don't care about that, but then she says 'so who was dude that you beat up'. Yep, she was following me that night and she pretty much had me in a position where all I could do was find out what she wanted and what she was going to do with that information. I was hoping she wouldn't go to the police. She tells me she's coming over to talk. At this point Stacie, I don't have a choice but to let her in. She gets in and it's all kinds of crazy going on. I mean she's like I should be with her and this that and the other. I tell her no and that's it. I tell her to keep it moving and then she threatens you." At this point in the story they are in front of Rashi's apartment building. He doesn't turn off the car and he doesn't attempt to get out, that part that pretty much tells what he does next is about to come out. "Stacie, she threatened you. She knew the only way that she could get under my skin was by threatening you. She said something like if I don't start talking to her or 'open the lines of communication' that something bad would happen to you. After that I kind of lost my temper and told her to get out. I mean she was there, and I told her and to get out and that if anything was to happen to you, she'd have to deal with me. So, Stace, that's the whole story woman. I mean I can't force you to stay and I don't want you to leave, so I'll let all of that soak in and if you want me to, I'll take you home now." He was hoping that she would say 'it's fine Rashi, I'm where I want to be' or something like that, but she didn't she just sat there and looked like she was deep in thought. So, he started to pull off.

"Rashi, I don't do drama like this. I mean I didn't know I was your first girlfriend and to be honest I don't usually date players either. You kept that from me, and I don't like that. You play women and you do your friends dirty as well, I mean I really don't know what to do here. You tell me all of this and I don't know it seems like you want me to leave."

"That's the thing Stacie, I want the opposite from you. I ain't never been in this position, so I don't know what I'm supposed to do, but I told you all of this so that you can make a choice. So that you don't feel cheated or feel like you didn't a fair shot at it. I want you woman, but at the same time I wouldn't force anything on you. Yeah, my life is complicated, but in the end, I honestly do care about you. So like I said I'll let all of this soak in, you have my number, you can call me whenever you make up your mind, I'm either here or at the shop, but you have all of my numbers, use them either way. You want to give this a try, or you don't, it's up to you, just keep me posted though." The rest of the ride was silent, and Rashi knew she had some things to think about.

Chapter 13

When the barbershop meeting the week before Christmas came, the whole crew was worried about Nehi. None of them had heard from him and the meeting in the shop was weird without him. Things were going down and they were always there for one another when things were getting this crazy. Preach told the guys his story first, he'd been coming off the bench lately, but not really doing much and it was taking a toll on him.

"Dude, I'm on the bench because of Carrie"

Rashi wasn't that close to Carrie, but he wasn't about to let Preach blame his cousin for his unfortunate season. "Preach, that's garbage son, I went to some of the games you started dude. You were trash out there. I was there with Stacie and we were ashamed to admit we knew you."

"Not like that son, I'm on the bench because I love her."

"What?" Rashad heard of love doing a lot of things, but he loved her in high school too, and he played his ass off then, he was not understanding this.

"Okay, I'm going to tell y'all why I got benched, and it ain't cause I played bad. I was actually forced to play bad. I did some foul shit and it caught up with me. I mean some really foul shit son."

"Like what?" Rashad was used to this coming from Rashi or even Nehi at times, but Preach doing something crazy wasn't even fathomable. "What happened that could have got you benched?"

"I cheated on Carrie."

Rashi was shocked. As many times as Preach could have cheated and never did. “Seriously bro, and the guilt is effecting your game son? I mean she isvmy cousin and all, but you gotta do what you gotta do to stay on that court son. I mean we ain’t telling and if you’ve got it out of your system, she’ll never know. Do your thing B.”

“It’s ain’t that easy Ra. It’s not about her finding out, the broad I was cheating with found out son. She’s a season ticket holder son, she saw me at the game and after the game I was with Carrie. She saw me and set me up. She invited me to dinner and all of that, when I got there she was waiting with dinner. Then she started in on the whole, ‘Chris I hate you, blah, blah, blah.”

“Chris?”

“Oh yeah, I didn’t want her to know who I was, so I told her my name was Chris. It was working for a while, but she found out.”

“Cause she was a ticket holder?” Rashad had a story to tell, but for now was into this one. Preach was on some Rashi type of stuff.

“That and I was in the newspaper. Yeah, I didn’t even think about that. She saw me in the newspaper and to make sure it was me, she memorized my birth mark on my leg. She was pretty smart about it.”

Rashi knew this sounded kind of crazy, no young girl pays that much attention to detail. If they did, he wouldn’t have gotten half the girls he met in the past, so he had to ask, “how old is she?”

“She’s like forty, bro. I mean I found her when I was off campus and calling myself playing it safe, I started messing around with her. She was never on campus, wasn’t calling me all the time and she could cook. I mean she wasn’t cutting into the time I was spending with Carrie, so it was all good.” Just talking about the story and Ms. CiCi was getting to Preach. He hated not playing ball like he knew he could, like he should be playing.

“So how is she forcing you to sit on the bench?” Rashi was there for one of the games, so he could believe that story. He’d never seen Preach play so badly before.

“She was on some revenge type stuff son. I mean I understand I played with her heart and I apologized, but that wasn’t enough for her. She calls herself a fan, but decided she’d rather bet against the school and win money. So, I was put in a position where I'm basically shaving points for her. I told her how this ain't just basketball she's playing with and how this is my life. She wasn't trying to hear that, she felt like since I lied to her before that I was lying about that too.

To top it off, she still has me sleeping with her on Sundays. I mean I figured playing horribly would be enough and that she would be happy, but now I have to sleep with her as well just to make sure that she keeps it quiet. I honestly don't know how you do it Ra. She's a handful and she's not trying to cool out at all. It's like she's enjoying seeing me suffer. Get this, she's made over 10G's and is still playing me. Why"

This was Rashi's area of expertise, so he had to say something. "Preach, she is enjoying this because it's killing you. You enjoyed what you were doing as Chris right? Well she's now in the driver's seat bro. Honestly, did you not think that when she found out that you would suffer. I'm sure you probably thought that she wouldn't find out, but in a situation like this you have to look at it from all the possible angles B. You have to know that getting caught is a 50/50 thing. If you don't get caught you did good work. If you do get caught, that doesn't mean you didn't do good work it just means that other things outside of your control happened. Like you said in this situation, she saw a newspaper, now I would have personally foreseen that, but this is your first time stepping out. Of course, you didn't plan for that. You know how they say 'all is fair in love and war' that's the same with situations that aren't love as well. No rules. She's an older chick, so she knows this, and that's why she's playing you. She's showing you that there are no rules and that she can do what she wants because she actually has you in a corner. This is how I approach any im in that involves multiple woman. I call it living in a circular room bro. You don't give them any options to catch you in a corner. You gotta think bigger than your immediate area. You're in Iowa and on the hoop team. You already know that when the season starts the spotlight is on the team. You live in a college town, so you not dealing with a chick on campus was smart. That's a good look Preach, but then you gotta realize that the school is the core of the city and you already know from playing high school ball that the school ain't the majority of the fans. It's the neighborhoods, it the community bro. So, what I'm saying is yeah, you did put some thought into this, but if you don't want to get your hands dirty or get hurt, you're going to have to think bigger."

Rashad and Preach were speechless, just listening and trying to take in the things that were being said. Not for later use, but because this was interesting. They were inside of Rashi's head and they'd known him for years and never actually been in his head like this. Getting to see first-hand how he thought.

"Don't get me wrong Preach, I'm not saying it cool to cheat on my cousin, cause quite frankly, it's not. At the same time though, I'm not in a position to tell you not to do that, look at me and look at the things I've been through with these women. I mean if she finds out, please don't tell her I knew cause I ain't trying to get into it with her over that. My biggest thing is though, even if you never do this again, you still gotta think about what's going on around you. My situation right now is terrible with Stace, because I really have no idea what she's going to do, or even how she feels about me. I have Dayna though, she's my fallback chick. I won't say I will not be a little bit hurt if Stace calls it quits, but I have a soft place to lay my head if she does. Y'all feel me?"

"So, what are you going to do?" Rashad wanted to go to the restroom but wanted to hear what was going to happen with this. "You going to let your whole season go to waste? Then next year they're looking for a new guard, to replace you?"

"I don't know yet, what do y'all think I should do?"

"Shad's right Preach, you don't pick your game up, you are going to be replaced. I mean you might think you're doing the best thing for Carrie but let's be real. If you wanted to do the best thing for Carrie, there would be no Chris. I mean I'm not a genius on boyfriend/girlfriend relations, but if you were happy, I doubt there would have been a Chris in the first place."

Rashad agreed with that. "True indeed son."

"Then I think I know what I have to do then, I gotta ball like this guy." He was pointing at Rashad, he'd been seeing his guy on ESPN and even though his season was going to hell, he was happy for Shad. "I mean I know it's going to make ole girl mad, but I gotta start looking out for me. I guess this means I'll be telling Carrie, huh? I don't want to, but I have to bro. I mean I can't keep looking like this. You just said you went to a game how bad did I look."

"You looked real bad Preach. I'm pretty sure Chris is more a lacrosse player than a hooper. I mean from what I can tell it looked like you were shaving points. I know your game though bro. I'm sure nobody else could have though because you were hustling and all of that, but I could just tell that you weren't hooping it up like we all know you can. I know it looked like you did your thing, but it wasn't Preach hooping. Maybe that was Chris as way."

"Anyhow, I'll be right back clowns, I gotta tell y'all what happened with me, Jackie and Caryl son." Rashad walked to the back of the shop he had to hit the restroom.

"So, you're telling Carrie? I guess you have to. She might blow her lid on you, or she might even accept it. I mean I don't know how love works or all that shit, but maybe she'll let you slide." Rashi didn't believe it, but whatever, this was his guy and he wanted him to get back to balling.

Rashad came back laughing. "Now what happened with Preach is crazy, but I need y'all to listen to this. Right now, at this very moment, I have two girlfriends, bro."

"What?" Preach actually felt better after sharing what happened with his guys and he really wanted to hear this. At least somebody else was going through something.

"Yeah son, so I don't know if you've been watching ESPN or not, but I've been on a few times now. It started that one game when I went for thirty-seven. I think that was where everything just started to become real funky. I mean I was with Caryl and I was spending time and everything, but as you know me, and Jackie have grown like closer and closer. It's almost every day, we chill after class, we chill before class, on Saturdays. Whenever we have a free moment, we spend that chilling. We hoop against each other and watch sports and all of that, so she's cool as hell to me. I honestly think of all things, her night getting into that scuffle with Big Josh, made her and I as close as we are. It was that night that we kissed, but I didn't smash because I had a girl at the time."

"Now you got two?" This shop visit was turning out pretty good to Rashi. He planned on telling the guys about him and Kionna, but his biggest concern coming in was Nehi. This was turning into something good though.

"What happened was, that night I was chilling with Jackie after the game. We go and kick it, but it's already kind of late, so we head back to the dorms. When we get there, we are watching TV or what not, but that damn lovesac bro. That thing is uncomfortable sometimes. So, my back gets to hurting and I ask for a massage."

"Oh, so basically you were asking to smash. That's funny, the first time I chilled with Stacie I pulled that can I get a massage thing, worked like a charm B."

"Well, clown, it didn't happen like that with me. First of all, getting a massage from her was like getting a massage from a gorilla. I mean talk about worse massage ever. Seriously son a massage from her is like the equivalent of being caned in a foreign country. Her hands felt like she'd been working on the railroad all the live long day."

They were having a laugh at Jackie's expense, so of course they all had to jump in Rashi was first as usual. "So you're saying you would have rather gotten a massage from Fred Flintstone? What about the maid on the Jetsons? You'd rather Robocop give you a massage rather than one of your girlfriends, bro?"

"Y'all clowns. I mean I was dealing with an old broad, but at least she used lotion on her hands."

"Whatever idiots, and yeah, I'd rather be whipped as a slave than get another one of those joints Preach. Anyhow after the massacre disguised as a massage, we ended up kissing. So, the kissing is leading to other things and next thing you know I'm half naked, she's half naked. We're going at it for real son, I'm pretty sure I'm about to smash this girl who was just basically punching me in the spine. I want to though, and of course my phone rings. I know who it is before I even look at the phone, it's after a game, it had to be Caryl. So, I answer it, and she's heard about the monster game I just had so I don't get rid of her just yet."

"You Idiot, it came on Sportscenter all night and the next morning." Rashi wanted to call him like Jackie did, but he'd just got into it with

Josh when he got home and saw it. So, he didn't call Shad that night about it.

"Well that comes into the story as well. So, I'm on the phone blowing it with Jackie. She was getting dressed cause I'm over here on the phone with Caryl trying to hear what she heard. At this point Jackie is ready to leave. I thought she was pissed, so I hang up with Caryl. I catch her at the door and she's like, 'don't worry about it Shad, it'll happen, talk to your girl.' I mean she's so cool about son, that I basically forget about the massage.

Jackie heads back to her dorm and what not. I'm call Caryl back and she decides that she wants to come over and kick it B. I know what this means, so you know I'm like of course, get your ass over here."

"Did you ask for a massage to make you feel better from that back breaker?"

"Ra, get off my girl like that. And what you laughing at Preach? Let me get back to the damn story clowns. So, she comes over. She's there like all of two minutes when of course, Jackie calls. I'm thinking, 'damn she saw Caryl', but she's calling cause she's excited for me. I pick up, she's screaming that I'm on ESPN. Well I did have thirty-seven, so duh. Anyhow Caryl think it's another chick yelling at me, so while I'm watching myself on ESPN, she turns the TV off." He paused because he was expecting some kind of reaction, but Rashi and Preach were just waiting on the rest of the story. "I get upset, but we make up. The next morning, I had class but it was crazy cause apparently quite a few people saw the report, and I didn't. I see Jackie, she's leaving her math class and she's like I have something for you. She has the Sportcenter on DVD. Then this fool calls" pointing at Rashi "says he's done what he said he'd do to Big Josh, and next thing you know we're back in my dorm. I tell her that I'm done with Caryl and that she's who I want to be with, and I smash. Well, we smash, it's a two-person thing."

"That story wasn't very funny, and it sounds like you lied to her. You're obviously still with Caryl so now you just have two girls." Preach didn't like this story because he'd be okay with a setup like that if Ms. CiCi would chill. Let him play and let Chris be Chris.

"That's cause it's not over clown. I'm talking to Ra, and he's like' text and tell her it's over.' Jackie on the other hand is like 'no, as a man you need to tell her in person.' Like a dummy I take Jackie's advice and I call her and ask can I come out there. I drive like a full hour to get to her and I get there she's extra fly son. I mean heels on, make up, just looking good as hell. I'm like why you all dressed up, and she hits me with, 'it's our four-month anniversary, I thought you forgot, but you didn't. You are here, and we're going to dinner and all of that. I end up feeding the girl, going on a long as walk, and talking to her about my favorite times with her. Needless to say, I didn't have a chance to tell her the real reason why I was there."

"Now that's funny." Preach and Ra were laughing hard at this. "This clown did all that driving to have dinner on his anniversary, that was sweet Shad."

"Shut up Preach. I planned on telling her, I didn't know we had a four-month anniversary coming up. We'd just had the three month the month before."

They were having a good time. So Rashi decided to make it even better by letting them in on the Christmas surprise he had in store. "I went all out this Christmas for all four of us. If anyone can actually get a hold of this clown Nehi we'll all be able to enjoy it. Dude I got us all tickets to NBA all-star weekend. I got us hotels and everything, two rooms though, and all we gotta do is drive. I mean we have tickets to everything. USA/International game, slam dunk, three-point contest all that stuff. If Nehi doesn't go, it's just us three son and I've wasted money on an extra ticket. At first, I was going to invite Stacie if dude didn't come, but she ain't speaking to me either."

"Why not?" Rashad hadn't heard this yet, so he knew that Preach hadn't.

"Oh, well Kionna, threatened her and it was kind of my fault."

"What? Why would Ki, Nehi's girl threaten Stacie? Oh, she's probably jealous Stacie was getting Nehi all those jobs huh?"

"Nope, I didn't tell y'all because I didn't think it would go as far as it did. After Nehi shot her the deuces, she started texting and calling me. I was cool with it, but I was dating Stacie. I didn't tell her cause as much trash as we were talking, I was sure that nothing would come from it. I start dealing with her, getting pics from her all of that. It was all done for fun though. I mean she's telling me she's done with Nehi so I didn't think it would be a big deal.

"What? After Aria?" Preach was visibly upset by this. "You're sitting there telling me that after the whole thing that went down with Aria, you did the same thing again? That's why Neo ain't talking to us, cause you did him dirty again? That's a dick move Ra"

"Ra, you smashed Kionna?"

"First of all, Preach, why do you call him Neo all the time? That's his DJ name, not his real name. Secondly, I didn't give Ki the pipe son. Her and I were friends and that was it. Yeah, it got a little close, but I wasn't trying to smash her. Your boy 'Neo' left her out to dry, so even if I had, it wouldn't have been his business anyway. He chose Big Aria and left her out here hurt so bad that she was calling me. She wasn't calling y'all crying and all of that, so I did what I figured Preach would do, I was there for her."

"I wouldn't have smashed."

"I didn't smash Kionna bro. Anyhow, like I was saying it's not like that, and for the record I didn't know she was nuts. That chick Kionna is crazy, and now I see why Nehi chose Aria."

"What happened?" Usually when Rashi said that a girl was crazy, it meant that he smashed and shot her the deuces and she reacted. He always called their reaction crazy, but Preach knew, especially now, that when you play with someone's heart they react. Crazy or not, they react the way they feel is right. "If you're saying she's crazy son, something had to happen as to where either you smashed or something. Nobody acts crazy when things are good. If you were just there for her like you're saying then, if anything she'd be more gracious than crazy."

"Okay, what happened was that we started off just basically talking about Nehi and his stupid decision to get rid of her for Aria. At the time I thought it was the wrong decision. Somehow that progressed to us talking about what we are looking for. Then that became something else as well. All of a sudden, she's hitting me like can I come over and all of that.

She didn't know I'd dealing with Stacie, and she decided do come to the shop acting like she wanted to see Nehi. She came to see me and that was crazy indicator number one. She got here, met Stacie, and then texted me talking crazy, that was crazy indicator number two. Then at the club that night she's dancing all on me trying to get me to leave a model for her, yeah that's crazy indicator number three. It gets worse though son, I mean I head to Vancouver I don't hear from her at all. She's like a ghost, so I naturally assume her and Nehi are Ki are working things out.

When I got back, I was spending my time with Stacie and Dayna. Nothing else was going on, I wasn't even talking to Ki like that anymore. How was I supposed to know that her crazy ass was still lurking? From the time I got back from Vancouver every day I was caking it with Stacie. We were going to basketball games, movies, shopping, and that was about it. When Stacie left out of town, I was with Dayna. We went to the game that this clown had thirty-seven points. She was there B. I don't know what for and to be honest I don't even think she knew you were playing Shad."

"Believe me clown, with the night I had, she knew I was playing. I mean I know you think she's crazy, but she ain't that crazy."

"Shad I'm serious clown. That's the night I ran into Josh clown. Remember? Well she was following me and guess what, she saw me run into him too. She tried to use it against me son. I mean she tried about every way she could to get me to smash her, then I told her why I wouldn't do it and it wasn't because of Stacie. It was because of Nehi. She thought I was holding this grudge or whatever cause I got a girlfriend, but she was dirty for how she tried to play me and Nehi against each other."

"Wait, how was she trying to get you to smash?" Rashad liked Ki, so this story was a little disturbing. He didn't know she was crazy.

"Oh, she came over. When she said she saw it, I asked what she wanted, and apparently, she wanted to come over. That's when she was trying to get me to smash her. I couldn't do it, so she gets to making threats and all of that son. I couldn't believe it. The threats against Stacie kind of worked against her though. They pissed me off, so I put her out. Told her that if anything happens to Stacie, then we have beef and I ain't talking rap beef. She knows I have like 45 sisters, bro, she ain't trying to get it twisted."

"So why is Stacie not speaking to you?" Preach liked that fact that Rashi didn't give in, he was thinking he should have done the same thing. He was going through all of this because he let some old ass lady punk him. Yeah, when he got back, he was fixing this. JuJuan West on the bench, that was nutty.

"Cause I told her everything and I haven't really heard from her since then. I mean I really told her everything. From the trip, to Aria, to Kionna, and I told her about the threats, and I guess she's thinking about it."

Rashad couldn't believe he'd told her everything. "Look at our boy finally becoming a man. Telling his girl the truth and all huh? Finally, son, you have a girlfriend that you care about. Yeah, she's breaking up with you."

Preach was right there to agree, "Yeah she is. With your history with women and the way you play games son, you might as well kill that. I mean that's just Karma. Come on Ra, you knew when you told her that this was it for you dude. It happens to us all."

"Well look here idiots, I ain't worried about it, she stay then it's a good look, she decides to leave, well then I guess it's deuces. I told y'all about Dayna. Yeah, if y'all were smart you would know what Dayna is, a back-up. Just in case this Stacie thing doesn't work out, I have something else on the side. Nothing wrong with being prepared is there? My plan is simple, if I don't hear from her by Christmas, then I'm bouncing I don't have the time or the patience to wait on her. I was honest with her about everything, except Dayna, so if she leaves then it wasn't meant to be. I notice y'all like to complain and try to go out of your way to please or keep your women happy. Look at you, you're on the bench cause you're scared of being dumped. And you, you didn't dump a girl cause it was your four month anniversary. Just so you know clown, anniversaries are a yearly thing that's what makes them special. If you were to stay with her for 5 years, would you idiots be celebrating your 60th anniversary? I thought not. So like I said, the ball is in her court. Whatever she decides, I'm good with. Anyhow, can we just get them heads cut and get ready go. I ain't trying to talk about Stacie all night, I'm sure she ain't talking about me."

Chapter 14

For Nehi, the last six months were like this for him, 'Eff the Crew'. He didn't say anything to them for Thanksgiving and Christmas passed without as much as a Merry Christmas from him. He didn't need them, he was making money, doing pretty good in school, and on top of that him and Aria were happy. Since the whole Kionna debacle, Nehi was focused on getting on with his life. His crew, in his opinion, abandoned him and now he was doing them the same way. They called and called, but he constantly deleted their messages. New Year's Eve which was supposed to be spent at the shop this year, he chilled with Aria downtown. He seriously wasn't trying to deal with them.

In Nehi's eyes, the so called 'crew' sided with Rashi about 100% of the time. From the Aria and Rashi thing, even to now with Ki, it just seemed no one really had his back. The funny thing to him was that the only thing keeping him even attached to them was Stacie. I mean he and Stacie didn't talk about what was going on with them, but she was dating Rashi. He was going to change that though, the only reason he hadn't done it before now was because he was letting his funds grow. He didn't want to ruin his hook-up. Stacie had to have a crush or something on him though, since around Thanksgiving, her work for him had almost tripled. Her emails since then seemed to be a little more intimate as well. Nothing freaky, but all of a sudden it was like she cared about him.

That idea alone made Nehi smile, the option to get Rashi back. He was a clown and a backstabber to Nehi and getting him back would be a good thing. In his mind though, if he got him back for all of that, the 'crew' would side with Rashi as usual though. He would have to hear about how he was wrong and how he shouldn't have done it out of revenge as to where Rashi was okay for sleeping with his girl. "Rashi did it to look out for him." What kind of bullshit was that, your best friend slept with our girl, and he was looking out for you. That's trash, and then a year later, the same thing? Yeah, he and Ki were broken up, but there are rules, at some point Rashi has to realize that.

Nehi had also been ignoring calls from Kionna. She played him, she acted like she wanted to see him, and basically used him to see that clown Rashi. He was sure that everyone knew just from the way they were acting, and this dude has a girlfriend. He wasn't calling her at first when they broke up because it just would have been uncomfortable and weird for both of them. She wasn't calling him either. During that time, they were basically strangers and he reached out, then she came embarrassed him and basically told him something that could have been said the first time he called.

Over the last few months though, he'd gotten close to his roommate and a few of his friends. He was the DJ, so he usually had money, so he found himself paying for a lot. He didn't mind though they filled the void of his friends. Rashi, Rashad, and Preach were in his past, these cats were his future now. Yeah, he'd probably not be as close, but he wouldn't be as hurt if the same thing happened. This is how Nehi was approaching everything until got a call from Aria on Friday night as he was about to go out with his new guys.

"Wassup woman?"

"Hey Nehi. What are you doing?"

"Getting ready to head out woman, what about you?"

"Nothing just thinking about you and decided to call." Aria began to cry. "Go enjoy yourself Nehi, we'll talk later."

Nehi heard her crying though so of course he wanted to know what the problem was. "What's wrong Aria? You okay? Did something happen when you were at home?" She'd been home lately with her family so Nehi figured something had to have happened there.

"No Nehi, we can just talk later. You go out and have fun with your friends and when you get back you can either come here or I'll come your way. Right now you just go and have fun."

Aria telling him to go and have fun was a rarity, so he really knew something was wrong. She was more open to him having fun now that he had new crew of friends, but this was a little weird. She called him, so apparently something was on her mind. "It's cool woman, I wasn't even doing anything big, what's wrong?

"Can we just talk about this later? It's not that important Nehi. I just have to go." She hung up. He called back a couple times, but the phone went straight to voicemail.

Nehi decided to go ahead with his plans and go out to the club. He tried to enjoy himself, but he just couldn't shake Aria. She was crying about something. As a good boyfriend it was his duty to find out what it was. On his way out of the club, he bumped into a girl on the dance floor. He knocked her drink out of her hand.

"My bad shorty. Want me to get you another?"

"Of course, and next time saying 'excuse me' might save us both a little time and money." She was joking and flashed Nehi a smile.

"Maybe I bumped you just so that I could see that smile, and then introduce myself, I'm Nehemiah."

"Okay, Nehemiah, I'm Leah. Nice to meet you."

"What were you drinking, Leah? I'll get myself one too and maybe we can go somewhere and talk a bit. I mean I really am sorry for knocking your drink over. It's the least I can do." Leah was a cutie, so at this point, the reason why he was leaving totally slipped his mind. "I can get us over in the booth, we can chill there a minute, and maybe get to know each other a little better."

"How can you get us in a VIP booth?"

"I'm a DJ, I work here a lot so I know a few people. So, once again Leah, what are you drinking?"

"Oh, vodka and pineapple."

"Then I'll be right back Leah. I know I keep saying your name, but I don't want to forget it. Just in case I come back and you're not in the booth anymore, I'll know the name of the one that got away. Leah." He was joking and like Biggie says 'once you grin, I'm in, game begins.' She was grinning at this point.

After Nehi got the drinks he got a booth where he and Leah sat and talked for a long time. She found out that he was a DJ. His favorite party starters were Notorious B.I.G. and Jay-Z, he was a south sider born and raised in Chicago. A full-time college student and apparently his friends weren't speaking to him. Oh, and he didn't have a girlfriend, Leah liked that.

Nehi found out Leah was half black half Cuban. She was from Miami, a college student as well. Her ID was real (his was fake, hence the drink, but he did pay $100 for it so it was good.) She was an education major and minored in criminal justice. She had a part-time job at a coffee shop. She was staying on the north side with some friends. She didn't have a guy right now either, she's recently broken up with a guy who lied about having a girlfriend. She hated liars.

Nehi and Leah talked all night, even when the light came on and the club was closing, they wanted to keep going. Nehi gave his new friends a ride, but he didn't want to end this night. It had been a while since he'd had sparks like this with a stranger. True he hadn't been looking lately, but he wasn't looking tonight either. "Leah, I have to take my guys home or whatnot, but we can meet at IHOP or something if you want woman."

Leah wasn't trying to leave the conversation either, so decided to be bold and said, "Can I just meet you at your place after you drop them off? We were surrounded by crowds all night I'd like to just to have you to myself sometime tonight. You know, just in case you're the one to get away."

Nehi really liked this girl, so of course he said. "Yeah we can do that. Give me like 30 or 45 minutes and I'll call you back with directions to my dorm."

"Okay Nehemiah, I guess we'll be chilling together later. Bye-bye."

"Deuces cutie."

Taking the guys home, the last thing on Nehi's mind was Aria and what was wrong with her today. Since he stopped talking to his real crew, every day was about her. He didn't want to admit it, but he was just getting tired of her. Everyday having conversations with her was like being tortured by a big, boring monster. Sometimes he just wanted to tell her to go and commit a crime so that she had something better to talk about. She had this whole 'I'm more mature' thing going on because she didn't take a year off from college and travel. After he dropped his guys off the first thing he did was text Leah, she had his undivided attention tonight. She might be exactly what he needs to go ahead and shoot Aria the deuces.

Right now though, at this very moment, the only thing on Nehi's mind was Leah.

Message to Leah:
Wassup woman, where are u?
Message from Leah:
At the Rock & Roll McDonald's, u want something?
Message to Leah:
Yeah, can u grab me a no. 1 I'll pay u when u get here
Message from Leah:
lol u don't have to pay me
Message to Leah:
So our first date is on u?
Message from Leah:
I know, u got the next one
Message to Leah:
So when u get here, u staying the nite?
Message from Leah:
Do you want me to?
Message to Leah:
U know I do, just want to make sure it's cool with you
Message from Leah:
If I do, will u look at me diff?
Message to Leah:
Leah, we're grown woman, anything that happens here is between me and u and anything that happens here I just want to be sure will happen again in the future
Message from Leah:

So I'm thinking I may stay the night, but I don't have anything to sleep in
Message to Leah:
I got u woman
Message from Leah:
How so?
Message to Leah:
We can both sleep naked j/k
Message from Leah:
Maybe we can
Message to Leah:
Don't play gurl
Message from Leah:
Lol
Message to Leah:
Pick up, I'm calling to guide you here, it's kinda complicated

Nehi told her how to get there, but the biggest thing on his mind as soon as he hung up was the Big One. He was hoping that Aria didn't just show up the morning unannounced. She didn't do that very often, but they hadn't really talked much that day and the last time they actually talked she was crying. He wasn't trying to have her crying one day and then crying the next for something else. He decided to call her before Leah got there to make sure that she didn't just pop up. It was 4:45 in the morning when he called, so he knew she was asleep. She answered sounding tired after three rings.

"Hello? You okay Nehi?"

"I'm fine, I was worried about you though. The state you were in earlier had me really trippin. I wanted to make sure you were good woman. I mean you never cry, and you were crying earlier. Did I do something?"

"No Nehemiah, but we do need to talk."

That made him nervous, but excited at the same time. What if she's crying because she wants to break up? He'd be okay with that. It could be something worse though, but he was hoping for the best. It never crossed his mind until now that that could be it. She might be crying because she feels guilty about dumping him. "I totally understand, what time are you going to church tomorrow?"

"I don't know, but I know I need to go."

"Okay, well can you hit me when you get out, I'll head to you was as soon as you call me."

"Yeah. I will call you as soon as I get back."

"Okay, and I'll head right over after then, and we can talk." That was handled, no Aria busting in and no lying to Leah. "I'll see you in the morning shorty. Deuces" Nehi hung up the phone feeling good. Aria was basically out of his hair, he wasn't hanging around Rashi, so Leah was safe, and she was on her way right now, so he was in a good mood. He had vinyl everywhere, so he had some cleaning to do.

When she got there he'd just picked up the last of the things he had lying around. Rashi hadn't been cutting his hair in a while, his new barber gave pretty good cuts, but the linings were a little off. He'd never actually felt conscience of this until this very moment though. He put on a fitted Sox cap.

"You wear a hat around the house at 5 in the morning?"

"I just got in, I took out the trash." He forgot that it was 5 am, now he was a little embarrassed. A cap at 5 am was just stupid. "Anyhow woman, what you want to do?"

"Can we watch a movie?"

"Of course, what do you want to see? I have a gang of movies in the bedroom so have a look and tell me what looks good. Want anything to eat or drink?" He took his hat off now, it was basically dark in the house anyway, what was she, a barber? If she noticed his hairline, she would be cutting his hair next week.

"You must be nervous. You know I have McDonalds right?"

In Nehi's head, all he could hear was 'STRIIIIIIKE TWO!!!!!' But he was trying to keep his cool. "Now nervous at all woman. I don't really do too much company and was just trying to be a good host. Anyways woman, what you want to see?"

"What's your favorite movie?"

"I don't even want to tell you, it's a funny movie, but it reminds me of me and my guys. I mean we don't skate, but we're a tight crew, well we used to be."

"What is it?"

"Let me just say, it's not my favorite movie, it's my favorite movie I like to watch at home when I'm just chillin, So when I tell you, I don't want you thinking I'm some kind of lame."

"Boy, what movie is it?"

"Okay, I'm going to tell you woman. It's ATL."

"I was expecting something else."

He already knew what she was going to say, but he asked anyway. "What movie did you expect?" He could have said it with her.

"Juice."

"Why would you pick that?" He knew the answer to that too, there were four of them and one was a DJ.

"Cause there are four of y'all, and you're a DJ, like GQ in Juice. I figured that would be the movie. I mean just from talking to you in the club, I got the Juice vibe. Just like in the movie, y'all aren't speaking and it just seemed like that to me."

"I feel ya, but I think ATL." Nehi sat down on the couch with Leah. "Anyhow, we can watch whatever you want tonight." He didn't really care what they watched he was just trying not to get that dreaded strike three.

"Can we just watch TV? I don't want to pick a movie, and then fall asleep. Don't want you mad at me."

"We can definitely do that, but it is like 5 in the morning, so nothing is really on. If we're going to watch TV though, and most likely go to sleep, then we may as well do it in my room." That had to be a hit, Nehi was looking for the home run.

"Okay, so now, those sleeping arrangements you were talking about? What are we sleeping in?"

'HOME RUN!!!!!' "Well, I always sleep naked, but if you want, feel free to sleep in one of my wife beaters. I mean that's up to you though." He was going to wife this chick, she was cute, funny, open-minded, and fun. "I don't even want the rest of this McDonald's, I'm sleepy all of a sudden."

"Whatever Nehemiah."

"I told you that you can call me Nehi, you don't have to call me Nehemiah every time you say my name."

"Doesn't everyone call you Nehi though?"

"Yeah."

"That's why I don't want to. I want to call you Nehemiah cause to me that's who you are. Maybe eventually I'll be able to say, 'my man Nehemiah.' She was serious and she could tell Nehemiah knew it. He started kissing her and lead her to his bedroom.

Later that morning Nehi was feeling good. He woke up next to Leah, who snored a little, but it was cute. She actually looked like she was glowing in her sleep. For the first time in a while, Nehi woke up with a smile on his face. Today was the day Aria dumped him, and the day that Leah became his girl. Hell, he was so happy about these new developments that he might even call the Crew, minus Rashi. Maybe not. Didn't need any new drama, plus right now it was time to do some acting. Some looking sad and pretending he wanted to still be with the Big A.

When Leah woke up, it was a little before noon. She didn't want a morning kiss, 'no toothbrush'. So, of course, Nehi found an extra he'd had and gave her that one. He told her that he had a couple of errands to run, but he definitely wanted brunch or something before they parted ways. They went to IHOP and decided to meet later in the day at Nehi's apartment at 5:30 or 6:00. Nehi didn't tell her about Aria though, she was about to be an ex. So she wasn't important, and Leah would know nothing of her. His main thing was to make sure he didn't say something like 'let's try it again' or 'let's give it another try.'

They parted ways and Nehi headed for Aria's. Feeling good, but trying not to be obvious about it. When he got there, Aria was sitting on the porch in the swing. He'd been here a million times as a shorty, growing up with Aria, so he just sat down next to her. "Sup woman?"

"Nothing Nehi. Been sitting here thinking, about some stuff."

"Like what?" Nehi was ready for it, actually looking forward to it. The whole 'us' thing was coming, and he'd just have to play it cool and leave without looking back.

"Like I might have to take a break from school. I don't want to, but it's looking like I'll have to."

"What?" Why would she need to take a break from school over a break-up? She was acting weird to him. "Why would you need to take a break from school Aria?"

"Nehi, that's why we need to talk, we both may need a break from school. My period was late Nehi and I thought that I'd just wait for it and maybe it would come later, but it didn't. I took a bunch of test Nehi, and I'm pregnant."

"What?"

"Nehi, I'm pregnant."

Nehi didn't mean to say this and he regretted it as soon as it left his lips, "by who?"

"What the fuck do you mean by who? You're a jerk Nehemiah. You know it's only been me and you for a while now. You know what, you deserve that crew of friends you have because you act just like all of them except for Preach. I've had your back since you stopped talking to them. I didn't even ask why. Now I'm going through something and you really ask me that. Who am I pregnant by? Nehemiah, I know you think you're some big shot DJ now and the world should bow down to you, but I just want to say Fuck you. I'll handle this alone. You're a piece a shit!"

"Sorry Aria, I have to go. I'll hit you later though and we can talk. I promise." He was still going to meet Leah today, but he had to call the Crew. His real Crew.

Aria was about to yell at him more, but she was so loud her mom came out and brought her into the house.

Chapter 15

"So let me get this right, this lame dodges us for like months, then he calls Preach talking about he needs an emergency meeting at the shop? Doesn't he have a new barber? Why doesn't he hold a meeting there?" Rashi was furious, Jujuan called him and Rashad telling him he'd heard from Nehi and that Nehi wanted to have an emergency meeting at the shop with the crew. "I bet this clown found out about the All-Star tickets and wants to get in tight again. Where was his punk ass at when you got benched? Or when Carrie dropped you like a bad habit? Was he there cheering when you got back on pace? Does he even know you were benched? Now he's late for the meeting he called us for? What about you Rashad, has he called you? Did he congratulate you for being named conference player of the month in December or any of that? I can't believe I'm here for this shit."

"Calm down Ra, he's still our guy." Rashad wanted to know what was up, he seriously doubted the All-Star weekend thing. "We're going to hear what he has to say and then handle it accordingly. We're still a crew, what do call us Ra, 'Supreme Clientele' right?

"Nope, dude he's a clown. I ain't talked to this dude since like October and he's been MIA. I don't care what he wants, he gets no love here. I dare him to sit his ass down in this chair like he wants a cut. I promise I'll give him leopard spots all over his head. I mean y'all can forgive dude all you want, but I got Kionna stalking me, Stacie barely talking to me, and I gave his ticket to Stacie just to get her to actually chill with me. So, if this about that or if he even mentions it, I'm putting him out the shop. He's a clown and always will be."

Jujuan knew what it was about, Nehi told him everything, but he promised him he wouldn't say anything. "Ra calm down bro, it might not be about that. What if something's happened, his mom is sick or something like that? You plan on punishing him over something like that? Yeah, he wasn't speaking to us, but that's still Nehi. If he's in trouble, we need to have his back. Look, if he's here about getting some All Star tickets, I say give the kid spots, but you need to realize that as much as he wasn't speaking to us, this has to be important."

Rashi thought about it, Jujuan did come all the way from Iowa for this, it had to be something. "Man, all I'm saying is we've been calling and calling him, and now he calls us and we're here for him. You don't think that Kionna stalking and threatening Stacie was important? I'm so tired of us catering to this dude, he was doing so fine without us, right? Why in the hell does he need us now?"

"Rashi, calm yo ass down. It's Nehi. Yeah, he ignored us, but he's still Nehi. He's going through something fool. I'm sure whatever it is, it was the other way around he'd come through for you. He didn't come through with Ki was because his girl was stalking you. Dude you and Nehi got a different kind of history. I can admit that I don't know why he didn't answer any of our calls, but he's Nehi. That's our guy, so Preach came, and like it or not clown, you came. So, you can sit there and act like you don't care, but at the end of the day, you're here."

Rashad had a point, but Rashi was still a little upset. "What if it's something that we could have helped prevent though? What if it's something that had he not been a jackass and talked to his friends he could have prevented. I mean I know Nehi is our guy and I would be there if it was something crazy, but he'd ignored us for months son. I don't hold grudges, but I feel like forget him. Y'all can sit here and act like, 'oh it's Nehi he needs our help' but we needed him more times than once over these last few months. He was nowhere to be found."

"Would he have to be dead or what? Rashi you can say what you want, Nehi has had your back a bunch in the past. He needed a break from you, and I guess from us. You have to respect that. You went to Vancouver and didn't call any of us."

"I was there for a couple weeks and when I got back, I came and saw both of you bums play. You might not have seen me Shad, but if anyone was to ask, 'oh and how are your guys?' I'd have still been able to say, they're good. Shad is killing here in the Chi and Jujuan not so great in Iowa. Give him time though, he's a dog. Nehi can't say that son, he shit on all of us. You too clown, yeah the Kionna thing might have made him mad, but had he not been communicating with Stacie, would we even know he was alive?"

"You got a point bro, but you can take that up with him when he gets here. All I'm saying is, whatever it is was enough for him to reach out. He knows that he hasn't spoken to us in a while, we don't need to remind him." Jujuan was trying his best not to say anything, but as mad as Rashi seemed he thought he would have to, until the shop door opened.

"Wassup y'all. Thanks for meeting me here. I have some stuff going on and I know we ain't talked in a while, but the shit has hit the fan son."

"Nehi, the shit has hit the fan for you huh? Did you call Preach for this meeting? Wonder why you didn't call me or Shad. As a matter of fact, I'm fine with you not calling me. Why not Shad? The shit has hit the fan for you? Dude ask Preach if it hit the fan for him. Him and Carrie aren't together, he was benched for like seven or eight games this year, and on top of that he almost lost his scholarship. Dude had a full-blown scandal out there and you know what he was saying like every day? "Where is Nehi. And where were you dude?" Rashi was really livid "What about Shad, this dude has two girlfriends right now. One is MIA because she most likely knows he's going to shoot her the deuces. Ain't nobody seen Caryl since Martin Luther King was shot. Yeah, you're looking crazy, but when people were calling you and all of that, you were ignoring us. Well let me catch you up, Rashad and Jackie, a couple. Couldn't break up with Caryl cause guess what, when he went to do it, it was their anniversary. Oh, and your ex is stalking me and trying to hurt Stacie. Yeah, the same Stacie who's steadily getting you gigs. I don't know what you think you can say right now that will make everything cool, but I'm done messing around with you. And look at that terrible lining, who's cutting your hair, Stevie Wonder?"

"My bad y'all." Nehi wasn't looking forward to this. The bombshell Aria just put on him was enough, and now this? When he talked to Preach everything seemed to be cool, but apparently, they weren't feeling him right now.

"Yo bad! Are you serious, dude it's been like six months, and all you can say is 'my bad y'all.'" Every time Rashi talked about Nehi and his silent treatment, the time frame was somehow exaggerated a little bit. "Dude, we've been through a lot and through it all, we've tried to include you. Every single time and now you call Preach and the whole world is supposed to collapse around you? One call is all it took, and everybody is in the shop like 'what's up with Ne?' Meanwhile people are calling you every damn time something happens. Preach is in another state and we know what's going on with him. You're down the street and we can't get a call, a text, or even an email from you. Nehi you're a clown B. We're real friends so we're here, but to me Nehi, you've shown that you're a clown and undependable. You won't hear from me again though, believe that, cause if it wasn't for whatever we're here for, your selfish ass would still be doing whatever you were doing to begin with."

"It ain't like that Ra. This is serious."

"Wait, so let me get this right cause I thought I just heard you say that this is serious. So, let me take a quick survey Nehi, I mean you and your serious situation must be crazy compared to our dull lives. All I need is a yes or no. I'll start with you Preach. Was you being benched a serious situation?"

"Yeah, but-"

"Yeah was enough, I'll stay here with you, what about that crazy chick Cierra who made you chose between basketball and Carrie, was that serious?"

"Yeah, but Rashi you gott-"

"Seriously Preach, right now, yeah is all I'm looking for. Nehi has a serious situation and I just want him to see that he's right compared to whatever he has going, of course our lives aren't worth a damn. I mean he's Neo right? So Preach once again, you being benched for the first time in your life, having to shave points. Was that serious?

"Yeah."

"Okay, and I ain't even going to go into the whole situation with Carrie and getting off the bench, I'll just assume those are serious too, but not 'Neo' serious. I mean if the girl I wanted to marry left me, I'm sure I would think it was serious. So, I'll just move on to Rashad. Shad, this girl Jackie, she someone you take seriously?

"Yeah." Rashad wasn't even going to try to get in a word. He already knew, just let Rashi get whatever he had on his mind off of his chest. So he just sat there and waited for the next question.

"This whole having to dump Caryl thing, something you taking serious or is it just a joke? Although you dated Caryl since like the first day you got back from the trip right, and now she's missing, so even if you didn't want to dump her you still wouldn't be able to talk to her. That's not important is it?

"Yeah."

"What about being on SportsCenter almost every night cause you're killing players left and right. Is that important Rashad?"

"Yeah."

"Okay, just checking and me, I just got your ex threatening the girl who gets you work. Yeah, she gets you work, and she's being stalked and threatened by your ex bro. And why is she stalking us? Nothing too serious, just the fact that you dumped her, I tried being nice to her and I wouldn't sleep with her cause she was your ex. She tried to play you and since I wasn't cool wit that, look what that got us. Oh, and something else not so serious, I had to handle the Big Josh situation. So, while you were ignoring your friends, we were in serious situations ourselves. Sorry we didn't call. Wait we did, but you were playing us. My girl is making sure you stay working and your ex is talking about hurting her, but you get to have it your way?"

"I didn't know it was like that."

"We know you didn't, we know you were playing us. What the hell are we here for anyway? What could have possibly come up that you decided to break your silence?"

Nehi didn't even want to say it at this point. "It's Aria yo. She's pregnant. I don't know what to do."

At this point there were three different reactions at the same time. Rashad couldn't believe it, he was immediately said, "What!?!" Jujuan shook his head and Rashi just started laughing. This was hilarious to him. Rashi's laugh seemed a little too loud. Kind of like a 'that's what you get' type of laugh. Rashad was the first one to something aside from 'what.'

"Is it yours? I ain't trying to say anything is wrong with you or her. She does have a history thought Ne. Is she trying to trap you? What did you when she told you that Ne?"

"I asked her by who. I'd just met this chick and was hoping to break up with Aria that day, and then she hit me with it. I wasn't expecting that, she was crying and all of that and when I asked by who, she lost it. I mean she flat out snapped. Her mom had to come out and I left then. I was looking forward to her talking about it was over, when she said that, I didn't know what to do."

"You sure she ain't just fat? I mean you know the Big A and she's more likely to have an actual bun in the oven, than a baby B." Rashi was making jokes and right now, Nehi didn't really feel like joking. "Big A and Nehi having a little one, that's crazy, of all the chicks in the world to knock up, DJ Neo knocks up the easy rider."

"Dude would you shut the hell up! If I knew you be like this I would have just-"

"Would have just what Nehi? Tell your new friends? Cry about it? What? You know this is how I roll I laugh when I want to laugh. Dude you're in my shop dummy, ain't nothing off limits. I can laugh at you knocking your girl up. You've been away from the crew too long if you think we're going to let this slide cause in your absence you grew a vagina. Nope, these dudes are shocked, I say that's what you get."

"Chill Ra. We all got situations, but none of us have a baby on the way." Preach knew that Rashi would have a lot to say. When he called to schedule this meeting a week ago, Rashi was talking about how he had a lot to say. Nehi was looking shocked right now, but what did he really expect? "Nehi, you called this meeting, you gotta take the good and the bad. We've had a gang of meeting without you and you're the new guy again."

"I don't even know what to say to you dude." Rashad was really in shock. He didn't know if anyone else was on the same page he was on, but he felt like maybe Nehi found out she was pregnant months ago and that's why he disappeared on them. "How far along is she?"

"I don't know Shad."

"How long ago did you find out?" Rashad was trying to do the math in his head. If he stopped talking to then around Thanksgiving and she got pregnant then, maybe she was like three or four months.

"About exactly a week ago. It's like 1 o'clock now, it was about one o'clock last Sunday when I went to her house."

"You're a dumbass Nehi. You let this chick trap you, now what, you going to marry her?" Rashi was over the funny part, now he was pissed, he told Nehi about Aria, but he still chose her. "Please don't tell me you're going to marry this silly ass girl?"

"Dude I told you I got a new chick son. I'm trying to get myself rid of Aria, but I can't shake that baby."

"If it's yours Neo." Preach mentioned it when he called on Tuesday earlier in the week and he was still standing by it now, "You need to make sure you get a test if y'all decide to keep it Neo."

"You better get that baby tested son. It could be everybody in the hood but yours. Dude I told you when you picked her to be careful, and like an idiot, you didn't. Ne, you a clown son. I feel no sympathy for you dude. I know you're going to end up marrying her and all of that, so I don't even have anything else to say." Rashi was done talking to Nehi about this, he just sat down in his barber chair and turned to face the mirrors.

"I agree with Preach Nehi, you do need to make sure she ain't trying to trap you B. I like Aria, but I don't really trust her like that. She's done some dirt in the past and I just wouldn't put it past her now." Rashad nodded his head toward Rashi. "She's done some unforgivable stuff, and you forgave her son. Do you trust that it's yours?"

"I don't know, but when I went to her house, I was expecting her to break up with me. I'd met Leah the day before and I'm feeling her.

I chilled this whole week with Leah, I don't even know if I should tell her about this or not. I mean if it's not mine, then not telling her works out pretty well for me, but what if it is? What if I find out that it's mine, then it's like I was hiding it from Leah."

"That's because you are. You're going to have to do like Rashi did and just tell the truth." Preach told Carrie the truth and although she broke up with him and he hated it, he was balling again, and he felt like, he cheated so he deserved to be dumped. "Look Neo, Ra is upset, but you know we have your back."

"I ain't close to being upset, I just don't care. If you're the father, you know I got your back, and you know I'll be his barber if it's a boy. I'll be his favorite uncle or her's if it's a girl. I just have nothing to say to you. We all had 'important' shit going on. I can't do it, they can, and I respect that, and we're still good Nehi, I just know that you're a joke. Selfish and on top of that, you left us out to dry. Oh, and I ain't cutting your hair. Let the clown who's been messing you up lately keep that going for you. Look here bro, you can come here when we meet and all of that, but I won't be calling you. You and Stacie talk, and I respect that, but you won't be hearing from me at all Ne. I called you like a hundred times, and nothing. You got yourself into this, I say get yourself out."

"That's your decision Ra, but this is a crazy situation. Dude she's pregnant, what am I supposed to do? I don't even want to be with her son." Nehi didn't expect Ra to spazz out like this, and how would you have reacted if the whole Kionna thing happened the other way around. She came here to see you cause she was trying to get at you."

"Yeah, but I told her that she was a clown for that. I told her that I had no interest in her and I told her that you're my guy and that since she did you wrong like she did that I wouldn't talk to her. She took that and decided that threatening me and my girl was the answer. I called your ass, like you called Preach and you know what happened? You did the opposite. I ain't even mad, I'm just done. We're cool, but as far as reaching out and all of that, I'll pass. What do you want us to do anyway? What was the purpose of this meeting?"

Preach stepped in cause he felt Rashi was taking it a little too far. "Dude, this is Nehi. Yeah, he shot us the deuces for a while, but we've been friends since forever dude. You need to cool out Ra."

"That's the thing, he's been friends with y'all for years, ever since the thing with me and his baby momma, he's been anything but a friend to me. I see the way he looks and acts when it comes to me, I don't say shit, because I was wrong. I know this, but a friend will forgive you right? I've apologized I don't know how many times, but this jackass goes and gets back with Aria right? Dude I tell my girl to give you jobs, even when you aren't speaking and acting like a chick, I still make sure you're good. Not even because I was sorry, because I'm done apologizing for that, but because you were my guy. Nehi keep paying for your cuts and I hope that baby is yours. Shad, take my keys and lock the shop when y'all leave. Deuces."

After Rashi left the shop was silent for a while. Rashad was the first one to say something, "anybody want a cut?" He was joking, but apparently, nobody wanted to joke just then. "Okay, so Nehi aside from knocking chicks up, I did hear you mention another girl, what was her name, Lena or something?"

"Leah."

"You told her about Aria yet? And her being pregnant?" Rashad was shocked by this. He always figured Rashi would knock somebody up way before any of them.

"I ain't stupid son, I like her. So nope, we've been chillin all week, every day at my crib just chillin. She comes out when I'm working and when I'm not she's cooking or going out to the movies with me. Plus, she's fun y'all. I mean real fun. I used to kick it with Aria and just dread the day, with her though, I mean it's all fun. I look forward to just being in her presence."

"What happens if it is yours then Nehi? You can't hide something like this and expect her to just forgive you. Ne, you are a clown these days. You even think about that? How about you tell her that an ex is pregnant, and you won't know if it's yours until she has it cause you are getting a test? She can't say you lied that way, and if it's not yours y'all still happy and what not, and if you find out it is, then y'all just deal with it when it happens. You don't want to ruin all chances of staying together by not telling her, then all of a sudden, you have a baby. That's the way wrong answer." Rashad was trying to get Nehi to do the right thing cause he didn't even believe that the baby was Nehi's.

"Do you even know if she's really pregnant? I mean she show you test or something you can confirm. When you called me this week, I was shocked, but not as shocked as I was when you told me what was going down. Neo, nothing personal, I just don't feel like you can trust Aria like that. I know it's the last thing you want to hear coming from me cause yeah, I did cheat on Carrie, but she has a history. Your being cautious is smart for one. For two, she made it like this. Shad is right too by the way you have to tell this new girl asap. I mean I should have told Carrie I was on some BS when I was, I lost almost half a season and my girl because I was lying. Seriously and this was just a basketball season. I'm trying to get her back and I'm working hard at it. I was benched, and the coaches were looking at me like I was just some bum. Now the thing about your new girl bro. A kid is forever, if and when she finds out about it, and that you hid it from her, ain't going to be just a half a season you're on the bench. You might be losing something special cause you're too stubborn to tell her what's good." Preach was preaching again, so decided to stop right here.

"So, both of y'all think I should say something huh?"

"Yeah." Preach was serious about his advice.

"I do. Nehi, if she's as good as you say she is, and all you want to do is chill with her, she needs to know. Damn, Ra mad as hell at you kid. I didn't want to say anything Nehi but your hairline does look like it's on a fifteen minute break." Rashad was going to ask Nehi about that but was glad he waited until Ra had left. "So who's been fading you up my dude?"

"This female barber I met up north. She's aiight."

"Nehi, are you not seeing your lining? She's taking it back more and more son. Looks like we might have to start calling you Neo five heads."

"Is it really that bad?"

Preach even had to say something about this cut. "Neo, your hairline is basically depressing. I mean I don't know why you stopped talking to us, but you should have called an emergency meeting after the first cut son. I mean she's messing you up, and Ra says he ain't hooking you up, so here's what you need to do. What's your new chick's name again?"

"Leah."

"Yeah, call Leah and tell her what's really good, let her know that y'all need to talk in person and then when you do see her in person, just be honest with her. And what's the barber's name?"

"Georgia."

"Yeah, when you get home, you just never call her again. I mean if you have her card, I'm going to need you to not only burn it, but stomp it a little, rip it up, flush it, and if you see her on the street, chop her."

Rashad and Nehi were laughing hard, Preach didn't usually go on rampages like that. "I told Jackie I'd be back on campus, y'all need to stay here and talk?"

"I hope not. Neo, you know our numbers, use them, and call Ra. Dude is mad, but you need a lining, you lining looks mad as well. Do that, keep us posted and I'll just see y'all nest week."

As they left the shop, Nehi went with Rashad after he locked up. Jujuan went the other way. He loved the shop meetings but hadn't been too honest in them lately. He was really missing Carrie. If he had to do it again, he'd have stayed on the bench and let Ms. CiCi just use him like she was already doing. Basketball right now wasn't the most important thing to him, but Carrie made it quite clear that she wasn't trying to be bothered by Jujuan. He was hoping this was a temporary thing and planned on being as honest and open with her as possible. He had to win her back. He was thinking about this a lot, so he didn't notice the young lady approach him on the corner.

"Nice haircut."

"Oh, thanks." Rashi had given him a cut the day before and he'd gotten some intricate designs. "They're designs I put in myself."

"Even the ones in the back?"

"Yeah, and by yeah, I mean no." She started laughing and that made Jujuan continue. "My guy did it, but they were my idea."

"Oh, so you come up with the designs and your barber makes them happen? That's cool. I'm Bridget by the way."

"Bridget, that's a cute name." What he meant to say was, 'wassup, I'm Jujuan.' What came out though was, "Oh, nice to meet you Bridget. I'm Chris …"

Lightning Source UK Ltd.
Milton Keynes UK
UKHW012053010321
379622UK00010B/996/J

9 781664 159440